She was shaking with need when he wrenched himself away from her, a question in his eyes.

"I've been holding this love inside for so long that I'm about to burst!" he said hoarsely.

Deep inside her head, the voice of reason screamed for her to move away from Perry. She took a shaky step backwards, certain that was what she should do, but a potent combination of need and want and love decimated her will. She couldn't think beyond this moment. Helplessly she nodded. "I want you too, Perry. I've got to have you."

Perry pulled her close once more to sear her lips with a burning kiss, and then taking her hand, he drew her into the cool interior of his villa. Imani kicked off her shoes. As the door slammed behind him, he lifted her into his arms and headed for the steps. "I can't make it up all those steps!" he growled in frustration.

Indigo Sensuous Love Stories

are published by

Genesis Press, Inc.
315 Third Avenue North
Columbus, MS 39701

The Love We Had

First Edition

The Love We Had

by

Natalie Dunbar

Genesis Press, Inc.

Acknowledgements

I'd like to thank my family for being loving, patient, and supportive while I worked on this book. An extra thanks goes to my husband, Chet, for his willingness to provide inspiration. I'd also like to thank my editor, Sidney, for helping focus the book better, and Karen White Owens, my critique partner for showing me that gangrene is a lot easier to deal with than brain tumors. A special thanks to Chris White for answering my questions about the experience of having a family member going through dialysis.

Chapter 1

Intent on checking her list and filling her grocery cart, Imani paused to listen to the happy gurgling sounds of the baby in the next aisle. It must be quite a little cutie to be spreading this much sunshine in the supermarket, she chuckled to herself as she placed a box of breakfast cereal into her cart. As she neared the end of the aisle, turned the corner, and started up the next, she anticipated seeing the little bundle of joy.

Focusing on the baby seater lodged on top of a bright yellow grocery cart on the left side of the aisle, she wasn't disappointed. Dressed in a Detroit Pistons sweat suit, a chubby baby with bright brown eyes and curly hair threw her a three-toothed-smile. Her heart melted when he extended a caramel-colored hand to her.

Cute! Cute! Cute! she thought, wanting to caress

those dimpled cheeks. Returning the smile, she approached. She loved babies. If things had worked out the way she'd hoped, her own baby would have been about this size. With that thought she spared a glance at the tall figure kneeling beside the basket and attempting to maneuver a tray of Chunky Gourmet baby food from the bottom shelf.

The muscles in her chest seized and she struggled to breathe. Perry! Her senses screamed as she stiffened in alarm. It couldn't be. No! She didn't want to believe her eyes. The man had his back to her, but she still recognized the long, wide-shouldered torso, and the classic shape of his head.

Her fingers were ice cold as she quickly wheeled her basket around, glancing once more at the little charmer. Jabbering happily, he had both arms extended as he waited for her to pick him up. Was this Perry's baby? she wondered. It looked just like him!

Shaking, Imani briskly headed the other way. She would never forget how sick she'd been when she was carrying Perry's baby or the fact that she could have died. The memory of his initial suggestion that she "take care of it" still reverberated in her thoughts. When he realized that she fully intended to have the baby, he seemed to support her decision, but once she lost the baby, she couldn't look into his eyes without seeing relief there. Shortly after she ended their relationship, there'd been pictures in all the gossip magazines of Perry with a pregnant starlet, along with rumors that the two were getting married.

Perry was busy lifting a tray of gourmet baby food from the bottom shelf when Jimmy started to cry. Turning his head in surprise, because Jimmy rarely cried, he saw a tall, slim, curvy woman in tight black pants and a short peach tank top. On elegant black sandals, she was almost running the other way. Imani!

No one else looked that good just shopping in the supermarket. His heart beat faster as a thrill of excitement ran through him and he nearly dropped the tray. It had been more than a year since she'd dumped him, but he thought about her every day. No woman had ever affected him so powerfully. He didn't need to lift the stylish cap from her head and see the trademark fall of shiny, black hair to know that it was Imani.

Maneuvering carefully, he got the tray into the bottom of the cart. Then he lifted Jimmy into his arms. "Imani!" he called as the figure reached the end of the aisle and whipped around the corner. There was no response. "Did she leave you? I know how it feels, man," he told the still crying Jimmy as he patted his back in a soothing manner and inhaled the pleasant scent of baby power and baby shampoo. "She left me too."

Perry found a tissue in the diaper bag, wiped the tears from the baby's face and eyelashes and then his nose. "Do you think we ought to go get her back?" Jimmy simply looked at him and began talking gibberish

3

again, but Perry already knew the answer to his question.

He and Imani had unfinished business. Placing Jimmy back in the basket, Perry took off after her.

Imani went all the way to the produce section at the other end of the store before she stopped to catch her breath. She'd heard him call her name, but how could she face him now? It hurt to see him with his baby. It should have been their baby! Covering her face, she fought tears and immobilizing pain.

Forget the past. He was not the man you thought he was and he never really loved you, she told herself, but her heart still ached. In all the time they'd been apart, she'd only just moved past a serious depression, while his life had to be ideal with a wife and that beautiful baby. What troubled her most was that deep inside she still harbored feelings for him, whether he deserved them or not.

Someone touched her arm. "Miss Celeste, are you all right? Do you need help?"

Dropping her hands, Imani shook her head, managing to smile at the stock boy. "No, Terrence. I've just got a headache."

"You sure?"

"Yes, I'm sure." Imani forced herself to take another look at her list to glean the produce items she needed. Briefly, she considered coming back at another time, but her mother's refrigerator needed restocking and she had several appointments scheduled for this week. If Perry insisted on talking to her, she was just going to have to handle it.

"Apples, bananas, and broccoli," she called out, forcing herself to concentrate as she snapped plastic bags from the roll and quickly gathered crisp red apples, golden bananas, and a thick, green bunch of broccoli. She checked the list again. "Cabbage, lettuce, and corn."

"Imani," a deep, provocative voice challenged her from behind. "We've been too much to each other for you to see me and run the other way."

At the sound of Perry's voice she took a calming breath and curved her lips into her trademark smile. He knew how easily she used that technique to hide her emotions, but she didn't care. When she turned, Perry Bonds stood there with the baby in his long arms.

The force of his bold, black brows emphasized the contours of his leaf brown eyes. The light in the supermarket played with the complex angles created by his jutting cheekbones, full cheeks and square chin to give him an attractiveness normally seen only on male models. He'd been working out again too, by the looks of the sculpted muscles shaping his arms and rise of milk chocolate skin peeking out of the open vee of his expensive sport short. There was a hungry look in his eyes that drew her and made her body tingle all over. Imani's mouth watered.

"Apparently I don't agree," she said, straightening her shoulders and lifting her head. "Seeing you brought back a lot of memories that I'm better off forgetting. How have you been?"

"Miserable. You're hard to replace and then there's the fact that I didn't want to."

At that she looked straight into his eyes and saw past his cocky expression. There was an inexplicable hint of sadness there. His words did not make sense, she reasoned, because if he were married to the starlet-harlot Rasheeda, he'd already replaced her, hadn't he? Perry had never been a cruel or vicious person, so why was he interested in seeing her now? Had his starlet proved to be less than wonderful?

"And how have you been?" he asked, obviously ignoring the fact that she'd failed to react to his statement.

"It took months for me to climb out of depression," she admitted frankly. "I had to see a doctor about it, but I'm a lot better now."

"I'm glad that you've recovered," he said with a warm sincerity that brought back memories of their past. He moved closer and she caught herself inhaling his fresh, familiar scent.

Seeing him standing in front her and hearing him talk of how irreplaceable she was, she thought of the pictures of the pretty starlet in the gossip magazines and the baby in his arms. The man had more balls than a bubblegum machine to be standing in her face trying to remind her of their past when he'd obviously been seeing someone else at the same time. Going for the jugular, Imani asked politely, "How's your wife?"

Giving her a strange look, Perry shook his head negatively. "I'm not married. You know it's only been a year since you broke our engagement."

The news hit her with the force of an earthquake. Imani swallowed hard and struggled for words to justify what she'd done when her world crumbled, leaving her helpless to cope. "It…it seemed right at the time."

Perry shot her a disbelieving look. "No, it was never right. It was just easier than dealing with the pain." The baby strained forward, his busy little fingers just managing to touch an apple. Sighing, Perry shifted the baby to his other hip.

Imani grabbed the handle of her grocery cart and held on. "What's your baby's name?"

Lifting him, Perry smiled and kissed the top of the baby's head. "This is my nephew Jimmy. Want to hold him?"

Imani stared, speechless. She could have fainted right there. She moved only when Perry dropped the squirming baby into her arms. Shifting him, with one hand supporting his bottom and the other his head, she felt his little knees grip her hip.

Perry shook his head in disgust. "You thought he was mine! Imani, you should know me better than that. I know there was talk in the gossip magazines about me and Rasheeda, but we were just friends. You can't believe everything you read and you know as well as I do that when you're in the limelight, people have plenty to say. They made up stuff about us. When there's no real news, they make it up."

At Perry's revelation, Imani felt as if a load had been lifted from her chest. She breathed a sigh of relief and then caught herself. What did it matter now? Her relationship with Perry was in the past. Cooing, the baby grabbed at her earring. "No, Jimmy," she said softly, catching the little hand and kissing it.

She glanced back at Perry and caught him watching her and the baby, hope and tenderness coloring his expression. "I'm sorry I jumped to conclusions," she told him.

"If you're really sorry, you can make it up to me," he said, folding his arms. "I'll make it easy."

She considered his statement. "What do you have in mind?"

"Have dinner with me." He watched her intently.

"I don't think so!" she said quickly. She likened the thought to jumping off a cliff. She had no control where Perry was concerned.

"Why not?" he asked, challenging her with his eyes.

"Because it won't do any good." She met his gaze. "It's over. It's been over for months."

"Then why do I still think about you?" he asked in a low tone.

Imani nuzzled the baby's soft cheek with her own,

fear growing within her as their encounter spun out of her control. In her secret heart she rejoiced at his words. She hadn't been able to stop thinking about him. But no one had ever hurt her as Perry had.

"Are you going to answer my question? If you really think it's over between us, then why do I still think about you?" he asked, repeating his question as he watched Jimmy play with her fingers and try to put them in his mouth.

"Maybe it's just force of habit." she answered.

"You know better than that." Perry touched her arm and she felt sensual heat radiating from his fingers to spread throughout her body. "If you won't have dinner with me, you could at least give me your phone number."

"Why?" she asked, throwing him a challenging look.

"So that I can stay in touch with you and see how you are. So that I can call you when nothing else gives me the peace I need to sleep at night. Can I do that?"

"Yes," Imani said, touched by something in his words and unable to deny the sincerity and need in his tone. She knew she shouldn't care, but she did. She gently placed Jimmy back into his arms and fished into her purse for one of her cards. With a gold pen, she wrote a number on the back. "I'll be at this number for a while," she explained.

"Thanks," Perry said, accepting the card.

Before either could say anything further, a couple of fans walked up and asked for Perry's autograph.

Imani seized the moment. "I've got to go. Take care."

"I'll take talk to you later," Perry called as he produced a pen.

She'd taken a few steps away when she came back to tuck a finger under Jimmy's double chin and kiss his cheek. She chuckled when he turned his little head and pressed his open mouth to her face in a parody of a kiss. "Good-bye, Jimmy."

As Imani stood in line and paid for her groceries, she tried to classify her feelings and failed. She felt glad, sad, excited, and scared all at the same time. Letting Perry back into her life would be a big risk. It wasn't as if she hadn't already learned this particular lesson. If you're still scared when he calls, you don't have to talk to him, she promised herself.

Perry signed the autographs and then casually headed towards the cash registers to get another glimpse of Imani. She was there all right, obviously unaware of all the attention she was getting from every male in the vicinity with that sexy outfit. The neckline of her shirt plunged enough to tantalize a man with the golden mounds of her breasts and its short length bared the band of skin above her tight pants. A diamond winked at him from her navel. Damn! he thought kicking himself, she's looking better than ever! What made things worse was that he couldn't rationalize the deep, sometimes gut-wrenchingly emotional tie they shared. It had hit him early in the relationship, but it had taken him a long time to acknowledge it. All his friends had dreamed of sleeping with her, but he'd been happy just being around her and letting things progress naturally.

Jimmy got his attention by grabbing at a box of crackers and knocking it to the floor. "All right, man, you can have some crackers," Perry told him as he tossed the box into the bottom of the basket. By the time he'd gathered the remaining items on his list, Imani had gone. He contented himself with watching her drive away in a red Mustang convertible as he stood in line to make his purchases.

On a whim, Perry stopped by the house of his friends Mariah and Ramón Richards on the way home. He'd attended the wedding of the lawyer and his modeling agency owner wife shortly after he and Imani broke up. As he walked up the winding drive of their Palmer Woods home with the baby in his arms, he realized that he should have called. Ramón and Mariah were still newlyweds, after all.

He'd just stepped onto the porch when the front door to the large brick mansion opened and Mariah stood in the opening with Ramón behind her, his arms locked around her waist. Still sporting the newlywed glow, they looked cozy.

"I can come back another time," Perry called, halting his steps.

"Don't be silly," Mariah answered, opening the door

and inviting him in. "We haven't seen you in a while."

"Yeah, well I got caught up in the game, and then I had that injury."

"Hey, we understand," Ramón said, "A man's got to make a living and it's even better when he enjoys it."

"Who's the cute little guy?" Mariah asked, reaching for Jimmy.

"This is my nephew Jimmy," Perry said, relinquishing his load.

"Hi there, sugar pop," Mariah cooed as she walked off with the baby.

"Want something to drink?" Ramón asked, leading him across the hardwood floor into the great room.

"I'll take a beer." Perry grabbed a handful of mixed nuts from the tray on the counter and settled onto one of the gray counter stools.

Ramón took two beers from the refrigerator and switched on the television. "So what's got you so excited?" Ramón asked with a grin.

"I saw Imani in the supermarket," Perry said, popping the top off his beer.

"That must have been hard," Ramón said, changing the channel to a basketball game.

"Yeah, I nearly was hard," Perry chuckled. "She is one beautiful woman and as stubborn as they come. When Jimmy first tried to talk to her, she got one look at me and took off in the opposite direction." He took a swig of his beer.

Ramón sat on the stool next to Perry. "Did you get her to talk to you?"

"Yeah, but she didn't like it. Did you know that she thought I was married? She also thought Jimmy was mine."

Ramón grinned. "Y'all got some strong genes in your family, man, because if I didn't know better, I'd think Jimmy was yours too! He looks just like you. How long are you baby-sitting?"

"Huh, my brother and his wife will be back by seven to get Jimmy. I've had fun playing daddy all day, but I'm ready to be a bachelor again." Perry took a few more swigs of beer and sighed. "So tell me, did you think I'd stepped off and gotten married too?"

Ramón shook his head. "Man, you need to keep up with your press. Right after you and Imani broke up there were a lot of articles in the gossip magazines about you and Rasheeda. It was before she had the baby and they were swearing that it was yours."

Hunching his shoulders at the counter, Perry remarked under his breath, "Imani has always been more than willing to believe the worst of me. Sometimes I wish I could just forget about her and go on about my business."

Ramón shot him a look of amused disbelief. "Man, quit. You know you love her and she loves you. You guys just need to work it out."

"So tell me this," Perry said, placing his empty beer

bottle on the counter, "did you and Mariah think I'd gotten Rasheeda pregnant?"

Again Ramón shook his head negatively. "No way. You'd already taken a lot from Imani while she was pregnant and then when she lost the baby things went from bad to worst. Only love could have kept you there for the brutal punishment she dished out."

Perry shrugged. "Hey, I'm no saint. I went to see her doctor. Imani had post-partum depression. I read up on it so I know she couldn't help herself. If I'd been the man I should have been, I wouldn't have let her drive me away."

"Don't blame yourself," Ramón advised, "you did the best you could."

"Yeah," Perry mumbled, momentarily checking the television screen to see how the college game was going.

The University of Michigan was slaughtering the other team. "You know, I'm surprised that Imani's not in Europe for that big show the designers are having. They love her there."

Mariah entered the room without the baby.

Perry turned to look in the direction she'd come from. "Where's Jimmy?"

"Jimmy's asleep in the center of our bed," Mariah said. "I've got pillows all around him to make sure he doesn't fall out."

"Thanks." Perry opened another beer.

"Something tells me that you'd make a great mother," Ramón said. His wife smiled softly.

Perry took a swig of cold beer. "So Imani's hanging around Detroit instead of making money on the runways in Europe.

"Her mother's sick, so she stayed to take care of her," Mariah explained.

"Oh." Perry's voice dropped. "Is it serious?"

"Yes." Mariah settled on one of the stools. "She's going through a tough time."

Perry stared into the depths of his glass. "I wish I could help."

Ramón and Mariah echoed the sentiment. There was a long, awkward silence. Then Ramón jumped up and got Mariah a glass of wine. "Here you go, sweetheart."

"Thanks." Mariah kissed Ramón 's lips. Suddenly they were sharing a deep, soulful kiss.

Lost in thought, Perry was silent for several moments. "I never thought Imani would forgive her mother for kicking her out when she was seventeen. Mrs. Celeste basically believed her new husband instead of her own child. The man was a dog. For years, Imani couldn't even talk about what happened without crying."

"Maybe they cleared the air, but I doubt it," Ramón told him. "When you're faced with losing a parent, you have to put some things on the back burner. Her mother is all the family she's got."

"I wish I still had my mama," Mariah said wistfully.

Ramón took Mariah by the hand and led her to the couch. "Come on and join us, Perry."

Grabbing his beer, Perry started to follow, but hesitated when he saw Ramón settle his wife into his lap. "You guys look like you need some time alone."

"Man, get over here and sit down," Ramón said. "We get all the time we need alone, but I still reserve the right to hold my wife in my own house whenever I get ready."

"I hear that," Perry answered with a grin. "How's business?"

"I don't have anything big going on right now, just a few felony cases, one with a minor who shot a playmate. However, the construction company has gone a long way on the new building for the modeling agency." Ramón played with his wife's hair.

"So when will the construction be complete?"

"It'll be at least another month," Mariah answered. "Then we'll have a big ribbon-cutting ceremony and a party."

Perry grinned. "I'll look forward to that. Will Imani be there?"

"Definitely," Ramón said. "It'll be a golden opportunity for you."

Perry finished the beer. "Well, keep me posted."

Imani parked her car in her mother's driveway and began unloading the groceries. Mr. Lewis, the middle-aged neighbor who lived next door, came out and helped her. She still felt a little strange when she used her key and opened the front door of the house where she had not been welcome for many years. She saw the solitary figure of her mother in the living room full of plastic-covered furniture. Her mother sat in the recliner, watching television.

Instead of focusing on her mother's face, ravaged by illness, Imani greeted her cheerfully and took the groceries back into the kitchen. Her mother politely returned the greeting. Mr. Lewis stopped to talk briefly with her mother and then followed Imani into the kitchen with more of the bags. While Imani paused to put some of the food away, he went back into the living room to talk to her mother.

"How's she doing?" Imani asked the private duty nurse who was in the kitchen warming soup.

"Pretty good today," the nurse told her. "I think she's feeling better. She ate lunch and she's asked for a little more soup. You know how hard it usually is to get her to eat."

Imani nodded. "That's good." Then she went back to the living room to join Mr. Lewis and her mother in conversation.

As their neighbor talked about his work in his garden, Imani saw that her mother looked calm and relaxed. After he left, she sat and tried to make conversation while her mother ate her soup. Before long, she fell silent, frustrated by her mother's short responses. Obviously her mother found it easier to talk with her neighbor than to talk with her only daughter. With the rhythmic clank of the stainless steel spoon hitting the side of the white ceramic bowl as a backdrop, Imani sank into thought.

"What's the matter?"

Her mother's question jolted her from her tangled thoughts about the encounter in the supermarket. Imani looked directly into her mother's face, which despite the wear from illness, still looked incredibly like her own. "Nothing," she replied.

"Did something bad happen in the supermarket or on the way back? You seem agitated."

Imani shrugged and said as nonchalantly as she could, "I ran into Perry Bonds."

The spoon dropped back into the soup bowl with a clatter and her mother wiped her mouth with the paper napkin. "No wonder you're upset. You never got over him, did you?"

Imani bristled. "You don't know anything about me and Perry. You and I weren't even speaking when Perry and I were together."

Her mother's voice rose. "I know that you loved that man. You've never bothered to get engaged to anyone else. You never slowed down long enough."

At a loss for words, Imani stared at her mother. The words hurt because deep in her heart she knew they were true. It didn't help to know that her mother knew and enjoyed twisting the knife. "Perry Bonds was just a dream I had…," Imani muttered under her breath. "You don't give your heart easily. You never have."

Imani rose. "I don't want to discuss this with you, Mama!" she said sharply and then caught herself. "I'm sorry. I didn't mean to raise my voice."

Her mother gave her a triumphant smile. "And that's how I know you still care for Perry. You never want to discuss the things you care about with me, and the things you do discuss are never anything to raise your voice over."

Gasping, Imani shook her head. "That's not true." Lifting her black brows, her mother tilted her head. "Isn't it?"

"No." Imani edged towards the stairs leading to her old bedroom. "I'm going to change and go for a run. Do you need anything?"

"No. I'm going to watch a movie and then take a nap."

Feeling a stab of guilt at having been gone for so long, already leaving again, and planning to go out tonight, Imani said, "Do you want me to stay and watch the movie with you?"

Her mother sighed. "No, Imani. You're chomping at the bit to escape this house and I know how you feel. Go on, I know you need your exercise."

Imani had reached her room and changed into her running outfit before her mother's words sank in. She promised herself that next time she'd stay and watch the movie with her mother. Then she met one of the other models from the McCleary Modeling Agency for a run in the park.

In the early evening hours, Imani was getting ready to shower and dress for her date when the phone rang. At the sound of Perry's voice she dropped down on the silk bedspread, her pulse racing. "Perry!"

"After seeing me in the supermarket, you must have known I'd call." His voice was low and provocative.

"I really didn't think about it," she answered, wanting to talk and yet wanting at the same time to end the conversation.

"Liar!" he chuckled, "you're just as shook as I am. Admit it."

"All right." She grabbed the heavy fall that nearly reached her waist, twisted it around one hand and pulled it over her shoulder. "But that doesn't mean I want to start all over again or act as if we'd never ended."

"What do you want?"

Perry's question repeated itself in her thoughts as she hesitated. "I—I don't know," she answered finally.

"I know what I want," he told her in a voice filled with conviction. "I want you and the love we had. Imani, we were good together."

Clutching the cordless phone, Imani felt an over-whelming ache inside. A tear slid down her cheek, touching the corner of her mouth in its path downward. Tasting the warm, saltiness on her tongue she said,

"That's not what I remember."

The silence lasted an eternity. "Ne-ne, I don't want to hurt you," Perry said softly. "Did I make you cry?"

"No," she lied, grabbing a tissue off the nightstand to pat her face. Perry was one of the few people who knew just how sensitive she was beneath the tough exterior she often projected.

"It was hard to stay away all these months. Do you want me to just forget about you? Leave you alone forever?"

The choked sound of Perry's voice stung Imani and she found herself holding her breath. She didn't want to hurt him either. Deep inside she admitted that she cared. "No, it's not what I want," she admitted aloud, "I—I just need more time and space."

"So you can forget about us?"

Imani cleared her throat. "So that I can cope."

Perry sighed. "I'll try to be patient."

"Thanks," she murmured.

"I will be seeing you," Perry said.

"Yes," she agreed. Then they said their good-byes and ended the conversation.

After hanging up the phone Imani stretched out on the bed and thought about Perry and the past. They'd come a long way from the two people who'd gone after each other on a dare and a bet. Two of his teammates had bet him that he didn't have the nerve to approach her and ask for a date. Because Perry had the reputation of being a loner who'd escaped some of the best laid feminine traps and she had never been in love, Imani's friends had dared her to make him fall in love with her. They'd both had a wild time and fallen hard for each other.

As she stripped and climbed into the shower, she resolved to straighten out the mess she'd made of her life. Maybe she needed someone safe and stable, someone who didn't make her crazy with suspicion and jealousy as Perry did, and someone with position and standing in the community and the financial means to complement her own. She chuckled in surprise when she realized that she'd actually described her friend Damon Kessler. Now all she had to do was convince herself to take him.

It was close to seven-thirty when Imani opened the door to the tall and elegant Judge Damon Kessler. Smiling into her handsome friend's sea green eyes, she gave him a big hug and kissed his cheek.

"You're beautiful," he said, taking her hand and scrutinizing her black lace- paneled dress. "And you smell good too."

Imani thanked him. As he'd requested, she'd worn a long, formal dress, but the alternating see thru panels made the dress seem more revealing than it actually was and the stretchy material hugged every curve. The neckline dipped low into the valley between her breasts and the conservative side split exposed a tantalizing bit of leg and ended inches above her knee. Her black lace evening shoes were barely there.

Damon cleared his throat, making a sort of strangling sound.

"Are you all right?" she asked with a grin.

"I'm trying to catch my breath 'cause I can barely breathe when I look at you," Damon told her.

Imani grinned. "The entire outfit's an Anthony LeFarge original."

He gave her outfit another penetrating stare and lowered his voice to ask, "Are you wearing anything under that? It doesn't look like it."

"Of course I am," Imani said with a provocative lift of her brows, "but I'm not saying how little."

He digested the information with a muted sigh.

"I like that suit," Imani continued, eyeing his formal black suit and lifting a hand to his shoulder to touch the rich material. "Isn't it Armani?"

"Yes it is." At her touch, Damon's glance caught hers and for a moment she imagined that in addition to friendship and affection she saw burning desire in his eyes. One blink of those green eyes and it was gone.

"I like all his suits," she murmured. Perry always wore Armani suits and looked fabulous in them. She didn't want to think about Perry so she thrust that thought to the back of her mind.

"How's your mother?" he asked, curving an arm around her shoulders.

"I think she's feeling better. Come and say hello."

Imani led her friend into the living room.

"How are you, Mrs. Celeste?" Leaning close, Damon Kessler kissed her mother's cheek.

"I'm actually feeling better, Judge," her mother replied, her face wreathed in a smile. It was no secret that she had a big crush on Judge Kessler. "This is my friend, Annie Elder. She's going to spend the night so that you and Imani don't have to rush back."

Damon nodded. "We appreciate that." Turning to Annie Elder, he took her hand and introduced himself. "So where are you two young people going?" Imani's mother asked.

Imani said nothing as she took a seat on the couch beside Damon. She'd already answered several variations of the same question earlier.

"There's a formal affair at the Ford Mansion for the Democratic Party's nominee for the Michigan Supreme Court," Damon informed them in his cultured voice.

"It sounds so exciting." Her mother's eyes sparkled.

"Maybe you could go out with us when you're feeling better," Damon offered.

"I couldn't do that." Mrs. Celeste blushed.

"Yes, you could, Mama," Imani said, "We'll make it a date."

"Then I'll look forward to it." Her mother beamed.

"I'll even find an escort for you," Imani added.

Her mother's expression sobered, determination hardening her facial expression. "That won't be necessary."

Imani shrugged, struggling to control her reaction. "Whatever you say."

Judge Kessler checked his watch. "We've got to get going."

As Imani and Damon stood up and said their good-byes, Imani wondered at her mother's change of mood at the mention of an escort. She knew that her mother had divorced her stepfather several years ago. Imani had found out the hard way that he'd had a thing for young girls and it had taken her years to get over the damage he'd caused in her life. She wondered, if he had turned her mother off men forever. When she and Judge Kessler drove off in his blue Mercedes, her thoughts turned back to her own problems.

Chapter 2

At the Ford Mansion, Imani and Damon worked their way through a long receiving line to meet the party's state supreme court nominee and then spent quite a bit of time circulating among Damon's many friends in the legal profession. Hours later they retired to their own table.

"You're unusually quiet tonight." Damon reached across the table to take Imani's hand and give it a squeeze.

"I had an exciting day, so I've got a lot to think about." Imani sipped her Margarita.

Damon gave her a sympathetic look. "Your mother?"

Imani fiddled with her straw. "No, although she gave

me enough to think about today, too."

"Then what?"

"I saw Perry in the supermarket and he had the cutest little baby in his arms."

Scooting his chair closer, Damon's shoulder brushed hers as he gave her hand another squeeze. "The child was his?"

Imani shook her head. "I thought it was. Today I found out that he's not married and he insists that he wasn't messing around with that starlet-harlot."

Damon chuckled. "Rasheeda?"

Nodding, Imani continued, "He wants to get back together."

"And what do you want?"

Imani shrugged. "Time and space to make up my mind for good. I still care about him but…"

"You're no longer certain that he's the one?"

"I don't know what to think."

Damon tapped the table with his fingertips. "Didn't he cheat on you while you were carrying his child?"

Imani found herself defending him. "I don't know that for certain."

"But early in the pregnancy, he did ask you to abort the baby?"

Imani stared down into the golden liquid filling her glass. "You know he did."

Damon's direct gaze demanded her attention. "Imani, I don't understand. You're so special and your beauty is not even half of what makes you so special. Perry's had his chance. He hurt you a lot. Don't you think it's time you moved on?"

This time she smiled. "You don't understand. I did move on. I've climbed out of my depression and I'm more mature, but it's hard to completely let go of the past. Before Perry, I'd never even been in love."

Damon's eyes narrowed. "So you still love him?"

"I—I don't know," Imani stammered, "but whatever it is, I don't want to ever go through it again."

"That sounds pretty final to me. You've no reason to think things would be any different this time around. I'm not trying to tell you what to do, but if it were me, I'd run for higher ground." Damon stood. "Want to dance?"

"Yes." Imani rose already rocking to the beat of the old Temptations tune, "Papa Was a Rolling Stone." At least ten years older than she, Damon had taught her all the dances that went with the golden oldies. She was always eager to show them off.

After a strenuous round of dancing, they returned to the table. Imani sank into her chair, fanning herself and calling for a fresh drink. "I shouldn't have let you talk me into wearing a long dress," she laughed, focusing on an attractive girl in a classic but seriously short dress that just barely covered the essentials. "I know she's cool."

"That's DeAndra," Damon said, getting to his feet.

"I don't know why she'd come to an important event like this dressed like that!"

"This is the 'teenager' you've been helping?" Imani asked incredulously.   Her lips curved in amusement. The young lady she saw didn't appear to need help from anyone. Although she was petite, she had a curvy little shape and walked with confidence.

"She's no longer a teenager, but she's still in law school," Damon said impatiently. "I hope no one from the law firm spots her."

"What law firm?" Imani asked curiously, knowing that her friend had dropped his load of clients as soon as he'd become a judge.

"Abrams, Abrams, and Wright."

"Hmmmh." Imani declined to comment at hearing the name of her friend Ramón Richard's law firm. Damon Kessler was still one of the partners and he only recommended the best students for the firm. She sat back in her chair to watch Damon as the girl arrived at their table.

"Hello, Judge Kessler," the girl said in a voice that managed to sound sweet and provocative at the same time. The short, wispy cut of her hair emphasized the delicate shape of her head and her big golden brown eyes. A straight little nose and full, sensual lips rounded out her appeal. As she stood on tiptoe to kiss Damon Kessler's cheek, the hem of her dress threatened to expose sacred territory. "I was hoping I'd see you here." Damon leaned close to DeAndra Blake. "I like to see a nice pair of legs as much as the next man and that metallic silk camisole you're wearing is very attractive, but what happened to the bottom of your dress?" he asked her in a low voice.

DeAndra merely laughed and said, "I thought you'd say something like that! You've got to understand that this is what people are wearing now."

"Really?" Damon tilted his head in amusement. "I suggest you look around the room and see exactly how many people are wearing dresses like yours now."

DeAndra's gaze slowly swept the hall until it returned to rest on Damon. "I guess I'm embarrassing the firm," she said in a more subdued tone.

Damon nodded. "Something like that. When you're socializing on a professional basis, it's always better to be conservative."

"I guess I should go." DeAndra's eyes never left the judge's face. From her rapt expression, Imani could tell that Damon Kessler's opinion meant a lot to her.

"Not just yet." The judge clasped her hand. "First I want you to meet my friend, Imani Celeste."

DeAndra greeted Imani, shook her hand, and said, "I've seen your pictures in newspapers and a lot of magazines."

Imani returned the greeting with a smile and said, "And I've heard a lot about you from Judge Kessler."

DeAndra's facial expression brightened as she turned to Judge Kessler. "You talk about me?"

Damon nodded gingerly. "Yes, when I just can't help

it. It's usually a sign of mounting frustration." He hugged DeAndra's shoulders affectionately for a moment. "Sit with us for a little while. Imani, do you mind?"

"Of course not." Imani accepted a fresh drink from the waiter and took a sip. "I'm still cooling off from all that dancing."

Damon motioned the waiter back. "What do you want to drink?" he asked DeAndra.

"A glass of Piesporter."

Damon narrowed his eyes.

"I'm over twenty-one," DeAndra said defensively.

He nodded slowly. "Yes, you are. Sometimes I forget." He gave the waiter the signal to get DeAndra's drink.

"Did you bring a date?" Imani asked DeAndra.

"Oh! I forgot!" DeAndra stood up and looked around the room again. Within minutes she was energetically waving at someone across the room.

"DeAndra," Damon called, his attention focused meaningfully on the disastrous effect her hand waving was having on the hemline of her excuse for a dress. When she didn't respond, he deepened his voice and drew out the syllables of her name.

DeAndra turned, saw where Damon was directing his attention and shrugged. Slowly she lowered her hand and straightened.

A fresh-faced young man of average height arrived

to stand by DeAndra. Grinning sheepishly, she apologized for leaving him, then introduced him to Damon and Imani as one of her fellow law clerks at the firm.

DeAndra's drink came shortly after they were seated, so the young man ordered a drink for himself and turned his attention to Imani.

"Imani," he gushed, "I never thought I'd see you in such a staid place."

"Staid?" Imani lifted an eyebrow.

"As in a bunch of stuffed shirts, nerds, and otherwise boring people with impressive titles," Damon answered for him.

The young man's face reddened. "Sir, I wasn't trying to say…"

"You wouldn't," Damon chuckled, "but that doesn't stop you from thinking it."

The waiter brought the young man's drink. Recovering a little, the young man turned to Imani again.

"Could…could I have your autograph?" At her nod, he produced a pen and started searching his pockets for a piece of paper.

Taking the pen, Imani wrote her name on the white cocktail napkin and gave it to him.

DeAndra finished her drink and retrieved her silk evening purse from the table. "I've got to go."

"It was nice meeting you both," Imani said politely as she started rocking to the beat of the Whispers' "Rock Steady."

The young man didn't move. Instead he eyed Imani hesitantly. "Could I have a dance first?"

"Sure." Imani rose and led the way to a clear spot on the dance floor. Instead of doing the dances she'd been using all evening, she asked him to show her some new dance steps. Soon they were burning up the dance floor and having a good time. When they got back to the table, Imani was so warm that she asked for a glass of water.

"Do you want to dance?" the young man asked DeAndra.

"No," DeAndra answered with a smile, "I think I should be getting back. If you're not ready to leave, I can get a taxi."

The young man rose. "I don't mind leaving now. Besides, we need to discuss that brief for tomorrow."

After the young couple left, Damon turned to Imani and said, "I enjoyed watching you dance with that boy, but it made me feel a little old."

"You're not old, Damon," Imani scooted her chair a little closer, "just more seasoned and distinguished. I like that in a man."

Damon took her hand and gave it a squeeze. "Well, since you put it like that…"

Imani chuckled. "I do. Besides, you're only thirty-six. You've got at least another twenty or thirty years before you should even think of being old. Are you sure DeAndra's not wearing you out?"

This time Damon chuckled. "Sometimes she is really too much, but I enjoy her zest and enthusiasm for life.

When I first met her she was in juvenile court for truancy and although she hadn't spent much time in school, she was smart as a whip. I did everything I could to challenge her. I even made her contribute to her own defense."

Imani caressed his hand affectionately. "I can see that you're proud of her."

Damon covered her hand with his other hand. "Yes, I am. She's come a long way. I think she'll make an excellent lawyer."

"Are you mentoring any others?"

"Oh yes. They call themselves Kessler's Clerks, despite the fact that I've found some of them positions in various firms in the area."

"I think it's great that you make time in your busy schedule to help some of the young people in the community."

Damon shrugged. "Just investing in the future. Are you still spending most of your Saturday mornings in the hospital ward with the AIDS babies?"

"Yes." Imani freed her hands to fiddle with the stem of her glass. "Sometimes it's so hard just to be with them, especially when they're real sick. They did nothing wrong and yet so many of them will never have a normal life."

Damon shot her a penetrating look. "Seeing Perry with that baby brought back a lot memories, huh?" he asked astutely.

Instead of answering, Imani sipped her drink.

In the background, a slow, romantic ballad began to play. Standing, Damon extended a hand. "Come on, let's dance."

On the floor, Imani went easily into Damon Kessler's arms. As they negotiated the dance floor she closed her eyes and found herself thinking of Perry. Damon was a good dancer, but Perry had been better. Perry had held her as if she were the most precious thing on earth and he was afraid she might break. Could she ever forget how special they'd been together when times had been good? It was true that she'd matured since she'd ended their relationship. Had she outgrown Perry?

When Imani came home that night, both her mother and Mrs. Elder were in their beds asleep. She was grateful for the chance to go out and have a good time with Damon, because despite the fact she could afford to hire help to care for her mother, she still put in a lot of her own time. Sometimes she felt herself slipping back into the well of depression she'd so recently escaped.

Later that week, Imani and her friend Roxanne were running at Belle Isle Park when Imani spotted a familiar figure coming towards them in black running shorts and a tank top. Her steps slowed. Still not quite ready to face Perry, her thoughts turned to escape. She wondered if he'd seen her.

Noting the direction in which Imani was looking,

Roxanne adjusted her tight shorts and said under her breath, "Oooh! Hunk on the horizon! Now there's a man who could spread my jam any day of the week."

"That's Perry!" Imani hissed.

"So much the better!" Roxanne continued, "You don't want him."

"That's not what I said," Imani snapped irritably.

"Yeah?" her friend challenged, "then how come you've got that standoffish look on your face?"

Tightening her lips and rolling her eyes at Roxanne, Imani didn't answer. Instead, she looked at Perry and tried to see him through Roxanne's eyes. At six feet, five inches, he towered just enough over her five feet, eleven inches, and the man was no bag of bones. The milk chocolate skin covering his chest, arms, and legs simply rippled with well-defined, sculpted muscles that made you yearn to spend the day exploring his assets. He was a mystery man too, with a hint of gold in those brown eyes. A woman could realize her dreams if she smoothed her fingers across the intricate planes and angles of his face and kissed those soft, full lips.

When he reached them, they greeted each other and Imani introduced Roxanne. "Perry," Imani said, "I'm surprised to see you here."

He gave her a slow smile. "I don't know why. This place has always been on my list of favorite places to run."

At his words Imani realized that his statement was

fact and wondered how that once well-known fact had slipped her mind. Judging from his expression, Perry obviously had his own idea.

He took her hand and clasped it. "It's good to see you. Did you just start your run or are you guys just finishing up?"

"We're in the middle."

"May I join you? Or would you rather I just run along behind you two? You'll hardly know I'm there." Imani knew better. She'd seen the way his stare left her face to linger on the swell of her breasts in the short gold tank top and the length of her legs in the matching shorts. She could still remember all the things he'd said about her 'bubble butt." He'd spent more than enough time kneading and massaging it. How could she run in silk shorts that barely covered the cheeks of her rear with him right behind her? She was a model, yes, and used to people looking at her, but she'd never been intimate with those people the way she'd been with Perry Bonds.

"I know that basketball season's over. Do you think you could keep up?" she asked, knowing he couldn't resist the challenge.

"Just watch me," he said confidently.

"We're just going to jog, right?" Roxanne asked.

"Yeah, but Imani's issued a challenge," Perry answered, "so I think your jog's about to get a little more aggressive."

"You're in good shape," Imani told Roxanne, "let's

go." She took off with a brisk jog and Perry and Roxanne were right with her.

For once, Imani had no time to people watch or enjoy the lush green grass and leafy bushes bordering the trails, the ducks floating effortlessly on the surface of the sparkling blue waters, or the occasional bird flying by. She concentrated on moving her legs, maintaining her pace, and regulating her breathing.

After a couple of miles, the muscles in her legs started to ache and her chest burned, but she was determined to give Perry a run for his money. She made it two thirds of the way through the next mile before she stopped and virtually fell down upon the grass to rest. Perry was at her side and Roxanne close on her heels.

Gasping, she opened her water bottle and greedily swallowed mouthfuls of the clear, refreshing liquid. She paused to slant a glance at Perry and Roxanne. Perry was drinking from his water bottle, a fine sheen of moisture on his forehead and chest. Imani refused to let herself even think about the things she and Perry would be doing now if they were still together. She turned her attention to Roxanne, who lay on the grass panting.

"Are you all right?" Imani asked Roxanne.

"Yeah." Roxanne turned on to her side and sat up. "But I think I'm through exercising for the next three days."

"I thought you were in better shape than that," Imani said with disappointment.

"If you need a partner before then, I'd be happy run with you," Perry offered.

"Thanks." Imani's voice lacked enthusiasm. "I'll call you."

Perry watched her with narrowed eyes.

Feeling the heat, she added, "I'll probably call the day after tomorrow."

"I'll look forward to it."

Imani said nothing as she massaged the sore muscles in her calves. She was angry with herself for showing off enough to cause pain.

"Let me do that." Before she could protest, Perry's warm, magic fingers were effectively working out the pain.

"Ow, ow, owl, oh!" she cried out as Perry worked at the knotted muscles in one leg, but soon found herself sighing. The man definitely knew what to do. After he used the same procedure on the other leg, she felt so relaxed that she stretched out on the grass.

"Should I return the favor?" Imani asked, eyeing his strong, athletic legs. She really didn't need the temptation that touching him so familiarly would cause.

"I don't really need a massage right now because I'm still in good shape," he quipped with a smile. "It hasn't been too long since the basketball season ended. Can I take a rain check?"

"Sure." Imani flipped her ponytail over her shoulder and pillowed her head on her arm. She didn't intend to be around to return the favor but she wasn't about to tell him that.

"Could you work the soreness out of my leg muscles too?" Roxanne asked in a voice that was entirely too innocent.

Perry gave her a slow smile. "Sure. I'd love to."

Imani felt the steam rising from her head. She could see right through Roxanne, but could Perry? she wondered. Men were such fools sometimes, she decided as she harrumphed to herself. Roxanne's breathy little o's and ahs got on Imani's nerves, bringing on genuine annoyance. Imani tried to lie on her side with her eyes closed and think about her upcoming assignments, but a particularly provocative sounding sigh caused her to open her eyes.

The contrast of Perry's milk chocolate-colored hand on Roxanne's golden tanned leg was riveting. Roxanne's eyes were sexy and flirtatious. His sparkled with amusement. Did either of them realize that she was still with them? Irrational jealousy burned like acid and ate at Imani's insides.

Turning her head, Imani strove to think about something else, but the little scene went on for ages. Finally she stood, unable to take anymore. "I'm ready to walk back to my car," she announced.

Immediately, Perry stood too, a knowing look in his eyes. "I'll go with you," he said to Imani. He turned to Roxanne. "Why don't you rest here and let Imani bring the car back to pick you up? Your muscles are still pretty tight."

Imani wondered that Perry could say that with a straight face. It should have been obvious that Roxanne was putting-on in a blatant attempt to flirt with him. Or was he really that gullible?

Roxanne's face colored the tiniest bit as she agreed. Then her glance slid to a point behind Imani and her eyes lit up. The girl was man crazy.

Imani could almost hear Roxanne saying, "Hunk on the horizon! Hunk on the horizon!" Turning in the bright sunshine, she headed back to her car, still feeling the weight of Perry's stare on her.

When they were out of Roxanne's sight, Perry touched Imani's elbow. "You weren't jealous, were you?" Perry's astute question startled Imani. Snorting with defensive laughter she quipped, "Dream on, Cookie."

"I must be dreaming," Perry snapped back, "because it's a beautiful day, we're together, enjoying each other and we're not arguing."

"That could be arranged." Imani glowered at him.

"I really bring out the best in you," Perry remarked, clipping his water bottle back to his waist.

"Why do you think I keep fighting the idea of us getting back together?" Flipping her ponytail behind her, she pushed damp tendrils of hair away from her face, "Do you think I like being so bitchy?"

"I know why," he said smugly. "You're afraid of me,

of us."

"No," Imani corrected him, conflicting emotions building within her, "I've just never been through such a difficult and emotional time in my life as when we were together except when Mama kicked me out and I had nowhere to go."

"But have you ever had a better love than ours?" Perry drew her beneath the shelter of a tree.

Imani set her back against the trunk. Blinking to stall the stinging threat of tears at the back of her eyelids, she drew a shaky sigh. "No, Perry." She grazed her bottom lip with her teeth. "But I need some peace and understanding in my life and I can't see us getting there."

"Okay, Ne-ne," he said in a low tone. Standing in front of her, he gently brushed stray wisps of hair from her face and kissed her eyelids.

Imani trembled from the contact, her senses scrambling. She'd always been like putty in Perry's capable hands.

"Even I know when to throw in the towel," he murmured, his fingers sliding gently from her temples to her cheeks. His beautiful leaf brown eyes were intense.

Imani tilted her face up, her eyes locking with his. She knew what was about to happen and a part of her rejoiced, eager to prove that it could not be as good as she remembered.

Perry bent toward her, his mouth covering hers in a hot passionate swirl. His tongue danced in her mouth, caressing and inciting an ache that had her quivering inside.

She leaned into him, her hands clutching the still damp swell of his biceps, tasting him, drinking him, yearning for something she'd been missing for a year. "Perry," she moaned when his lips left hers. Her arms locked about his waist.

He held her in his arms for a moment, his long fingers stroking her hair.

Imani snuggled against him, absorbing his strength and vitality. It felt like heaven.

Then he dropped his arms, took a step back, and scanned her features. "Take care of yourself."

Imani watched him turn and walk away. "I will," she promised. As she walked to her car alone, she wondered why she felt so bereft. Yes, she was still attracted to him, but she'd gotten what she wanted, hadn't she?

By the time Imani got her car and drove back to the spot where she'd left Roxanne, the sun had gone in, casting a gray tint on the previously bright day. Now it looked as if it would rain.

"Where's Perry?" Roxanne asked as she got into Imani's sports car.

"He had to go." Driving off, Imani gave as little information as possible. "Did you talk to that guy who was running by?"

"Yes, but he was nothing like your Perry." Roxanne clicked her seatbelt. "Let me know when you're done."

"We're done," Imani said evenly.

Roxanne stared at her. "Then you must be hiding someone because except for your pal Judge Kessler, no one I've seen you with comes close."

Imani shrugged. "I don't really need anyone right now. Can we talk about something besides my love life?" Roxanne smiled. "Did the change in the weather get to you?"

Imani nodded, her attention on the road. As the first few drops of rain hit the windshield, she realized that she felt like crying. It made her more determined than ever to forget about the past.

Judge Damon Kessler arrived at the restaurant on time for his prearranged appointment with DeAndra Blake and found her sitting at a window in the sunshine poring over a legal brief. She looked like a taller, prettier version of actress Jada Pinkett. Spotting him, she stood, took his hand and kissed his cheek, her young and delicately featured face sparkling with excitement. He wasn't so old that he didn't appreciate the sight of her shapely legs in her short but otherwise conservative navy suit, or the provocative scent of her cologne. DeAndra had always pushed the limits of conservatism and always would. He'd realized long ago that some day she was going to make some lucky man an exciting wife.

"I'm sorry to ask you to read this brief at the last minute like this, but I have to give it to Ramón Richards by three o'clock today and I really need it to be the best," she began when he was seated.

"I'm sure that what you've prepared will be fine," he replied, "you're the most promising student I've mentored." Pointing to the legal papers she'd been studying he asked, "Is that the brief?"

"Yes," she answered, placing it in his hands.

Without another word, he plunged into reading the document that stated an opinion and cited various cases and precedents for the sentencing of children in cases involving murder.

The waiter arrived at the table and DeAndra ordered a glass of wine. When he ordered coffee, she amended her order to coffee.

Damon could feel the weight and energy of her eyes upon him as he read the brief. It was excellent, truly inspired. He was on page three when the coffee arrived so he stopped to add cream and sugar and take a few sips. DeAndra gave him an anxious smile. "Well? What do you think?"

Damon set his cup down. "No complaints or criticisms so far." Then he read on, his mind delving deep into the arguments she presented. When he'd finished, he sat back and considered her.

DeAndra sat clutching her coffee cup and nervously biting her lower lip. This time she didn't prompt him for his opinion, but the hopeful expression on her pretty face gave him every assurance that she was all but holding her breath in anticipation of his evaluation.

"Excellent work," he said finally. "Your arguments are compelling and your choice of precedents supports them."

DeAndra gave a heartfelt sigh. "Whew! Thank you."

"The work speaks for itself," he said seriously. Then he gave her two more precedents to support her arguments.

Producing a little notebook and a pen, she quickly wrote the information down.

Damon finished his coffee and checked his watch. "I should be going."

DeAndra reached over to place a soft hand on his. "I—I was hoping you'd stay and have lunch with me, my treat, because I really appreciate all you've done for me…"

Scanning her features, Damon wondered at the fact that she still seemed a bit flustered. He'd praised her work. Any lawyer worth his salt would have. So what was bothering her? "DeAndra, I have to be back at court before one o'clock and you don't owe me a thing."

"I want to have lunch with you," she admitted artlessly.

Damon's mind considered all the reasons why this attractive young law student would want to have lunch with him. She didn't need to impress him; she already had, several times over. He was already mentoring her and her future looked successful. He was thirty-seven-years old, thirteen years older than DeAndra, and much older than any of the young men he'd ever seen her with. "Is there something else you'd like to discuss?"

"I'd enjoy your company."

He'd been planning to grab some fast food on the way back to court and review some records, but there was nothing urgent. More than a little curious, he nodded. "I'll stay for a sandwich."

The waiter placed glasses of water on the table and gave them menus.

After they'd ordered, she remarked, "You know, you used to spend a lot more time with me."

Memories played in Damon's mind, causing him to smile. "You needed someone to spend a lot of time with you. It didn't take long for me to realize that a lot of what you did in the past was done for attention."

She returned his smile. "And because I could get away with it."

"That too." Damon relaxed against the back of his chair.

Her eyes sparkled with a faraway look. "I'll never forget the first time I saw you. You were so handsome and successful. When they assigned you to my case, I was in heaven. Then when you had the nerve to make me work on my own defense, I resented it like hell, but no one else would even consider helping me. My aunt had given up on me a long time ago."

"She just didn't know what she had," Damon assured her. "You were a diamond in the rough, and one of the smartest, most intelligent kids I'd ever run across."

"I'm not a kid anymore," she said softly.

"No, you've grown into a beautiful young woman with a promising future in the legal profession." Damon accepted his corned beef sandwich from the waiter and put his napkin in his lap. "I have to keep reminding myself of that fact."

"I noticed." DeAndra accepted and checked her club sandwich.

The fragrant aroma of corned beef drifted in the air, causing Damon's mouth to water as he lifted half of the thick, grilled sandwich and took a bite. He hadn't realized he was that hungry.

"Did you know I had a serious crush on you?" DeAndra asked between bites of her club sandwich.

Remembering some of her antics, Damon chuckled. "I suspected."

"You were my hero," she said, her mahogany brown eyes intense, "the man of my dreams. I idolized you. No one I knew grew up to go to college and become a lawyer. A lot of people I knew then never even lived long enough to grow up."

Finishing half his sandwich, he wiped his fingers on the napkin and lifted the other half of his sandwich from the plate. "You've more than thanked me for my efforts by realizing the potential I saw in you, DeAndra. What's going on in your life now?"

Her eyes were magnetic and compelling. "I'm in love with an older man and he doesn't even know I'm alive." Startled, Damon considered her words in silence. "Did I start a tradition?" he asked finally.

She looked a little nervous and uncomfortable. "Yes, you did," she answered seriously.

"Is he in the legal profession?"

DeAndra nodded. "And he's about your age."

"I don't know how I can help you with that," Damon told her honestly, still getting used to the idea that his little DeAndra was lusting after an older man.

"Tell me what you think of girls my age and men your age getting together romantically," she said.

Damon shrugged. "You've met my friend, Imani," he said with a smile. "She couldn't be more than two or three years older than you, but she's mature for her age and she's pretty worldly. If you're talking about someone like Imani, age doesn't matter."

Swallowing another bite of her sandwich, she asked, "You don't think I'm mature for my age?"

"I think you've grown a lot, but you've still got a ways to go before I'd consider you mature. Enjoy your youth, DeAndra. On you it's very attractive."

"I guess that's a compliment," she said as she finished her sandwich and wiped her mouth and fingers on the napkin. Her eyes darkened. "Are you in love with Imani?"

Again Damon smiled at the thought of his gorgeous friend. "I don't know. Maybe. But we're not talking about me, are we?"

"No." DeAndra looked uncomfortable.

Damon checked his watch. "DeAndra, I've got to go. Ramón will be happy with the work you've done." Pulling out his wallet he tossed a twenty on the table. "This should take care of everything."

DeAndra grabbed the twenty and thrust it back at him. "No, this is my treat."

"If you insist." Damon shrugged, throwing her a tolerant look.

"Yes. I do." DeAndra dug a twenty out of her purse and placed it on the table.

Damon stuffed his twenty back into his wallet. As he stood and turned to go, he said, "Good luck with your older man."

"Thanks." DeAndra's voice lacked energy and enthusiasm. "And thanks for your help," she called after him.

Chapter 3

Perry parked outside the new offices for the McCleary Modeling Agency and got out of his car. In the warm, spring air filled with laughter and music, he walked past the banner touting the ribbon-cutting celebration to push open the front door. Mariah McCleary Richards spotted him immediately and came to greet him with a smile.

"I was wondering when you'd show up." She gave Perry a hug as she accepted his kiss on her cheek. "You've only got about an hour of daylight left to get out there and enjoy the view."

"It's good to see you, Mariah." Perry scanned the room, looking past several groups of people talking, laughing and dancing for a glimpse of Imani.

"Good to see you too. If you're looking for Imani,"

Mariah said carefully, "she's out front waiting for a ride on the boat of my father-in-law. Avery's been taking groups of people down past Belle Isle, over near Chene Park and close to the Canadian border."

"Where's Ramón?"

Mariah grinned ruefully. "He's out back harassing the catering guys. The shrimp, chicken, and shish kebabs weren't enough for him, so he insisted on making his barbequed ribs."

"With the special sauce?" Perry asked, his mouth watering at the thought of Ramón's trademark barbeque sauce.

"You've got it. I made him promise to save me a couple of bones."

"I think I'll go see how he's doing," Perry said as he turned and headed for the door. "See you later."

Out front a group of people were milling around close to the dock. It wasn't hard to spot Imani in a daring blue jean jumpsuit with several woven strips cut out and the edges coated with gold. Three-inch heels added to her height and the black silk of her hair floated like a cloud around her face and shoulders.

Just looking at her, Perry felt his temperature rise. He'd almost talked himself out of coming because of the things she'd said in the park, but Ramón and Mariah were his friends too. And he had promised to come and help them celebrate the opening of McCleary Modeling Agency's new site on the banks of the Detroit River.

The pleasant expression in those exotically-slanted eyes of hers changed to one filled with determination and defiance when she caught sight of him watching her. They stared at each other until Imani put a hand on one hip and made an elaborate turn. She was ready to do battle and wouldn't be making it easy for him to spend time with her.

Who says you have to? Perry asked himself as he continued following the curve of the wraparound deck to the back of the building. He was used to women chasing him, and it wasn't just because of his position on the basketball team or his lucrative salary.

Some of the people in the rear of the building were dancing to music from the live Caribbean band. Lynn Ware, Mariah's newly promoted assistant, and Anthony LeFarge, her Italian designer boyfriend, sat at a table between the stage and the grill talking quietly. Perry greeted them on his way to the grill.

"We haven't seen you in a while," Lynn said as he kissed her cheek. "How have you been?"

"Fine, I've just been lying low since the season ended."

Anthony shook his hand. "How's the injury?"

"I can't complain. I just have a twinge every now and then."

"I think Imani's missed you," Lynn said carefully. "She's just coming back to herself after everything that's happened."

"Let's not talk about Imani." Perry shifted his feet and worked to keep some of the frustration out of his face and voice. "You guys doing all right?"

Lynn nodded politely and Anthony said he couldn't complain. Promising to come back later to sit with them, Perry headed for the grill.

At one grill a couple of guys in white chef hats and jackets were grilling shish kebabs, shrimp, chicken, and steak. At the other, Ramón Richards was working in a white chef's hat with the words 'Chef Estupendo' print- ed on the front in large black letters and a large apron with the words 'Chef Estupendo Fantastico Hermoso' printed on the front.

"Hey Ramón," Perry began after they'd greeted each other, "I don't know much Spanish, but does your hat say 'chief stupid'?"

"Okay smart ass!" Ramón laughed. "You really don't know much Spanish and you obviously can't read. This chef stuff is a gift from my mom. My hat translates into 'Super Chef' and this apron says 'fantastically handsome super chef. "Got that?"

"I guess." Perry examined the meat on the grill. "I'm looking forward to some fantastic, super barbequed ribs." Ramón gave him a paper plate. "Well, you've come to the right place." Spearing a rack of ribs with a fork, he took a knife and cut five bones off the short end. "Good enough?"

"It's a good start." Perry helped himself to some of

the bread on the table near the grill.

"Need a drink to go with that?"

Perry turned to see a tall, attractive woman holding two beers and offering him one. "I wouldn't mind," he said with a smile as he accepted the drink.

"I've been sitting over there," she said, pointing to a small table on the grass. "Would you like to join me?"

"It sounds like a good idea," he answered, following her to the table. After they'd introduced themselves, he was surprised to discover that instead of being a model as he'd assumed, she was a lawyer who worked for Ramón 's firm. Although he really wasn't interested in her personally, Perry enjoyed talking to a beautiful woman for a change without having to actively pursue her or put up with her temper tantrums.

After about an hour, he got up and went to sit with Lynn and Anthony. It didn't take long for him to notice that the sexual tension between the two of them was so thick you could have cut it with a knife. It was in the way Lynn's eyes lit up when she looked at Anthony and the way he responded. You'd have thought he was in heaven.

Not liking the direction of his thoughts, Perry looked back at the grill. Mariah and Ramón were playing around and teasing each other. When they shared a tender kiss, Perry looked away. Maybe it was time to go home.

"Perry! I was hoping to see you here." Roxanne,

Imani's running partner and Tina, another one of the agency's models, sat down for some conversation. Despite his protests, they drew him back inside the building to dance to the live rhythm and blues band and the musical selections of one of Detroit's hottest DJs.

Gyrating, posturing, and dancing to the upbeat music, Perry enjoyed himself. Between the two women, he lasted only an hour before they all retired to a table on the edge of the dance floor for refreshments.

He'd already downed a glass of punch when he spotted Imani watching him from the other side of the dance floor. Although her facial expression was calm enough, anger and jealousy glittered in her eyes. Suddenly all the fun he'd had so far paled in comparison to what used to be, what could still be.

When Imani realized that she'd been caught watching him, she quickly turned away and began responding to the man at her table who'd been talking to her all along.

Perry took it all in stride. He was through trying to get Imani's attention. Long ago he'd realized that the best things come to those who wait. The problem was that he'd never been able to take his time and wait with Imani. He promised himself that this time he'd wait until she realized that she still loved him.

As the hours flew by, more and more of the guests left. He refused an offer to accompany Roxanne and the other model to an after hours club. Because he had nothing more interesting to do, Perry stayed and enjoyed the music, refreshments, and pleasant company. Before he realized it, there was no one left but himself, Mariah, Ramón, and Imani.

Shuffling a deck of cards, Ramón sat down at Perry's table. "Want to play some Bid Whist?"

"Yeah, but I'd rather play partners," Perry answered.

"Let's see if Mariah will play."

When Mariah agreed, she brought Imani with her and they decided to play the men against the women. Sitting directly across from Ramón, Perry shared a corner of the table with Imani. For the first time all evening he was close enough to smell the light musk scent of her perfume. As she scooted her chair closer to the table, an errant lock of her hair brushed against his arm. Unable to resist, he slowly turned to look at her.

The dramatic fringe of her lashes lifted to expose her sherry brown eyes, filled with challenge.

Ignoring her facial expression, he smiled and complimented her on her appearance.

Her lush, currant-colored lips momentarily formed a pout and then she murmured her thanks.

As expected, Ramón and Perry quickly won the first two games. Then wounded pride forced Mariah and Imani to get serious with their playing style. Both women were delirious when they won the third and fourth games.

The fifth game was a battle. Ramón bid a five, but

57

Imani won the bid with a five special. Mariah sighed meaningfully as Imani turned over the cards in the kitty and made her selection. The women won the first three hands easily, but then Ramón put the men in the game with an ace of spades and then the two of spades. Mariah produced another ace, bringing the ladies up to a total of four books.

"One more to go," Imani said, easing out a three of clubs. She smiled when she saw that Perry's card wasn't the same suit. That smile disappeared when Ramón produced a two of clubs.

"Sorry, babe!" Mariah slapped the ace of clubs on top of the pile.

"We won!" Both women gave each other the high five and danced around the table.

"Should we take it back? Come on, one more game?" Ramón asked Perry.

Perry stood. "No, man. I'm a little tired. Time to go home and hit the sheets."

Imani stood too, yawning and obviously tired, but still looking beautiful. "The car is in the shop so I came with a friend. I'm going to call a taxi."

"It's really not necessary," Perry told her, "I can drop you off at your mother's on my way home."

"No, I'd rather take a taxi," Imani said stubbornly.

"We'll drop you off on our way home," Ramón said in a voice that brooked no input as he rose from the table.

"Ramón, it's not on your way home and you know

it," Imani returned shortly. "I don't want to put you and Mariah to any trouble."

"It is definitely on my way home and it wouldn't be any trouble," Perry said in a voice oozing with patience, "but if you feel uncomfortable…"

Imani slanted him a glance filled with annoyance. Perry had no doubts that she felt she was being manipulated. "Just let me get my purse," she said in a resigned tone.

Perry and Ramón exchanged meaningful glances.

"This could be your chance," Ramón told Perry as soon as Mariah unlocked her office door and the women disappeared inside.

Perry tightened his jaw. "No," he told Ramón, "I'm not chasing her this time. I'm not playing her game. If she wants a different life with someone else, she's welcome to it."

"Sometimes you have to show people that you're the one they really want," Ramón said in a voice filled with the wisdom of experience.

"Yeah," Perry said as he pulled his keys from a pants pocket, "and I'm not going there. Imani's given me the boot for the last time."

"Man, you know she's crazy about you." Ramón lowered his voice as they heard sounds of the women returning.

"That remains to be seen," Perry said succinctly as the women reentered the room and started the round of hugs and kisses that went with good-bye.

In the car on the way home, Perry was silent for the first solid fifteen minutes.

"How's your mother?" Imani asked, breaking the silence.

"She's fine," he answered in a neutral tone. "She's been asking about you."

"Oh?" Imani's voice lilted with surprise. "Maybe I'll call her."

"Don't," he said quietly.

"Why not? We always got along real well."

"It would give her hope, make her think she's still got a chance of making you her daughter-in-law," he said, turning to give her a look filled with criticism as they stopped at a red light.

"Oh." Imani's disappointment colored her voice and she stared at him uncomfortably. "I guess I wasn't thinking."

"How's your mother?" he asked, ignoring the little voice inside that told him that he should care less.

"M-Mama's dying." Imani blinked several times, then turned to look out the window. "She's got high blood pressure, a heart condition, and failing kidneys. The only way I found out was because Reverend Allister, the minister of her church, thought I should know. Can you imagine that?" Imani asked in a choked voice.

"No, I can't." Perry opened the case between their seats to reveal the box of tissues he kept there, but kept his eyes steadfastly trained on the road. The last thing he needed to see was Imani crying.

"I was angry for years about the way she treated me, about the way she wouldn't listen when she kicked me out of the house, but I-I still loved her." Her voice rose and fell with emotion.

Perry heard the sounds of her gathering tissues from the box and blowing her nose. In the past, he would have pulled over to the side of the road to comfort her, but now he kept driving. Imani wanted nothing from him and it was time he faced that fact.

"I still love Mama." Imani drew out a long, tearful sigh. "She's all I've got."

In another time and place, he would have told Imani that she had him, because he still loved her, but Perry kept his mouth ruthlessly shut. It hurt to sit and listen to Imani's pain, but he knew that she needed to talk to someone.

"Six months," Imani mumbled as he pulled up outside of her mother's house, "a year if she's lucky. Perry, what am I going to do?"

Looking at her in the car illuminated by the nearby streetlight and seeing the teardrops caught in the fringe of her lashes, the dewy look in her exotic eyes and the slight trembling of her lush mouth, Perry could come up with only one word. "Survive."

Imani's eyes widened and then she reached for him, pulling him closer and stretching her body across the seat to place her hands on his shoulders and her face on his chest. She trembled.

Perry's heart did a tap dance, a rush of pleasure radiating through him at the touch of her body. He ached for her. Reining himself in, he decided not to hug her because he wouldn't be able to stop there. Instead, he patted her back awkwardly until she calmed enough for him to pull away, get out of the car, and come around to the passenger door.

Letting him help her out of the car, Imani balanced effortlessly on three-inch heels as he walked her up the stairs. Outside the front door she turned to him, her eyes filled with need. "Please Perry," she cried in a near whisper, "I just need a hug."

He opened his arms and she fell into them, her head on his chest, her arms winding themselves around his neck. Her scent tantalized his senses as he held the warm softness of her body as if he would never let her go. She was his. He wanted and needed to be with her, to love and protect her forever.

Hugging him tighter and tighter, her soft breasts pressed against him, Imani rubbed her face alongside his chest. Her soft sighs and the heartfelt noises she made in her throat caused a roaring sensation in his ears as he felt the pull of happier times.

Perry's fingers trailed down her temple and his lips bestowed a kiss there. His hands slid up and down the curve of her back, gripping her tiny waist. "Imani," he whispered, throwing caution and resolve to the wind, "You're not alone. I still love you."

She stiffened in his arms, slowly dropping hers. Smothering a groan she stepped back out of his embrace, shaking her head. "That's not what this is about," she said, a sharp aggressiveness creeping into her tone. "I-I'm upset right now. Yes, I've made some mistakes, but I can't go back to that one. Can you understand that?"

Perry clenched his fists at his sides, his eyes full of Imani's blazing eyes and the furious set of her lips. An answering feeling of frustration sprung up within him and forced its way to the surface. "No, Imani!" he said so vehemently that she startled, "I'm tired of this bullshit!" Then he took a few moments to control himself. "I don't understand and I don't agree, but it really doesn't matter, does it?" he continued in a lower, more controlled voice. "The next time I see you in the supermarket, you won't have to run. I'll just pretend I didn't see you and it'll be the truth because you're no longer the woman I fell in love with, the woman I've always considered the love of my life."

Pivoting, Perry turned and headed back down the steps. At the bottom, he paused to add over his shoulder, "I'll be in my car until you get in the house."

He saw Imani staring after him, her face a mask of indecision before she turned and huffed her way into the house. When her front door closed, Perry tried to see it as a door slamming closed forever on his past with Imani.

Perry spent the rest of his way home berating himself for tossing out his rules of engagement. He was supposed to drop her off and keep things on a civil level. It didn't matter that he'd weakened when she'd raised those tear-filled ebony eyes and asked for a hug. He'd known that she wasn't herself.

"It really is time to move on," he sighed as he stopped at a red light. At twenty-eight, he felt like a veteran in the dating wars and was not looking forward to future combat. He'd never really understood women. But for a time it'd seemed that he and Imani shared a special understanding in addition to a powerful attraction to each other. Even now, he blamed himself for the negative turn their relationship had taken because of his initial response when she'd told him of her pregnancy. He'd never been married and was fighting increasingly complex and emotional ties to Imani at the time, so who could blame him for suggesting abortion to give them a chance to sort out their feelings? She'd never forgiven him for that, and losing the baby had made things too painful to deal with.

He thought of his brother Phil and his wife Cherise, and a familiar pang of jealousy hit him. They were ecstatically happy together and their baby, Jimmy, had simply added icing to the cake. Why couldn't life have been as easy for him? Before Imani, he'd been somewhat cynical in his views on women and hadn't expected much in the way of relationships. Now he had a standard that would be hard to beat and he really didn't want to try. Sighing again, Perry turned into the driveway of his Palmer Woods home.

Weeks later Imani dressed carefully for her date with Damon Kessler. She poured herself into a slinky black sheath that hugged every curve, the jewel-shaped neckline dipping low to reveal her cleavage. Change was in the air and she couldn't help noticing it. He'd been different with her for several weeks now, kissing her more often and more passionately. She hadn't discouraged him because she liked Damon and knew him well. She even loved him a little. They'd been friends before Perry, but not nearly as close as now. Damon Kessler was the sort of man she'd always dreamed of marrying: stable, distinguished, a pillar in the community, yet fun loving, handsome, and kind. He was the type of man her mother had always wanted for her. She asked herself, Why did you ever let Perry Bonds move you off the path you'd set for yourself?

Damon arrived on time for their date and gave Imani a hug. Then he spent several moments just looking at her, his green eyes intense, before he told her that she was beautiful and complimented her on her clothing and appearance. Cupping her face in his hands, he kissed her deeply and passionately.

Imani leaned into him, enjoying the kiss because she genuinely liked the man. With her head against his chest, she felt the tension strumming throughout his body and realized that the kiss had really moved him. On the contrary, she felt relaxed, her mood pleasant. She was never going back to the aching, earth shattering, and addictive kisses she'd shared with Perry and that suited her just fine.

She smiled at Damon and his eyes darkened with desire.

"It's a good thing you're staying here with your mom," he murmured under his breath, "because when you look at me like that, I could forget about the damned show and stay here with you."

Imani laughed. "You know you really want to see that show. You've been planning this for months."

Damon took her hands and kissed them. "That's true, but you could easily make me forget about it. You could make me forget my own name."

Leaning towards him, she kissed his cheek, then kissed him on the lips. "I don't want to make you forget anything. Shouldn't we be leaving?"

He checked his watch. "Yes. It's almost eight o'clock. Let's go," he said, opening the door and leading Imani out of it.

The show at the Fisher Theatre was a musical mystery that had Imani perched on the edge of her seat with excitement and guessing till the end. When the curtain went up, they stood in Damon's private box and gave the cast a standing ovation.

After the show, Damon took Imani to Charlie's Crab

in Troy for a late romantic dinner and cocktails at a booth in the back. A live band played a musical version of an old hit in the background. Listening closely, she recognized the tune, "Will You Still Love Me Tomorrow?" As she sipped her wine, Damon took her free hand.

"Over the past few weeks I've gotten closer to you than I ever dreamed possible," Damon began, his eyes filled with emotion. "Do you know that I love you?"

"I hoped," she replied honestly.

"Well, I do love you," he continued, his hands caressing hers. "You're genuine, smart, beautiful, and sophisticated, everything I've ever wanted in a woman. Being around you simply makes my day and when I'm not around you, it's as if the sun doesn't shine. Will you marry me?"

"Oh Damon!" She threw her arms around his neck, hugging him tightly as she waged a war with herself. This was what she wanted, the life and love she'd have, the kind of man she'd never have to wonder and worry about, and yet she hesitated. Deep down inside, a weak little part of her still longed for Perry Bonds, and no matter how hard she tried, she hadn't been able to kill it.

"I'd make a good father and I love children. We could have as many as you want." He stroked her cheek. "You're shaking Imani. Are you going to turn me down?"

"No!" she managed, thrusting the weak part of herself to the background, "but I want a long engagement." Damon tilted her chin up and looked into her eyes. "How long?" he asked gravely.

"A year? We could spend the time planning the wedding and then I would be ready..."

Damon's thumb caressed the soft skin on her hand. "To sleep with me?" Damon finished for her in a low voice.

"Yes." Imani searched his face, trying to guess his thoughts. "I'm sorry, Damon. I-I'm just not ready yet."

"I suspected as much." Damon bent his head in disappointment.

"Maybe we should wait until I'm ready for everything," she suggested. "I don't want to hurt you or cause you pain."

"No," Damon insisted stubbornly, "I'd rather know that you belong to me, even if we haven't been intimate. I love you, Imani. Don't you love me at all?"

"Of course I do." She tugged his head down and pressed a gentle kiss to his lips. Then she scooted close and pulled his arm around her. "It's just that I've gone through a lot and even though my body has recovered, I still feel wounded in mind and spirit."

"Will you marry me?" Damon asked again, gathering her close to the warmth of his body.

"Yes," she answered, her smile widening when he produced a black velvet box and opened it to reveal a two-carat diamond solitaire surrounded by a cluster of smaller diamonds.

"Then you've made me very happy," he said, curving the other arm around her to place the ring on her finger. "It's beautiful, Damon." Imani fought inexplicable tears as the diamonds sparkled and flashed brilliantly. "Thank you."

Damon's arms tightened around her. "No, thank you, my love. We're going to be gloriously happy. We're going to buy a house on the lake and we're going to have a houseful of beautiful, intelligent kids that we'll spoil ridiculously, and you'll only have to work if you want to."

"Sounds like a dream," Imani murmured, trying to picture the house and the children and marveling that one of the chubby little babies was not unlike Perry's nephew Jimmy.

"It's my dream," Damon told her.

"It's our dream now." Imani lifted her glass. "Let's drink to us."

They heard the musical sound of Damon's beeper just as they set their glasses back on the table.

"Do you think it's an emergency?" Imani asked in concern. Damon's beeper rarely went off.

He pressed a button and stared at the display for a moment. "No, it's probably nothing serious. It's DeAndra Blake. I wonder what she wants…"

Imani gave Damon a tolerant smile. "Me too."

It was late when Imani let herself into the silent house. Locking the front door, she glanced at the mail in the basket on the table and froze when she recognized the distinctive envelope from Henry Ford Hospital.

She'd been expecting the bill, but hoping against hope that the hospital would take its time billing her and that the amount would be something she could afford. Gritting her teeth, she tore open the envelope and stared at the cold figures on the page. Imani mouthed the words in dismay. Thirteen thousand dollars

Last month's medical bills had amounted to twenty-five thousand dollars and the insurance had paid next to nothing. Her mother had no way of paying on her own and Imani had been dipping into the money she'd saved to live on when she became too old to model and would be forced to retire. She couldn't afford to continue like this. What was she going to do? In the short term, she could always take more assignments, but because her mother needed her, she could only work so much.

Seeking to shake the worry from her thoughts, she focused on the ring on her finger as she headed for bed. When she passed the kitchen, she heard a soft, muffled sound. Stiffening, she slowly pushed open the kitchen door. Her mother sat at the kitchen table drinking tea in her old blue robe.

"Mama!" Imani exclaimed in surprise. "Are you feeling all right?"

Her mother nodded, her long braid bobbing behind her. "I couldn't sleep. It seems that the better I feel, the less I can sleep."

Imani strolled over to the refrigerator and opened it. "Want something to go with that tea?" she asked, staring at the contents.

"No, I'm fine," her mother retorted, "and I don't need you to serve me. Sit down and talk to me."

Imani pulled out a chair and sat down. "Mama, I got engaged tonight."

Her mother gave her a soft smile. "I knew it was coming. So you and your Perry finally made up."

"No, Mama." Imani threw her mother an incredulous look. "Perry and I are through. Damon Kessler proposed tonight and I said yes."

"Why?" her mother asked, scanning her face.

"Because we love each other, why else?"

"You don't think you could be running from Perry?" her mother asked, her sherry brown eyes clearer than they'd been in months.

"Mama, you've never even met the man," Imani snapped irritably.

"I didn't need to. We weren't speaking when you were seeing him on a regular basis, but don't think I wasn't following the two of you in the magazines and newspapers. You were so happy that you sparkled like a precious diamond and risked your life to carry his baby."

Imani's hands twisted in her lap. "I don't want to talk about Perry, Mama."

"Then let's talk about you and Judge Kessler. I know that you're good friends and all, but that's not the kind of love to carry a marriage. You wouldn't be doing him any favors and I'm speaking from experience."

Experience? Mama was speaking from experience? At this tantalizing bit of information, Imani stared at her mother. "What do you mean?" she asked, thinking of her mother's wild and handsome second husband, with whom Imani had clashed on numerous occasions. He had also been instrumental in getting Imani kicked out of the house.

Near the end, he'd gotten so bold that Imani hadn't been able to pass without him trying to touch her. She would never forget how frantic she'd been when he'd finally caught her. Refusing to follow the memory to its conclusion, she forced her thoughts back to her mother. "Are you talking about Louis?"

Mama twisted her lip stubbornly. "I've said all I'm going to." She reached for Imani's hand. "Let me see your ring."

Imani laid her hand across her mother's palm, smiling at the thought of the wonderful future she'd have with Damon.

"It's a lovely ring and it set him back a bit too." She turned Imani's hand in the light. "I figured the man had good taste and I was right. When are you getting married?"

"About a year from now."

"Why are you waiting so long? With your connections you could have the wedding of the year in just a couple of months."

Imani retrieved her hand, lowering her eyelids to hide her annoyance. She had a feeling that her mother knew why she wasn't racing to the altar. "Which one is it, Mama?" she asked. "Am I running away from Perry or dragging my feet to the altar with Damon?"

Mama raised her eyebrows and said, "You know, I've let some things slide, but I'm not too sick to get up from here and smack you down for disrespecting me."

Imani sighed. "Sorry, Mama."

"Now as far as what you doing with this getting married to the judge, who knows? The man's all right with me. I just hope you can live with him." All at once she seemed to fold in on herself to look old and tired.

Standing, Imani said, "Are you about ready to get back to bed?"

Mama nodded and Imani helped her up and walked her to her room.

Chapter 4

His ankle ached. It was enough to awaken Perry and send him scurrying to the kitchen for a glass of water and one of his pain pills. Once he'd downed the pill, he sat at the oak counter in the neutral-colored great room to look out past the deck into his backyard.

The steady patter of falling rain formed a soothing rhythm on the wooden deck, soaking into the dark green grass and vivid red and hot pink roses adorning his yard. Unlike most people, he liked the rain because it always made him stop and think about his life and where he was going.

He knew he wasn't getting any younger. That's why he'd scheduled a lunch appointment with his agent to discuss opportunities for increasing his income. He'd also scheduled an appointment with his financial advisor for later in the week. Now he needed to work on getting his personal life back on track.

Noting that it was nearly nine, and that he'd promised to play a few basketball games with his buddies, he got up and fried bacon and eggs. Then he put wheat bread in the toaster and made coffee. As he sat and ate alone at the counter, he realized that he was lonely.

In bygone days he would have been cooking for two while Imani set the table with those fancy plates, silverware, and napkins she liked, and instead of spreading the wheat toast with jam, he would have eaten bagels and croissants. Afterward they would have taken off to do something physical or slipped back into his bedroom to spend hours making love. Frustrated, Perry shut off all thoughts of Imani.

Why hadn't he gone to Vegas for the weekend with his teammates? he wondered. As he finished his meal and straightened up the kitchen, he resolved to put more effort into replacing Imani.

Hours later, feeling more relaxed with a couple of scrimmage games under his belt, Perry sat in the Union Street restaurant talking to his sports agent. "I know that I'm not a household name like Mike or Grant, but I'd like to get into being a rep for somebody," he said. "I've seen guys do cars, sportswear, vacations, airlines, cereal...I can't remember all the products."

"It's—doable," his agent said with a grin. "You were having a record season till you injured that ankle."

Perry nodded. "Tell me about it. When I think of all I could have done…"

"Don't sweat it. You're okay now and you've got a year left on your contract. I think they'll renew and we'll go for more money." His agent made a few quick notes on his Palm Pilot.

"And in the meantime?" Perry asked, seeking a commitment.

"In the meantime I'll make some calls and beat the bushes. In the early part of last season Top Pro Sportswear was looking for someone."

"Sounds good." Perry downed his second glass of water. As he started to put the glass down, his attention shifted to the tall, beautiful woman in a short, figure-skimming sheath entering the restaurant with an older, distinguished-looking man. He could tell when she spotted him because her distinctive, long-legged walk in that purple dress slowed almost imperceptibly.

"After all that's happened, it still looks good to you, eh?" his agent cracked, quieting when Perry threw him a quelling glance.

This was one time Perry wanted to be ignored. Just seeing the only woman he had ever proposed to with another man made his body vibrate with suppressed violence and frustration.

As the woman neared their table, Perry's pulse sped up and he caught a whiff of her delicate musk perfume. Beneath the table his hand clenched. He placed it behind him as he stood up.

"Perry," she said, managing to look tough yet vulnerable at the same time, "I wasn't expecting to see you here. How have you been?"

"I'm fine," he replied coolly, "What have you been up to?"

"Would you believe that I got engaged?" Imani blurted out. "It wasn't something I expected. I'd like you to meet my fiancé, the Honorable Judge Damon Kessler."

Perry couldn't breathe and his ears were ringing. He felt as if five of his fellow Pistons had fallen on his chest all at once. Forcing air through his lungs, he shook Kessler's hand, congratulated the couple, and murmured polite nothings that he didn't mean.

Perry could see that Kessler was no fool. He caught a hint of sympathy in the other man's eyes as they shook hands and saw Kessler shoot a probing glance at Imani, who was pretty nervous for someone who was supposed to be gloriously happy.

Something sparkled on Imani's long, elegant fingers. Perry wondered how he'd missed the obvious. Despite everything he'd said about giving up, he likened this moment to someone drawing the deadbolt on a door that was already closed. "Is that your ring?" he choked out.

Imani nodded, hesitating in the resulting silence, but finally lifting her hand to display a healthy-sized diamond solitaire surrounded by smaller stones.

Against his better judgment, Perry took her hand and

pretended to examine her ring. At the contact, heat radiated throughout his body. Would he always feel the intimate connection with her? He felt Imani trembling. "The ring suits you," he said, releasing her hand. "It's good that you've finally found someone who can make you happy."

The lids lowered over Imani's exotic eyes and lifted to reveal the liquid sheen of moisture as she thanked him and said her good-byes. Then Kessler led her away.

"She's a beautiful lady, but you, you poor bastard, are just wallowing in it," Perry's agent remarked.

"Not anymore." Perry sat down and took a long draught of his iced tea. "I'd say that being engaged to be married is pretty final."

"Huh." His agent let his glance drift over to the table at the window in the front of the room where Imani and the judge were ordering their meals. "It ain't over till the fat lady sings."

"Really?" Perry pulled a few bills from his pocket and tossed them on the table. "I don't plan to stick around to hear her." He stood and gathered his camera case and sports bag.

"Where are you going?" his agent asked.

Perry shrugged. "I don't know. They're having one of those festivals downtown on the waterfront and I thought I might get a few good pictures. Want to come?"

"No, I've got to see another client." The agent closed his briefcase and got to his feet. "I'll give you a call next week and let you know how I'm doing, okay?"

"Sounds good," Perry said as they turned and headed for the door. "I'd like to get something started before the season begins again."

At the table by the window Imani and Damon watched Perry and his agent pass the window on their way to their cars.

"He still has feelings for you," Damon remarked, his green eyes lingering on her face and assessing her, his fingers fiddling with her ring.

"Yes," she acknowledged, "I'm the one who ended things."

"I know that you really loved him. That's pretty obvious." Damon shifted in his seat. I see that he still makes you nervous."

Imani slanted him a coy glance. "Are you jealous?"

Damon shook his head. "No. I know you too well."

"Then what's the problem?"

"I actually felt sympathy for him."

Imani raised an eyebrow. She couldn't allow herself to acknowledge the sympathy she felt for Perry. It amazed her that Damon also sympathized with her ex. "Do you think I should give him another chance?"

"No." Again, the weight of his eyes lingered on her face. "I just hope you know what you're doing."

"I do." Imani smiled. "You're a wonderful man, the kind of man I've always wanted."

Damon left his chair to sit close to her on the padded

leather bench. "Well, now you've got me."

Laying her head against his shoulder, Imani closed her eyes and wished she could still the inner trembling that had started when Perry touched her. She looked forward to the day when she would see Perry Bonds and remain unaffected.

As their meal arrived, Damon's phone chimed. Apparently annoyed, he pulled it out, checked the number on the display, and then put it back in his pocket.

"Who was it?" Imani inquired.

"Just DeAndra." Damon put his napkin in his lap and picked up his fork. "Lately she's always calling and trying to get my opinion on her briefs, her career, and even her love life."

"I know that she admires you," Imani told him. "Have you ever thought it might be more than that?"

Damon chuckled. "She's admitted that she had a crush on me years ago, but now she's in love with someone else. It's someone my age."

"Is it someone in the legal profession?"

"Yes." He shoveled a forkful of pasta into his mouth.

"And you're sure that it's not you?" Imani picked and ate the dried Michigan cherries from her salad with her fork.

He nodded and chewed in silence.

"I'd just love to know who he is," Imani murmured as she continued to eat her salad.

Perry drove to downtown Detroit and parked in a lot

on one of the side streets that led to Jefferson Avenue. With his new camera slung across his shoulder, he walked to the park on the waterfront. As he neared the ethnic festival, the sounds of a rhythm and blues band filled the moist air. People danced and sang along while vendors plied their wares.

Sitting in the stands in front of the stage for hours, he listened to music and people watched. He almost laughed aloud when a brother got caught out with another woman. Both women verbally ripped him to shreds in front of God and everybody and then went their separate ways.

After a while, he took out his camera and snapped pictures of the performers and interesting people in the crowd, using the knowledge he'd gained in the photography class he'd taken years ago. Then he strolled around the different stands looking at the wares and taking pleasure in the crowd. People were enjoying themselves too much to recognize him and it felt good. A mix of English, Spanish, Arabic, and Polish stimulated his ears. Stopping at one stand, he bought a barbeque sandwich and a cup of lemonade, and took them to a stone bench facing the Detroit River to eat. Surging around him, people ate, drank, and partied. When he'd finished his sandwich, he snapped a few pictures of the Canadian shoreline and the restaurants, marinas, and lights on the American shore.

It was close to eight o'clock when Perry drove back to

his home and crawled into bed, satisfied with all that he'd accomplished and glad that his hobby had taken his mind off Imani. Tomorrow he'd get up and run, play a few games with his buddies and start looking for a new girlfriend.

Her mother was fast asleep when Imani tipped in and sent the sitter home. Locking the door behind the woman, she tried to ignore the two new envelopes on the mail tray with the distinctive insignia of Henry Ford Hospital. Mama's health seemed to be improving. Shouldn't the bills start decreasing or at least stop coming so often?

Halfway up the stairs to her room Imani turned around and went back for the mail. Ripping open the envelopes, she anxiously scanned the documents. "Diagnostic tests, blood tests, therapy, tests, consultation..." Imani's teeth grazed her lip.

She mentally added the figures and stuffed the papers into a pocket with a sigh. The bills totaled another twenty thousand dollars. She needed to make more money, fast. What was she going to do?

Her stomach gurgled and burned as she climbed the stairs. In her room she thought of her assignments and calculated the expected income. It wasn't enough to cover the new bills and replace the funds she'd already taken from her nest egg. She went to bed with her spirit swimming in a sea of worry and panic.

In the middle of the night she awakened in the darkness to get down on her knees by the side of the bed to pray. Her heart opened up and the words tumbled from her mouth in an angst-filled flood. Afterward, she climbed back into bed and drifted into a calming sleep.

Two days later Imani hurriedly stripped and stepped into the hot shower. She'd spent a grueling day at her so-called glamorous job in a skimpy swimsuit with an igloo and a lot of ice. They'd sprayed so much water that she'd thought she'd drown. Now she couldn't seem to get warm.

To distract herself, she turned on the television while she got ready for bed. She was watching a Revlon commercial when an incredibly simple idea came to mind. Why not lend her name and face to a signature line of cosmetics? Why not start her own line of cosmetics for women of color?

Excited, Imani called her employer, Mariah McCleary Richards, and left a message on her tape. Then she pulled out her yellow pages and looked at all the companies listed under laboratories and cosmetics. Sadly, the companies listed under laboratories were all involved in medical testing and the only company listed under cosmetics was Avon. Undaunted, Imani went to sleep with visions of dollar signs dancing through her head.

Going into the office for an early appointment with Mariah two days later, Imani was still excited. She spoke briefly with Lynn Ware, the agency owner's virginal assistant and Anthony LeFarge, her hot Italian boyfriend who still shared office space with the agency. Lynn glowed with happiness while Anthony virtually smoldered with sensual emotion, and they used every excuse possible to touch one another. It didn't take a doctor to know that they hadn't got around to doing the dirty deed. Imani knew that Lynn was pretty religious and had been under her mother's thumb for years. Moving to Detroit and having Anthony LeFarge as her boyfriend was probably the only way she had ever gotten out of line with her mother's expectations.

When Lynn and Anthony disappeared into Lynn's office, Imani checked her watch as she stood in the reception area. Almost nine-thirty. She heard the sound of a door closing, signaling that Mariah's nine o'clock had left by the rear door.

"You can go in now," the receptionist told Imani.

Mariah opened her office door before Imani reached it.

"Mornin' Imani, how are you?" Mariah greeted Imani with a bright smile.

Just then the outer door banged shut behind a handsome man in a blue designer suit carrying an armful of vibrant red roses. "Hey, gorgeous!"

"Ramón!" Mariah's eyes glittered with pleasure and excitement. "I didn't think you'd leave the office to come over here. I know you have to be—"

Ramón Richards strode past Imani to grab his wife

and stop her mid-sentence with a passionate kiss. Virtually oblivious to their audience, Mariah softened against him, tilting her face up to return his kiss with fiery abandon. Ending the kiss, he covered her face with ardent kisses and presented her with the roses he'd been holding behind her back. "These are for you, my love, my sweetheart, and the soon-to-be mother of my children."

"Thank you." Mariah's eyes shone with tears as she pressed a gentle kiss to his lips.

As Imani witnessed their emotional display of love, a rush of painful longing filled her. She'd only felt this kind of love for Perry Bonds and it had never been returned with the depth and commitment she needed. Ramón and Mariah had gone through a very painful time to get to their current happiness. Ramón had been almost killed in a car crash outside the courthouse before love and need triumphed over Mariah's fears.

"Cancel all your appointments between eleven and one, because you're having lunch with me," Ramón ordered as he gathered Mariah close with one arm and nuzzled her cheek.

"I'll ask Lynn to take my appointments," Mariah said.

In the background, Imani heard the door to Lynn's office open and Lynn and Anthony's voices as they talked in low tones.

Ramón turned to face Imani and the new receptionist, so happy he could barely talk coherently. "In case you guys haven't heard, we just found out this morning. Mariah's pregnant! We're expecting our first child!"

"Oh!" Imani rushed forward to hug Mariah. "Congratulations. I'm so happy for you guys!"

"Thanks. I'm still in a state of blissful shock," Mariah gushed. She turned to accept congratulations from the receptionist.

"Congratulations!" Imani told Ramón with a fervent hug. "I know this is part of your dream."

Ramón dipped and did a silly little dance. "I'm still dancing on air!"

"Mariah, ahhh!" Looking thoroughly kissed right as she stood outside her office with Anthony, Lynn Ware ran screaming to Mariah to give her a hug, and rock her from side to side. "This is fantastic. I can just about visualize a little MariahRamón. You're going to have a beautiful baby."

Anthony stepped forward as he finished shaking Ramón's hand and congratulating him to hug Mariah hard. "Congratulations! I've never attempted designs for babies, but you can count on me to come up with one of the most stylish maternity outfits you ever saw!"

"Thanks, Anthony," Mariah said. She took Ramón's hand.

"I've got to get to court," Ramón told her, "but I'll be back for lunch."

After Ramón left for court, Lynn went back to her

office and Anthony disappeared into the west wing of the building. Mariah found a large, white column vase for the roses and placed them on the conference table in her office. Then she invited Imani in.

"I'm sorry it's taken me a few days to get to you," Mariah said with a smile. "I haven't been feeling very well lately, but I had no idea!"

"I can see why you two are on top of the world," Imani said, ignoring the roaring sound in her ears and the dry, cottony taste in her mouth. Standing, she went to the conference table, filled a glass with water, and drank it. "Would you like some water?"

Mariah shook her head. "You know I made a few calls to shake the bushes on getting you a contract with one of the cosmetics companies. It'll be at least a week before I hear back from my contacts, but the really big contracts have gone to the big super models and a lot of the others have gone to very new faces who weren't billing at the rates you demand."

"No one's leaping at the chance to sign me, huh?" Imani asked sarcastically as she returned to Mariah's guest chair.

"Not for cosmetics," Mariah told her, "but they'd love to have you in that round of shows in Europe and you've been lucky enough to be offered a spot in the *Sports Illustrated Swimsuit Edition* if you want it."

"I want it." Imani leaned forward in her chair. "That'll get my name and face out there even more."

"And the shows in Europe?"

"I'm not sure I can get away for two weeks. I'll have to talk to my mother."

"How is your mother?" Mariah asked softly.

"As well as could be expected." Imani's hands clenched in her lap. "They think she's got less than six months because they can't control her blood pressure, her heart is weak, and her kidneys are failing."

"They've been wrong before."

Imani nodded. "That's what's keeping me going. I'm just trying to take one day at a time."

Mariah patted Imani's arm. "You've been pushing yourself very hard."

"I've had to. Mama's too young for Medicare and her insurance pays next to nothing. Thank God I've been saving my money."

"What about the retirement you've been saving for?" Imani shrugged, steeling herself against the sympathy in Mariah's eyes. She couldn't afford to feel sorry for herself and start crying now. "I don't know. I have to take care of my mother. When I can no longer get assignments, maybe I'll go back to school, get a job, and rebuild it. I'll do what I have to."

"I'm sure you'll be fine," Mariah said soothingly. "I'll get the *Sports Illustrated* details. If you're going on the European fashion circuit you'll need to leave as soon as possible."

"I'll discuss it with my mother tonight," Imani promised, certain it wouldn't be possible. Running off to Europe was something she wanted to do because there she'd be in exotic surroundings with other people in the same profession who really didn't know her. She could lose the self she was now, the self she didn't like very much. Imani gave herself a mental shake. Where had that thought come from?

At dinner that night her mother looked as healthy as ever in a flowered print lounging outfit Imani had given her. When Imani brought up the shows in Europe, she urged her to go. "Annie's taking me for those two dialysis appointments," she told Imani, "so you don't have to worry about me. I'll still be here when you get back." "Besides," she said fixing Imani with a penetrating stare, "I think you need to get away for a while."

Surprised, Imani fairly bristled. "I'm fine, Mama."

"No, you're not. You're sad and worried."

"I'm not sad, Mama," Imani said, working to keep the annoyance out of her tone, "I'm happy. I'm engaged to a wonderful man."

Her mother didn't bother to reply. Instead she sighed heavily and rolled her eyes.

Wishing Mama would quit trying to analyze her, Imani didn't make the mistake of engaging her mother in further conversation on the subject of Damon Kessler. Mama had already gotten it into her head that he wasn't the man for Imani.

Her mother drew the piece of apple pie closer, cutting into it with her fork. "If you're worried about all the bills, they'll all be paid when I die."

Imani drew in a quick breath. "What are you talking about?"

"I've got an insurance policy for two hundred thousand dollars. I've been paying on it for years. You're the beneficiary."

"I-I don't need your money, Mama. You already use most of your check for the doctor bills."

Jaw tightening, her mother raised her voice, "Well, I need to pay my own bills as much as I'm able, so you will use the money from the insurance policy, won't you?" Imani nodded. "Yes."

"And I'll look forward to seeing pictures of my daughter strutting around in some of those fancy clothes nobody can afford to buy."

Imani smiled at her mother. Going on the European fashion tour was going to be like a vacation.

Later that night Damon came and took Imani to the Comedy Club. Between shows she gave him the news. "What's wrong?" she asked when he was silent.

"I guess it's selfish, but I'd like you here with me."

"I'll only be gone for a couple of weeks," Imani said soothingly.

"It'll be a long couple of weeks." Damon moved closer. "Too bad I can't go with you."

She could barely imagine having Damon with her in Europe and knew she wouldn't be able to handle it, so she said nothing. Instead, she put her head on his shoulder.

"I thought we were getting closer," Damon said, putting an arm around her.

"We are." Imani stared into his sea green eyes. "I'll come back to you, I promise."

At that he chuckled and trailed a finger down her cheek. "You've already promised to marry me."

Imani threw him a daring look. "Do you think I'm lying?"

Damon pulled her closer. "No, I'm just going to miss you."

"I'll call you every day," she told him.

The European Fashion Tour was everything Imani could have wished for. She didn't have to worry about anyone but herself and she spent a few hours each day modeling fabulous clothes as she strutted down a runway. Every night they partied and she was content to dance and drink with the people there and go back to her hotel alone. On the two weekends she even managed to get in some sight-seeing.

In a New York office Perry Bonds pulled an expensive gold pen from the inner pocket of his gray, custom-made suit and wrote his signature at the bottom of a contract.

Beaming, the man across from him extended his hand. "We're all excited about this arrangement at Top Pro Sportswear and Apparel. I'm sure this will be a very lucrative and successful association for all parties concerned."

Perry shook his hand and watched his agent follow suit. "I'm sure it will."

The company rep continued, "One of the ad campaigns we're considering will focus on you and a female companion. We've narrowed our selection down to three models. Of course, the chemistry between the two of you will be the most important thing. Think great sports athlete with a beautiful woman on his arm... Who wouldn't want that sort of life?"

"I wouldn't mind it myself," Perry murmured.

"We'd like you to take a look at each of the finalists. There's a short biography on the back of the eight by tens." The man gave Perry a file. "Take your time reviewing the file."

Opening the folder, Perry's glanced at the first picture and the sight impacted him with the force of a punch to the stomach. Imani's exotic eyes stared back at him. Playing it cool, he glanced through the other pictures of her. In most, she modeled European designer fashions.

As Perry viewed the pictures, the company representative provided additional information. "Those are from the European Fashion Tour that ended just last month. She was a big hit in that."

Perry nodded, swallowing hard. Viewing the last couple of pictures heated his blood. Imani lay in the sun on a sandy beach. One shapely leg was drawn up at a right angle to her body and the other stretched out to the approaching surf. He followed the length of her legs to the semi-translucent leopard print bikini that barely covered the essentials. Her waist curved inward, her voluptuous breasts spread out like a feast. He could almost make out her nipples beneath the damp material. Forcing his eyes upward he took in her long, damp hair, luscious lips and the provocative expression on her face.

"That picture's a hot one, isn't it?"

The company representative's voice cut into Perry's thoughts, forcing him back to the task at hand. He was hard and glad he didn't' have to get up anytime soon. "Mmm-hmmm," he answered.

"Those last two pictures are going to be part of the upcoming *Sports Illustrated Swimsuit Edition*. The first is my vote for the cover."

"Mine too." Perry forced himself on to the next picture. Imani stood by a waterfall, one foot stretched behind her to emphasize her rounded derriere. The suit was another skimpy bikini masquerading as a one piece. A wide vee opened between her breasts, slanting and narrowing until it reached the bottom. The entire garment was made of a gauzy, semi-transparent material that was doubled or lined in the areas covering her breasts and crotch.

Hot in his custom suit, but not about to let anyone see him loosening his tie or undoing any buttons, Perry moved on to the next model. She had a more curvaceous body than Imani and a face like the girl next door, but she didn't affect him the way Imani had.

The last model was as beautiful and exotic-looking as Imani and was built like a dream. She was the kind of woman who attracted him and he sensed that that the chemistry would work. Common sense urged him to select this model and skip dealing with Imani, yet he hesitated. The last time he'd talked to Ramon and Mariah, they'd told him that she was working hard and taking extra assignments to cover her mother's medical bills. No matter how angry he was with Imani or determined to stay away from her, he still cared.

"You don't have to decide today," the company representative told him, "We'd planned to have the ladies in to snap a few pictures with you and see how it goes. We hope to have all the ads "

"Great." Perry folded his copy of the contract and put it in a pocket. Closing the folder and placing it under one arm, he stood and shook the company representative's hand again. "It's a pleasure doing business with you."

Outside the Top Pro Sportswear and Apparel office building, Perry loosened his tie and shrugged out of his jacket.

"How about a nice cold glass of water?" his agent asked, a wise expression on his face.

Perry didn't bother to answer.

Breathing in the scent of disinfectant, Imani entered her mother's house, closed the door, and scanned the mail tray. For once, she found a reason to smile. There were two checks waiting from the McCleary Modeling Agency and she knew that the amounts were more than generous because they included her income from the work she'd done for the European Fashion Tour, and the income from the glorious weekend she'd spent in the Caribbean working for *Sports Illustrated*. The money would go a long way towards replacing the funds she'd used to pay her mother's medical bills.

Placing the checks in the outside pocket of her purse, she strolled into the living room. Her mother sat in the black leather recliner watching her soap operas. Absently kissing her on the forehead, Imani sat down on the plastic-covered couch.

"Have you seen today's paper?" her mother asked when the station played a commercial.

"No." Imani leaned her head back against the pillows. "Why do you ask?"

"There's a feature on your friend Perry."

Imani shivered, a chill running down her spine. "He's getting married," she guessed.

"I don't know about that, but he just made a deal with Top Pro Sportswear and Apparel." Her mother waved a folded section of the newspaper at Imani.

"Read it for yourself."

Accepting the folded paper Imani read:

> Detroit Pistons forward Perry Bonds
> has just signed a ten million dollar deal
> with Top Pro Sportswear and Apparel.
>
> Paired with one of three models,
> Bonds will be shown on the basketball
> court and in other sports activities, and
> featured in and around town and several
> exotic locales wearing Top Pro clothing.
> An interesting note: One of the models
> is ex-girlfriend Imani Celeste, most
> recently seen on European runways and
> rumored to be on the cover of the
> upcoming issue of the *Sports Illustrated
> Swimsuit Edition.*

Imani's stomach fluttered uncertainly. Although Mariah had mentioned submitting her portfolio for a contract with Top Pro, she'd failed to mention that Perry was involved. That piece of information made all the difference in the world. Working with Perry would be next to impossible, especially since she was engaged to Damon.

Imani forced herself to breathe. They won't pick you, she reasoned, Perry won't let them. No matter what she wanted, she needed them to select her because if Perry was getting ten million, she had to at least be getting something close to one million. She really couldn't afford to turn away from a lucrative assignment like this, not when her mother was so sick. She glanced up from the paper to find Mama watching her.

"Do you think they'll pick you?"

"I don't know," she answered honestly. "Perry could nip that in the bud."

Raising her eyebrows, Mama smiled. "Would he?"

"If I were him, I wouldn't want to deal with me," Imani admitted, thinking of the way she'd ended her engagement to Perry, then allowed him to hope, only to turn around and accept Damon Kessler's marriage proposal.

"Then it's a good thing he isn't you, isn't it?"

Inclining her head, Imani sank into a cycle of worry until late that night when it occurred to her that there was no action she could take. The ball was in Perry's court and until he made his play, she could only wait. If she landed the assignment, she would keep things on a professional level.

Chapter 5

"Are you all right?" Imani stared at the modeling agency owner, Mariah McCleary Richards, who sat nibbling saltine crackers and drinking hot, decaffeinated tea. She was pale beneath her caramel brown coloring.

Mariah lifted bleary eyes. "No. My stomach's heaving and I haven't really had anything to eat yet." She gripped the edge of the oak desk. "I'm so nauseous I could cry."

Sympathy filled Imani's thoughts. She'd spent many a day just as sick as Mariah when she'd carried Perry's baby. Glancing at the white leather couch occupying a corner of the room near the window she said, "Why don't you lie down?"

Mariah forced down another mouthful of tea. "I was trying to get through all the business."

Imani smiled. "We're done, aren't we? We've reviewed my assignments."

"And you haven't forgotten the photo shoot this afternoon?" Sympathy lingered in Mariah's expression.

"Not hardly," Imani snorted. "It's going to be difficult, but I can do it." She stood and took Mariah's arm. "Here, let me help you over to the couch."

Mariah rose, leaning over the wastepaper basket with a serious case of the dry heaves. When she finished, a tear escaped the corner of one eye to slide down her cheek.

Pressing a tissue in her hand, Imani helped her to the couch. "Maybe you should go home."

Mariah stretched out on the couch with a sigh. "If I'm not better in the next hour, I will." She dabbed at the tear. "Ramón tried hard to get me to stay home today. He's been babying me something awful."

"He's a nice man," Imani murmured, remembering how much her friend had helped her during her problem pregnancy.

"Yes, he is," Mariah agreed. "I wouldn't trade him for the world."

Amid a lot of commotion in the outer office, a knock sounded on the door. Without waiting for a response, the door burst open and Ramón Richards stood in the opening with a carryout bag. Mariah's secretary stood right behind him. "I told him you were in a meeting," she explained apologetically, "but when he heard it was with

Ms. Celeste, he barged right in."

"Damned straight," Ramón chuckled, "Imani and I are old friends." He turned to Imani. "Looking good, girl. You don't mind if I interrupt, do you?"

Imani grinned. "Of course not. We were just finishing anyway. That's why Mariah's on the couch."

Striding into the room, Ramón placed his bag on the conference table and approached the couch. "Hello gorgeous! Feeling dizzy?" he asked, carefully perching himself on the edge of the couch.

"Nauseous," Mariah moaned.

"I think you should go home." Ramón stroked her cheeks and forehead with gentle fingers.

"I think you should be in court," Mariah shot right back.

"We're recessed until one o'clock," he said. "So I came to have lunch with you. I brought you some soup."

"What kind?"

"Chicken noodle."

"I can't eat right now." Mariah sighed.

"It'll be here for you to eat later," he said soothingly, his head dipping to drop a kiss on her lips.

This is what I missed with Perry, Imani reflected silently as she watched.

Ramón gently urged his wife onto her stomach.

Mariah grunted. "I wish you could take a turn carrying this baby."

"Me too, sweetheart." Ramón rubbed her back.

"What's going on?" he asked, turning to Imani.

"Photo shoot with Perry in about two hours." Imani stood and gathered her purse.

Ramón's brows lifted. "He made the decision already?"

"No. They're taking pictures of Perry with each of us to help make the decision." Imani's hands tightened reflexively on the handle of her Coach bag.

"If you want it, you've got it," Ramón told her confidently.

"Sometimes I don't know what I want." Imani moved away from the chair, surprised that she'd revealed so much of her thoughts.

"That's the problem, isn't it?" Ramón quipped with a wise look in his eyes.

Giving Ramón her best don't-mess-with-me facial expression, Imani shook her head and said her goodbyes. "Mariah, feel better, okay? Ramón, take care. See you guys later."

Leaving the office, Imani stopped for a quick salad at the Parthenon in Greektown and then drove herself to the local studio where the photo shoot was being held. Riding up in the elevator with her heart hammering in her chest, she reminded herself that she was a professional and she wasn't going to get angry, no matter what Perry did.

When Imani walked into the studio office with her makeup case, the first person she saw was Perry, standing near the reception desk talking to another gentleman. She felt her legs shake a little as she forced air through her lungs. Now that the basketball season was over, he'd let his hair grow into a flattering cut that emphasized his classic features. He'd also put a few pounds on his tall, slender frame. His gold and brown Top Pro warm up suit matched his leaf brown eyes and accentuated his wide shoulders and trim waist. When he greeted her, his expression was calm and his brown eyes sized her up and dismissed her without a visible shred of emotion.

Imani returned his greeting politely, feeling as if she'd been slapped, but she kept smiling. She didn't understand why Perry's attitude still mattered. She was engaged to Damon Kessler.

The other man stepped forward and introduced himself. "I want to congratulate you on those shots you did for the *Sports Illustrated Swimsuit Edition*," he told her, "especially the cover. I'm going to get mine coated with plastic."

"It was a nice cover," Perry added casually from his place at the reception desk. His sensual mouth curved into a polite smile.

"Thank you. I can get you a signed copy," Imani said to the company representative, giving him her trademark smile.

"Hey, I'd like that!" the man said enthusiastically.

Perry merely shrugged his shoulders. Clearly he felt she was yesterday's news.

Turning, the company representative pointed to a door. "They're waiting for you in there. For the first photo we're going for a casual look."

As Imani headed for the door, it opened and a small, dark-haired woman gestured her into the wardrobe room.

They'd selected three outfits that coordinated with Perry's for Imani to choose from. She examined the outfits, fingering the material and holding them up to her body in the mirror. Deciding on a gold and brown tweed jacket with matching pants and a color-coordinated gold top with a loosely rolled neck, Imani stripped and slipped into them. She added gold socks, coordinating jewelry from a manila envelope that had been attached to the outfit's hanger, and tennis shoes from the nearby rack.

Another woman entered the area to brush Imani's hair, pull it into a ponytail, and coil a braided strand around it. Then the makeup artist made her face up.

Perry's eyes narrowed momentarily as Imani reentered the studio, reducing her to the size of an ant. Their glances met and held, then he casually turned away. She sensed that he was still angry with her.

Do you want him to ignore you or cause a scene? she asked herself. A ripple of anguish surged through her, and the weak, helpless voice at the back of her thoughts cried, I can't do this! Imani straightened her shoulders and hardened her heart. She'd made her decision and promised herself that Perry would never hurt her again.

The Love We Had

The photographer explained his concept for the session and then had them pose at a white-covered table set with candles and fine china in a set mimicking an intimate French restaurant.

She caught a hint of the spicy aroma of his cologne on his milk chocolate-colored skin and unbidden memories filled her thoughts. Her pulse sped up. The scent had never failed to drive her crazy in the late hours of the night. She bit down on the inside of her lip.

Following the photographer's instructions, Imani sat on the edge of her chair, leaning forward to smile at Perry as if he were the moon and the stars, all she could ever desire. At the moment, it wasn't far from the truth. An almost tangible warm, sexual magnetism surrounded him, enveloping and dazzling her despite her best efforts to remain remote.

Something in his eyes caught fire and he smiled back with a daring, devastatingly sensual edge to all the warmth and charm that had made him irresistible.

Accustomed to using whatever inspiration was available to get herself into the desired mood for a photo shoot, Imani fought the effects of Perry's attention. Still, molten heat stirred within her, melting her insides to a tantalizing ache that centered between her legs and energized the tips of her fingers. She wanted to touch him. She found herself wondering, How long has it been since I made love with Perry?

"Fantastic!" the photographer crowed, snapping off

three pictures in rapid succession. "Same look, same mood, but offer her the glass of wine," he instructed Perry. Surveying the result for a moment, he added, "Imani, place your hand on his, as if you're accepting the glass."

Not giving herself a chance to hesitate, she followed the photographer's directions. She felt a throbbing current of electricity when her hand touched Perry's. A fantasy played in Imani's mind:

Perry leaned even closer and placed his hot mouth on hers in a searing kiss that left no doubts of his intentions. Shaping the classic curve of his head with her fingers, she relished the soft, wavy texture of his hair on her fingers and pressed herself against the hard warmth of his body. Moaning with pleasure, she savored the feel of his tongue mating with hers in a slow sensuous slide. His fingers trailed down her face, across her neck to caress her aching breasts through the tweed fabric of her jacket. Dispensing with the jacket, he lifted the bottom of the gold top to expose her naked breasts…

"Imani?" The photographer's voice cut into her daydream.

"Mmmh?" Blinking, she saw that both the photographer and Perry were staring at her. "Excuse me. I guess I was daydreaming. What did you say?"

"I said that what I've shot so far is great. You two have good chemistry going for you. We'll call and let you know about our selection next week."

"Thanks." Imani reclined against the back of the chair as the photographer started gathering his equipment.

"Daydreaming?" Perry murmured, his eyes smoldering. "Want to talk about it?"

In spite of herself Imani blushed. She used to tell Perry all her dreams and fantasies and then they'd act them out. Sometimes they'd even filmed them for their private pleasure.

"That good, huh?"

"It's not what you think," she lied, feeling his proximity all along the surface of her skin.

He chuckled. "It doesn't matter." Turning abruptly, he headed for one of the dressing rooms.

The studio door opened and an attractive woman with a short, chic haircut strolled into the room. "They said you were finished shooting," she said.

"We are," Perry answered, turning to take in the tall, voluptuous figure in the short red suit.

Nice face, good body, nice legs, Imani sized the other woman up. She was just the sort of woman Perry liked. When Imani considered the way Perry had reappeared in her life so determined to renew their relationship, it shouldn't have been so easy to replace her.

The woman walked over to Perry and pulled his head down for a kiss. "I made reservations for five o'clock. Do you have to change clothes?"

Perry grinned. "Not really. They're giving me a

wardrobe of Top Pro clothing. Does this look okay for dinner?"

Returning his grin she answered, "You look fine. You always do." She hooked her arm into his and then turned to face Imani as though noticing her for the first time.

"This is Imani Celeste, one of the models we're considering for the ad campaign," Perry said. "Imani, this is my friend Dr. Cynthia Williams."

Both women greeted each other politely.

"What is your specialty?" Imani asked, all too aware of the fact that Perry liked brainy women. She knew she wasn't stupid, but no one would ever call her brainy. She'd managed to get a degree in business from Wayne State University after several years' hard work, but she could never imagine herself focusing long and hard enough to get a doctorate degree.

"Sports medicine. I've been helping Perry with his ankle and he's been helping me get into shape." She shook Imani's hand. "Good luck with the ad campaign."

"Thanks," Imani murmured, "and if another woman's opinion makes any difference, you appear to be in good shape already."

Perry laughed. "I tell her that all the time. Personally, I like women with a little meat on their bones."

Imani felt her face burn. As a model she scrupulously watched her weight because the camera added pounds to her figure. Despite his words to the contrary, she'd always worried that Perry found her too thin, that he thought she didn't have enough meat on her bones.

Dr. Williams hugged Perry's arm to her chest. "You are a paragon among men. We'd better get going. It was nice meeting you, Imani."

Murmuring the polite response, Imani headed for the dressing room. Her head hurt and she felt chilled. Could she be coming down with a summer cold?

Changing back into her clothes and washing the makeup from her face, Imani thought about all that had happened at the photo shoot. Despite her engagement to Damon Kessler, she was still attracted to Perry. She hated that fact, but shouldn't have been surprised. After some wild, troubled, and turbulent teen years, she'd learned to keep to herself until she'd met Perry. She'd become a different person then, and only Perry knew just what a toll the past had taken on her.

You've got to stop comparing yourself with his women, Imani advised herself. You're no longer one of them. And if you get the contract, you'll have to avoid spending time alone with Perry. How difficult could that be?

Further north, at the Rochester Steakhouse, Perry and Dr. Williams placed their orders and settled back to talk. Piano music created a contemporary atmosphere. The restaurant hummed with the low buzz of private conversation and the fragrant scent of beef wafted through the air.

"That was your ex at the studio?" Dr. Williams asked in a matter of fact tone.

Perry nodded. "Yes. How did you know?"

"If I hadn't been following the romance in the gossip magazines and newspapers last year, I'd still know from the way you both tried so hard not to look at one another and the chemistry in the air. You guys were heating up the room."

Perry huffed. "Now you're imagining things."
"Am I? You're in love with her."

"I was," Perry admitted. "She's engaged to someone else now."

"So you've moved on?"

"I've been trying to. Are you going to help me?" Perry raised an eyebrow.

"Any way I can," Cynthia answered in a husky tone. She wet her lips and smiled at Perry.

Late that night Perry sat up after tossing and turning for hours. Thrusting aside the sheets, he got up and walked around the house in the dark. Glancing out his front window, he saw that nothing moved on the silent, tree-lined streets. A quarter moon gave everything a pale, surreal glow.

Replacing the blinds, Perry padded into the kitchen to make himself a cup of hot chocolate. Before he realized what he was doing, he'd added whipped cream and a cherry on top, the way Imani used to when he found it hard to sleep.

Shrugging it off, he went into the den and switched on ESPN. Settling into a plush velvet recliner with his drink, he tried to concentrate on the featured heavy-weight boxing match. Fifteen minutes later he was flip-ping through the satellite television channels restlessly. When he stopped on a channel that featured a couple rolling around on a bed, he realized just how horny and tense he was.

Perry stood and went to the watercolor portrait of his mother. Lifting it off the wall, he punched in a code on the exposed display. Tensely watching the door swing open, he pushed past the stack of stocks, bonds, and cash to the row of videotapes in the back. His fingers clenched the next to last tape in the group and he pulled it out. He didn't stop to think about what he was doing as he removed the tape from its cover and placed it into the VCR.

Imani's laughter filled the room. On the large pro-jection screen Perry saw himself dancing around the room with her and acting a fool as they practiced the ballroom dance steps they'd just learned. They stopped to kiss in a corner of the room...

In the next section of the tape Imani stood in front of the camera dressed in a red silk teddy complete with garters, stockings, and high heels. A red lace cape, com-plete with hood, covered her head and shoulders. Lifting the basket filled with champagne, cognac, appetizers, and fruit, she fixed the camera with a provocative look and cooed, "I'm Little Red and I'm on the way to Grandma's house. Want to come along?"

Perry watched as the story progressed. Discovering that Grandma had gone shopping, he, the big bad wolf in a G-string, gray cape, and wolf's head, goaded Little Red into sharing Grandma's basket of goodies with him. Removing her high heels, he pulled Little Red close to ease the stockings down her long legs and strip the silk teddy from her curvaceous body. Then he kissed every inch of her silky flesh until she screamed with pleasure. He spent the next hour enjoying Little Red on Grandma's king-sized bed.

By the time Imani's little taped fantasy ended, Perry had released all his tension. Feeling more than a little mellow, he placed the tape back in the safe and washed up in the bathroom before returning to bed.

With a sigh he covered himself with the crisp cotton sheets. In all the months they'd been apart he'd never so much as thought of the tapes and he'd never told anyone about them. It bothered him that seeing her at the photo shoot had weakened him enough to make viewing the tapes necessary. It was time he made new memories with someone else.

As he drifted off to sleep he promised himself that the next time Cynthia Williams invited him to spend the night, he would take her up on it.

Damon Kessler switched on his phone and checked

his voicemail. The three calls from DeAndra Blake got his attention. She was definitely in danger of becoming a pest with her incessant calls at the most inopportune moments.

He'd had a long, rough day in court with a controversial case involving a serial murderer and was looking at two more hours at least of reading legal briefs. Damon Kessler stared at his phone. His patience had worn through hours ago.

In the time it took to dial her cell phone number he attempted to calm down, but as he spoke into the receiver, frustration overwhelmed him and colored his voice. DeAndra's voice was unnaturally low and subdued as she answered.

"DeAndra," he began, "You've got to stop calling and paging me so much. I get a lot of satisfaction from helping young people achieve their goals in the legal profession, but I'm also a very busy man. Is there a valid reason for all these calls?"

"Yes. I really need to talk to you. Please come."

Listening to the choked sound of her voice, he realized that something had gone dreadfully wrong. "Where are you?"

When he heard the east side of Detroit address, he was on his feet in a flash. Didn't her grandmother stay over there somewhere?

Damon arrived at the address DeAndra gave him in time to see the coroner's wagon pull away. She stood on the small wooden porch wiping away tears with the back of her hand and crying brokenly. Apparently none of the neighbors standing in their front yards felt comfortable enough to approach her.

Getting out of the car and climbing the rickety steps of the little wooden A-frame, Damon approached her. "DeAndra, who did they take away?"

She turned watery red eyes on him, her teeth chattering. "Granny," she sobbed, "Granny's dead."`

Damon blinked in the afternoon sun, noting that the wagon had already turned the corner. This was only the second time in all the years he'd known DeAndra that he'd seen her cry. He gathered her slight form into his arms, his fingers stroking the short silky hair at the base of her neck. "Let's go inside."

Once he'd nudged her inside the neat little house, Damon closed and locked the door. Then he led her to the couch and simply held her until the tears stopped. "Can you talk about it?" he asked when she'd calmed. DeAndra lifted tear-swollen lids and nodded.

"What happened?"

"She wasn't feeling well, so she slept late," she croaked hoarsely. "When I looked in on her, she asked me for a cup of tea. When I brought it to her she wouldn't wake up!" The pitch of her voice rose painfully. "She was gone!"

"Had she been sick for a while?" he asked gently.

Blowing her nose, she nodded. "And she was eighty-six years old. But I thought she had a lot of good years left." DeAndra ended on a hiccupping sigh. The tears began again.

One of her small, cold hands held his so tightly that he winced. Using his other hand he loosened her grip and rubbed her fingers in an effort to warm them. In the doorway to the left he saw a kitchen. "I'm going to make you some tea."

"Don't leave me!" DeAndra held on to him with both hands.

"I won't." Damon stood with her clinging to his hands. "You can come with me." He inched awkwardly towards the kitchen with her and urged her into one of the yellow, plastic-padded chairs at the table.

While she slumped across the table, Damon heated water and made sweet, lemon-flavored tea. Then he set the cup in front of her and settled into the adjacent chair. "Did you call the coroner's office?" he asked, noticing that her hands shook slightly as she lifted the cup to lips. "Yes." She blew across the surface of the hot liquid and took a small sip.

"What about your mother and your brothers?"

"I—couldn't." She turned wide and watery eyes on him. "The only reason I called the coroner's office was because I knew that she wasn't going to wake up. I couldn't stand to look at her any more."

He touched her shoulder gently. "I think I know how you feel. My dad died suddenly when I was twelve. I was devastated."

"D-did you get over it?"

Damon stared down at the table, remembering the pain as if it had been yesterday. "It took years, and things have never been the same. We were very close." With her hands holding on to the lifeline of her teacup, she swallowed. "Granny was the only one in my whole family who understood me. She loved me."

"Do you want me to call your family?" Damon offered.

DeAndra nodded slowly.

Using DeAndra's address book, Damon made the necessary calls. Then he urged DeAndra to lie down while they waited for her family to arrive. Unwilling to be alone, she stretched out on the couch with a quilt while Damon sat in the chair by the fireplace.

She'd just fallen asleep when the doorbell rang. Damon opened the door to Mrs. Blake and one of her oldest sons.

"Thank you for calling us, Judge Kessler." Mrs. Blake turned red-rimmed eyes on Damon. "I knew Mama was sick, but I never thought…" She started crying.

Her son put his arms around her, murmuring softly until she was able to speak again.

"She was so feisty and independent that we couldn't care for her the way we wanted," Mrs. Blake continued in a strangled voice, as she walked into her mother's home. "DeAndra's the only one she'd see on a regular basis." Her eyes scanned the room, stopping on DeAndra's prone figure on the couch. "Is she—"

"Yes, she's asleep. She's still pretty upset."

"We'll take care of Dee." DeAndra's brother approached the couch.

"Damon?" DeAndra sat up on the couch looking lost.

"I'm still here." Damon approached the couch, "And so is your family."

"It must have been hard for you to be all alone with Granny like that," DeAndra's brother said, dropping down on the couch and putting his arms around her."

She nodded, tears slipping down her face.

Sensing that it was time to leave, Damon gathered his things. "If you need to talk, you know the number," he told DeAndra with a gentle touch to her shoulder. "If I'm busy, I'll call you as soon as I can."

Damon drove home in a reflective mood. His time with DeAndra had drawn him away from the worries associated with his job and made him remember how he'd felt when his father died. He was determined to provide any support she needed.

Imani entered the house feeling so tired and irritated she asked the nurse to stay for another hour. The photo session with Perry had taken a lot out of her. Before she could slink upstairs to rest, her mother called out from the living room.

"Imani, how'd it go?"

Dragging herself into the living room, Imani answered reluctantly, "Okay. The pictures will be nice." Her mother pressed the mute button on her television remote, her face animated despite the yellowish tinge to her coloring. "What did Perry say?"

Imani stalled, not wanting to think about the photo session, let alone relive it for her mother's curiosity. "Mama, I don't feel like talking about it."

"That's right!" her mother snapped, "I forgot that you don't feel like discussing anything important with me."

Rubbing a throbbing temple, Imani pleaded, "Mama, please! That's not it. I'm not feeling too good right now and I'm not up to going over how bad it was." "All right." Her mother used the remote to reactivate the sound of the television and sat back in her chair with her arms folded and a sanctimonious expression on her face. Anger vibrated through Imani. "You know, it's not as if you discuss anything important with me either."

Her mother snorted angrily. "Just what have you been trying to discuss?"

"I've asked about Louis several times now, and you've just ignored me."

Imani's mother blanched beneath her yellowish

beige coloring. "Maybe it just surprises me that you're so interested in the fate of someone so instrumental in getting you kicked out of the house at seventeen." Her jaw clenched stubbornly.

"Oh no, Mama, I think that's the best reason of all. How could I ever forget Louis and—and…" Imani's voice trailed off.

Her mother stewed in silence for several moments, her fingers fumbling with the remote. "We're divorced," she said finally. "What else is there to say?"

"Don't you want to know what really happened the night that—"

"No, I don't." Mrs. Celeste's voice overpowered Imani's. "I've had too many years to think about it. Nothing you could add would make me feel any better." Imani stared at her mother in injured amazement, but she kept silent out of respect for her mother's weakened physical condition. *What about me? Don't you want me to feel better about the past?*

Her mother clutched the remote in stony silence. She refused to look at Imani.

"I'm going upstairs." Imani turned abruptly and went upstairs to her room, but today her room seemed more like a prison than a haven. When she looked at the frilly bed and the girlish white furniture, all she could see was Louis's handsome face smirking at her as it had all those years ago.

Balling her fists, Imani closed her eyes. She'd had

years of counseling to help her get over the past, so why did she feel like crying? Louis had been an awful, manipulative man with a handsome face and a deceptively civilized manner. It was time she stopped letting him hurt her and her mother.

Easing herself down on the bed, she dialed Damon's house. When voice mail answered, she tried his cell phone. Again she got his voice mail. Damon rarely missed her calls. Fleetingly, she wondered if he'd been in an accident. Then common sense kicked in and she decided that he was probably overloaded with work.

Imani dialed the number for the agency she used and made arrangements for someone to sit with her mother when the nurse left. Then she got in her car and simply drove for an hour. When she'd calmed enough to notice her surroundings, she realized that she was a street away from her apartment. It felt odd to pull up to valet parking and let them take her car for the first time in months. Instead of taking the elevator, she climbed the curving wooden stairs to the second floor and crossed the thick gray carpet to her door. Sunshine and dust filled her apartment. Needing something to do, she cleaned it, vacuuming the thick vanilla carpet and dusting and polishing the expensive contemporary furniture.

While placing an envelope in one of the drawers in the coffee table she found the picture of Perry. His smile, friendly, generous, and loving yet sexy and so unlike the ones he offered earlier in the day, captured her. For a full

119

five minutes she fervently wished she could talk to Perry about her feelings and hear his opinion. Except for the time when she'd been pregnant, he'd always seemed to understand her and know just what to say. Then reality set in and she realized that there was too much separating them now.

Closing the drawer on Perry's picture, she thought of Ramón Richards who had been her friend and confidant for years. He was probably home fussing over his pregnant wife Mariah, who hadn't been able to keep anything down lately. Imani refused to intrude on their time together. That left her currently unavailable fiancé, Damon Kessler.

If I'm going to marry Damon Kessler, he should be the one I discuss my feelings with, Imani realized. I'm going to have to get a lot closer to him.

"I tried to reach him," she muttered under her breath. Checking the nightstand in her bedroom, she found her book of prayers. Then she stretched out on the bench in the bay window facing the river to read and pray. The sunlight filtering through the polarized glass warmed her skin and made her sleepy.

Hours later, the tinkling sound of the cell phone broke the silence in the room. Imani sat up in the warm darkness. She'd fallen asleep in the window. As the musical notes sounded again, she switched on the phone.

Damon's voice filled her ear. "Imani, I see you've been trying to reach me. Is everything all right?"

"I guess." Imani shrugged. "I had a headache and I've had a bad day. Between the photo shoot with Perry and an argument with Mama, I just wanted to run away."

"Sorry, I wasn't there for you."

"I am too. Where were you?"

"DeAndra's grandmother died and she was pretty torn up about it."

Imani leaned forward and turned on the lamp with a sigh. "I can imagine how she feels."

"I couldn't leave her like that, so I called her family and then stayed with her until they arrived."

Imani nodded in agreement. "You did a good thing."

"But I failed you."

She shrugged. "I'll survive, Damon."

"I know that. You're a very independent woman. I just want to be with you when you need me." His voice lowered suggestively. "Want me to come over?"

She considered it. "No. I'm fine now. I fell asleep and it must have helped."

Damon changed tactics. "Where are you anyway? I called your house and you weren't there."

Easing down on her side, she stretched out on the window seat again. "I'm at my apartment."

"Then maybe I should come over," Damon said. "I could provide lots of personal care."

"Damon, I'm fine," Imani protested.

"Not ready yet, huh?"

"No." Imani felt pressured. Despite her feelings for Damon, she wasn't as free with herself as she'd been in the wild days.

"Will you ever be?"

"Do you seriously doubt it?" she challenged.

"No," Damon huffed. "If I did, I'd break the engagement in a heartbeat." His voice softened. "I just get a little impatient because I really want to be with you. I love you."

"I love you too," she told him, while silently assuring herself that even though this love was not as consuming as her love for Perry had been, it was just as real. "See you at dinner tomorrow?"

"I can't wait," he said wistfully.

Chapter 6

Perry arrived on time for his meeting with Top Pro Sportswear and Apparel. He took a seat on the geo-metrically-patterned couch by the expansive plate glass window and relaxed with a bottle of mineral water.

When the company representative appeared, he was clearly excited. "All the pictures from the photo shoots turned out great, but some were simply spectacular. Can you guess which?"

Perry threw him a wary glance. "The pictures of me and Imani Celeste."

The man grinned. "You've got it!"

Perry shifted uncomfortably in his seat. He didn't need to see the pictures to know that he still had feelings for Imani and that it probably added an extra spark to the photos. He'd simply made a decision not to wallow in the pain of being around her and knowing that she belonged to someone else. "Has Imani been selected for the campaign?"

"That's up to you, bro. What do you say?"

"I want to see the pictures."

Five minutes later Perry sat at a desk scanning the stack of pictures. Each of the models was beautiful and seemed natural in the poses with him, but the pictures of him with Imani sparkled. He tore his eyes away from the photos and surprised himself by saying, "Looks like Imani Celeste is the one."

"Things seemed a little tense between you two. Is that your final answer?"

Perry returned his gaze steadily, not amused by the obvious reference to a famous line on "Who Wants to Be A Millionaire?" "Unless you want to second guess my decision."

"No. We'll give her the news this afternoon and make the announcement tomorrow."

"I'd like to talk to her first," Perry told him.

"Sure, be our guest."

A couple of hours later, Perry sat in a booth upstairs in the Traffic Jam restaurant in Detroit, waiting for Imani. He knew that Top Pro had called and asked her to meet him for lunch to discuss her future with Top Pro Sportswear and Apparel. They were also footing the bill. He watched dozens of professionally dressed people climb the stairs to sit in the area for lunch. The mellow sounds of a jazz radio station were audible above the buzz of many conversations. Automatically scanning the wine list, he opted for bottled water in deference to the basketball camp he had scheduled at a local high school for later in the afternoon. Knowing that Imani would probably be nervous, he ordered her a glass of Piesporter. Looking stunning in a burgundy silk jersey sundress that skimmed the curves of her body, Imani climbed the stairs· with undeniable grace. As she glided towards his table in matching heels, Perry's facial expression was calm, but something resonated deep inside him. He wondered if he would ever be able to look at her without feeling that she belonged to him.

After they exchanged greetings, she slung the waving length of her hair over one shoulder, slid into the booth, and leaned forward, her almond-tilted eyes sparkling. "Have I been selected for the ad campaign?"

"After we've had this talk, your selection will be final," Perry told her.

"Yes!" With a wide smile, Imani lifted a fisted hand and brought it down in victory. "I've had mixed feelings about this one, but I need to do it for a lot of reasons." Perry sipped bottled water. "I figured that."

As she watched him, a little of the sparkle left her eyes. Glancing away momentarily, she seemed to notice the glass of Piesporter. "Is this for me?"

"Yes, I thought you'd want a glass of wine."

"Thanks." She took a few sips and threw him an

expectant glance.

The waiter appeared and Perry ordered the beef tenderloin bouché and Imani ordered the Traverse City dried cherry and pecan salad.

"What's this about?" Imani asked when the waiter walked away with their orders.

"I thought we should talk and clear the air if we're going to be working together," Perry told her.

"You're right." Imani swallowed. "Perry, I'm sorry about the way I broke the news of my engagement. I—"

"I've accepted your engagement to Judge Kessler," Perry interrupted. "There's no need to apologize about the way I found out about it.

Imani's sensual mouth opened as if to make a statement and then closed again.

Perry caught a hint of nervousness in her eyes as she lifted her glass and took another sip. "We tried to make it as a couple and we failed. It happens to people all the time. It doesn't have to make us adversaries. It doesn't mean we can't be civil to each other."

"So you've gotten over your feelings…"

"I've lowered my expectations and I try not to focus on the past," Perry told her confidently. "As far as I'm concerned, everything ended when you got engaged to Kessler. You're in love with him aren't you?"

"Yes," Imani nodded.

Perry noted her lack of enthusiasm but kept a tight

hold on his emotions. "Then let's leave the past behind us."

Imani's eyes were strangely shiny. "Can we at least be friends?"

"No," he said more vehemently than he intended. "There's nothing friendly about the way I feel about you."

Imani recoiled from his statement. "I know that I hurt you, but I never thought you'd hate me." She looked away, blinking.

"I don't hate you," he said, wanting to touch her, to comfort her, but she'd given that job to Damon Kessler. She faced him, the vulnerable expression fading and he was glad that she'd won her battle with the tears. He could keep his distance when she was hard and unreasonable, but not if she cried.

Scanning her face, Perry kept his voice even. "But what I feel is no longer your concern. I pride myself on being a professional. We can work together. If I didn't think so, I wouldn't have selected you for the campaign. The shots of you and me were the best because we still have a lot of chemistry between us, but the others were good."

"I see." Her voice was just above a whisper as she stared down at the table, her fingers playing with the stem of her glass. "So what are the ground rules?"

"Do we need them?"

She shrugged, risking a quick glance at him. "As long

as we're clearing the air."

"How about agreeing that whatever we do in front of the camera for the campaign is just that."

Imani's lips tightened. "I couldn't agree more. Anything else?"

"Why don't we agree to be as pleasant and agreeable as possible?"

Rolling her eyes at him, she asked, "What are you talking about? I'm always easy to get along with."

Perry stifled a grin. "There's a certain time every month when you're not." Imani's monthly bouts with PMS were legendary.

"You're not always easy to get along with either!" she snapped.

Perry nodded. "That's why we're coming to an agreement."

"All right then," she murmured huffily as the waiter brought their food.

They ate most of their meal in relative silence. Perry finished first and sat drinking decaffeinated coffee while Imani finished. She spent more time pushing the food around on her plate than she did putting it in her mouth.

He wasn't surprised because Imani could barely eat when she was nervous, excited, or upset.

"How's your mother?" he asked when she finally laid her fork to rest.

"Good right now. Everything seems to be in a holding pattern."

"What does her doctor say?"

"He's still standing by the original estimate, but he doesn't know what he's talking about."

Perry listened sympathetically, silently fearing that the doctor was right. He knew that except for her mother, Imani had no family. That fact had been a contributing factor to her initial decision to keep the baby. He now knew that the baby would have been good for both of them.

"Anything else?" she asked Perry as the waiter cleared the table.

"You'll get the call later this afternoon," Perry answered, "and then Top Pro's scheduling a press conference for the day after tomorrow."

Perry paid the waiter and walked out with Imani. He stopped short of accompanying her to her car, but he watched her get in. As he took the Lodge Freeway home, he congratulated himself for remaining somewhat detached. He didn't plan on being one of Imani's pawns. Now all he had to do was to stay focused until he really didn't give a damn. He was looking forward to that day. As Imani drove home, she congratulated herself on getting the job. She was glad that Perry had set the ground rules because she was having trouble sorting her feelings out and didn't need the added stress of Perry pursuing her. She found herself reliving the entire lunch, word for word, especially the part where Perry said there was nothing friendly about the way he felt about her.

When something slid down her cheek, she realized she was crying. Disgusted with herself, she grabbed a tissue and took care of it. She didn't want Perry back, did she? No way. And she didn't need his friendship either. He'd always abandoned her when she really needed him and she'd never been able to fully trust in his love.

Two days later Imani got up early and took her mother to the clinic for dialysis. Afterward, she rushed home and left her mother with a companion while she dashed over to the Top Pro Corporate Offices for the press conference.

Because she'd washed her hair and only wore moisturizer on her face, it didn't take long for the crew to make up her face and style her hair into a high ponytail that fanned out to frame her face. Then they changed her nail polish to match the black and white outfit that they'd selected.

Apparently Imani had missed the Top Pro Company's announcement to the press because when she stepped into the press conference room, she saw Perry and the Top Pro representative in the middle of a group of reporters. Perry's handsome head lifted as she approached and his sensual lips spread into a smile of pure male appreciation and welcome that warmed her all over. She responded with a smile of her own as she made her way over to accept his extended hand.

"Gentlemen, this is my partner for the duration of this campaign, Miss Imani Celeste."

The group moved closer to surround them, shooting questions at Imani.

"Imani, saw your picture on the cover of Sports *Illustrated's Swimsuit Edition.* Nice shots!"

"Thank you," she murmured graciously.

"Miss Celeste, weren't you at one time engaged to Perry Bonds?"

"Yes."

"May we assume that the engagement is back on?"

"No," Perry and Imani answered in unison.

"But the romance is back."

"No," they both answered again.

"I'm engaged to Judge Damon Kessler," Imani said above the noise of the crowd.

"He's a good man," someone said. "Have you guys set a date?"

"No, we haven't."

"If you were my fiancée, I couldn't see letting you fly all over the country to romantic settings with the notorious Perry Bonds, who's also an ex-boyfriend!"

"Good thing I'm not your fiancée, isn't it?" Imani smiled charmingly. "My fiancé knows I can handle myself."

Imani and Perry fielded questions for another ten minutes, and then everyone took pictures of them signing their contracts and then a pose of them together.

The two of them left the pressroom together, smiling. Turning to make a comment about the press, Imani saw Perry abruptly disappear into a dressing room. All the warmth she'd felt from the camaraderie they'd shared vanished. She stood looking after him, feeling stupid. When he'd said they'd play it up for the camera and have nothing personal to say to each other afterward, he'd obviously meant it.

Imani arrived home, feeling physically and mentally exhausted. Not used to interacting with the press, she'd worn herself out trying to respond positively. Hopefully she'd get better at it as the campaign continued.

At home, she stopped to see how her mother was feeling. Her mother seemed fine, but Imani never made it past the living room couch. Lying on the couch as she talked to her mother, she sank into the soft cushions and fell asleep.

Much later, Imani felt one end of the couch dip with an added weight and then a pair of warms lips brushed her forehead. Opening her eyes, she saw Damon smiling down at her. She couldn't believe she'd slept through the doorbell ringing and her mother's friend answering the door.

"I thought we were going to dinner."

Imani sat up yawning. "Me too. What time is it?"

"Eight o'clock."

"Why didn't you wake me?"

"You looked like you needed your sleep."

"I did," Imani yawned again, "but now I'm starving."

"We can still go get something to eat," Damon offered.

"Have you seen Imani's Top Pro press conference?" her mother asked brightly from her side of the room.

"No, I haven't." Damon and Imani turned to scan the television screen.

"I'm taping it off the local station right now!" Mama said proudly.

"You guys seem awfully chummy," Damon commented as they watched Imani accept Perry's extended hand.

Imani shook her head. "Just acting for the camera." She was glad that the station was showing only a few highlights from the conference. Just as she started to relax the reporter explained her previous engagement to Perry and her current engagement to Damon. When all was said and done, the reporter made Damon seem awfully gullible.

"Maybe we should rethink your participation on the Top Pro contract," Damon remarked.

Imani put an arm around his shoulders and kissed his cheek. "Relax. You have nothing to worry about. Besides, you're a judge, you know it's an iron-tight contract."

"I suppose."

"You know."

Damon simply shrugged.

"If you could see the way he acted after we left the room, you wouldn't give all this hype another thought," Imani continued.

"How did he act after you left the room?"

Imani drew in a slow breath. "As if he didn't know me at all."

"Can you blame him?"

"No," Imani answered, tired of kicking herself for the way she'd handled her relationship with Perry.

Damon squeezed her hand and murmured, "How did you want him to act?"

"I just hoped we could be friends."

"Personally, I'm glad that's not an option."

"Don't you trust me, Damon?"

"You, yes. It's Perry that I don't trust. He's going to try to get you back. I know I would."

"I've already gone through the trying-to-get-back-together stage with Perry, and it failed," Imani said, deciding not to tell Damon about her lunch with Perry. He'd definitely misunderstand.

Damon snorted skeptically. "If it were me, I'd keep on trying."

Imani let the subject drop and hoped Damon would do the same.

As her mother used the remote to click off her VCR, Damon asked, "Can you be ready in about ten minutes?"

Imani yawned and stretched again. "Would you mind if I fixed us something here? I'm still exhausted."

"I just want to eat. What did you have in mind?"

"Soup? I've got the frozen soup vegetables in the freezer and there's chicken in the fridge."

"Sounds good. It's hard to believe that I've known you for years and never eaten your cooking. I didn't know you could cook."

"I wouldn't raise a child who couldn't take care of herself," Imani's mother put in. "Imani's a great cook and she used some of those trips to Europe to get gourmet cooking lessons. She can cook anything."

"I'm looking forward to this meal." Damon stood and offered a hand to Imani.

"Nothing fancy, you understand," Imani said, letting him help her up.

"I like home cooking in all its forms."

Imani turned towards the kitchen. "All right then, follow me."

"Aye, aye, sir." Damon followed her to the kitchen in a mock military fashion.

"Are you coming, Mama?" Imani called over her shoulder.

"No, I believe I'll sit here and watch this show, but I want some of that soup."

"I'll bring you a bowl," Damon told her.

In the kitchen, Imani set Damon to chopping onions while she assembled her ingredients. When his cell

135

phone rang, she saw him checking the number on the display. Noticing that he didn't pick it up, she asked, "Who is it?"

"It's just DeAndra. She's still trying to get over losing her grandmother. I'll give her a call on my way home."

"How's the rest of her family coping?" Imani asked, an unsettled feeling in her stomach. DeAndra Blake called Damon far too much to suit Imani.

"As well as could be expected. I promised to help DeAndra through this. You don't mind do you?"

"No, of course not," she lied, deciding to give the situation time to blow over.

A week later, Imani smoothed a hand down her red satin shorts and turned in the mirror to assess the look of the matching sleeveless top. The outfit flattered her figure and had pockets for her keys and change. Checking the height of her snowy white socks, she lifted one and then the other Top Pro running shoe-clad foot. She decided that she liked most of the Top Pro clothing.

The makeup artist applied light makeup and the hairstylist pulled a sweatband over her head and painstakingly braided her hair into a thick plait that hung down the middle of her back, almost reaching her waist. Stepping out of the dressing room into the warm morning sunshine, Imani feasted her eyes on Perry. He was definitely masculine looking. The white running shorts and muscle top with red accents didn't seem to cover enough of his buff brown body. His chest was impressive and the rope-like definition of his sculpted biceps gleamed in the sunlight. She glimpsed his flat stomach and trim waist when he raised his arms in a stretch. Her mouth watered. Perry looked good enough to grace her pin up calendar every month in the year. When he bent down to touch his toes, Imani forced herself to look away from those long lean-muscled legs and his well-shaped rear.

What's wrong with you? she asked herself, not quite believing that she was drooling over a man she'd given up for good, a man who'd disappointed her more than once. It didn't matter that he was the only man she'd ever loved with a passion she couldn't deny. She could get over that. Resolutely, Imani began her own stretching exercises. Angling her body from side to side, she stretched her legs. She glanced up and found Perry watching her, his sexy brown eyes sparkling with desire, and her mind echoed with all the hot, passionate things he'd ever said to her. A delicious shiver of desire rocked Imani. Despite the crew setting up the cameras and the people clearing the area they would run in, it was as if they were alone. It took everything she had to look away.

"Why don't you guys jog a bit to loosen up? Your movements will look smoother when we shoot and it'll make it easier to get through it," their director said.

Still working to ignore Perry's distracting presence, Imani shot off, determinedly not thinking about him until she realized that his footsteps started echoing much later than hers. She felt the weight of his eyes on her and knew he was watching the movement of her legs, thighs, and buttocks. When they'd been together, he'd loved that view of her body, his rapt attention never failing to arouse her. When she turned her head to look over her shoulder, she saw that he was about thirty feet behind her. Was she imagining thinly veiled excitement in his eyes? Slowing down so that he could catch up with her, Imani tried to remain calm. "You're making me uncomfortable," she said when he reached her.

"You're a beautiful woman, Imani. You used to like me to look at you. You said it turned you on," Perry told her in a husky voice.

"I wasn't engaged to Damon then," she replied, stating the obvious.

Perry shot her a simmering glance. "Well, I like the way you've been looking at me. It still turns me on."

She drew in a quick breath, the blood rushing to her face. "I haven't—"

"Don't bother denying it," he rasped, "I know when you're hot for me. If you weren't engaged to Damon, we'd be getting it on right now in that forest area over there or one of the dressing rooms."

Imani gasped, going hot and shivery all over at his words. She was hot for him, her body tingling and her mind filling with erotic pictures of the two of them making love. Perry was the most passionate lover she'd ever had. Swallowing hard, she turned and took off running back towards the crew. Calm down, calm down, calm down, she told herself as she ran. You can do this.

"We're about ready to start," the director told her.

When Perry joined them, Imani didn't look at him. Instead, she concentrated on the director's instructions. "I want you two to jog the track with the camera following you along. This is something you do several times a week and you're both in great shape, so there'll be no visible signs of strain. I want you to talk and laugh easily as you jog. We won't record what you're saying, but we want you look natural. Start when I yell action."

Perry and Imani nodded. In an effort to cool off, Imani pictured herself skiing down a snow-covered mountain, as the wardrobe and makeup crew checked their hair, make-up, and clothing. She felt the pat of a soft makeup puff against the little beards of sweat breaking out on her nose. She didn't want to think about the other places on her body that were wet.

"Action!"

They took off with an easy jog. Forcing a smile on her face, Imani thought of the pleasant sensation of the sunlight on her skin.

"I saw Jimmy yesterday," Perry said.

Surprised that he wasn't still trying to titillate and tease her, Imani turned her head to look at him, a bright, natural smile shaping her lips at the thought of the baby.

"How is he?"

"Getting big. Yeah, I know he was already a big baby, but he's getting a little taller. And he's got five teeth now."

"He is such a sweet little baby." She sighed. "I wish I could see him."

"You can. I'm going to be baby-sitting again this weekend and I could drop by your mother's house with him."

Imani gave the camera her profile as she looked down the track. "I don't think that's a good idea."

"Scared?"

Imani turned her head to flash him a brilliant smile. "Just being cautious."

"Then I guess you'll have to catch us in the grocery store."

Inclining her head she answered, "I guess so." She knew then that she simply wasn't going to see Jimmy.

"Cut!" the director yelled. "Take fifteen while we review the tape."

Slowing their steps, they walked back to the area where most of the filming crew stood. Helping himself to two large yellow cups, Perry poured glasses of cold, fresh-squeezed lemonade for Imani and himself.

Accepting one of the cups from Perry, Imani murmured her thanks and cautiously followed him over to one of the picnic tables. Her senses screamed, "Wrong move!" But she was determined to hold her own.

Settling himself a conservative distance away from

her at the picnic table, Perry casually asked, "Have you and Damon set a date for the wedding?"

"No, we haven't," she answered stiffly, hoping he wouldn't continue this conversation.

Perry leaned towards her and asked in a low voice, "You haven't slept with him, have you? That's why you're so vulnerable."

Imani glared at him incredulously, amazed that he read her so easily. "I'm not going to discuss my sex life with you."

"You don't have to. I can see what's going on or rather what's not going on by the way you're behaving. You're still carrying around all of that baggage from your stepfather…"

"Stop it." Imani stood up, feeling angry and frustrated. "I hoped you wouldn't make it difficult for me to work with you." Setting the lemonade down on the table, she went into the air-conditioned trailer and slammed the door. When the break was over, she came out and started jogging along the track as the director suggested.

"I'm sorry," Perry said when he caught up to her. "This is hard for me too."

Imani saw sincerity in his facial expression. "I guess we'll just have to give each other space."

Near the end of the session Dr. Williams, Perry's friend, arrived dressed in a turquoise halter-top and short shorts. Waiting quietly in the background until the session was over, she approached Perry and gave him a showy kiss.

Just happening to glance in their direction, Imani noticed that his hands stayed chastely at her waist instead of straying down to cup the curve of her hips the way they often had with her. She wondered if that meant that he was less turned on by Dr. Cynthia Williams than it appeared. Perry was a hands-on type of guy. When the happy couple finally left for a picnic at Kensington, Imani relaxed.

On the way home, Imani gave herself a pep talk and tried to convince herself that setting up a romantic evening with her fiancé was the thing to do. It would cure all the problems she was having with Perry. Spending the night with Damon would also cure the hot, achy feeling that had overtaken her when she'd feasted her eyes on Perry that morning and stayed with her all day long. Was sex really the answer? Making love, she corrected herself.

At home, she ignored her feeling of relief at her discovery that Damon was unavailable. She drew herself a tub full of bubble bath and put on a Marvin Gaye CD. Easing out of her clothes, she slipped into the bathtub. Eyes closed, she relaxed in the warm bubbles and imagined that her man was in the tub with her. By the time Marvin Gayle started singing "Sexual Healing," she was imagining that her man sat behind her in the tub, giving her a sensuous body massage. When the man in her fantasy turned her head for his kiss, she realized that he was

Perry. Abruptly, she sat up straight in the tub, rinsing off the suds. Perry had really gotten to her today. Standing, she grabbed one of the large blue towels, dried herself, and smoothed lotion into her skin. Donning a sheer black nightgown, she regretfully turned Marvin Gaye's music off. There would be no sexual healing in her future anytime soon.

Chapter 7

Imani's feet hurt from walking around in high heels all evening and she couldn't wait to get out of her tight minidress, but she sat next to Damon on the plush cream couch in his home, trying to appear calm and relaxed. She hadn't been with a man since she'd lost the baby. Was she really ready now? For the fourth time she reassured herself that she hadn't finally agreed to sleep with Damon because of Perry's teasing and overconfident remarks earlier in the day.

In the background Johnny Gill crooned, "My, my, my, you sho' look good tonight." Soft ambient light enveloped Damon as he poured golden wine into the two delicate crystal glasses on his coffee table. He presented her with a glass, nodded at her murmured thanks. "To us."

Imani repeated his toast and absently sipped from the glass, wishing she could get rid of the nervous energy strumming just below the surface of her thoughts.

"Seems like the concert put you in a mellow mood." Damon's words drew her attention and she saw that anticipation of their first night together colored his smile. "I love Will Downing," Imani told him, "and dinner at Company was delicious."

"And I love you. Are you ready for the encore?"

Nodding, Imani tensed a little as he bent down to grasp her left ankle.

"Relax." Damon smiled, lifting her leg and scooting down to the end of the couch. He placed her foot in his lap and removed the offending high heel. "It took me long enough to get to this special moment. I'm not going to rush now." He carefully set her shoe on the luxurious cream carpet and began massaging the bottom of her foot.

Stifling an urge to pull down her short dress, Imani tried to relax. She jumped, feeling unexpectedly ticklish at the feel of Damon's hands on her foot. No one had massaged her feet since she'd broken up with Perry last year. She'd made massage appointments at the spa, but always seemed to miss them.

Imani tilted her head back against the arm of the sofa. "Can you get the top of my foot too?"

"I'm willing and able." Depressing the skin, his thumbs drummed their way up to her ankle.

Imani smiled, still trying to get a flow of sensation coursing through her body. She felt Damon remove her remaining shoe and start on her other foot.

"How am I doing?" he asked in a suggestively low voice. His fingers patiently manipulated each of her sensitive toes.

Imani placed her hands on his and swung her legs out of his lap, shifting to fold them beneath her. Somehow she couldn't relax enough to enjoy Damon's foot massage. "Let's try something else."

"I can think of other parts of you that need massaging." Advancing towards her on his knees, Damon brushed his lips on hers, his mouth opening in a warm, moist kiss.

Sighing, she ran her hands along the length of his back.

"Mmmh-hmmm!" He pulled away momentarily to rid himself of his dress shirt.

The muscle shirt he wore hugged and flattered the masculine contours of his body. "Nice chest." Imani trailed her fingers across his pects. "No one just looking at you would ever dream that they were drooling over a judge."

"I've been working out to make it just right for you." "Well, I like what I see. You've got a satisfied customer here." Imani pulled his head down for a kiss.

"Oh darling, I haven't begun to satisfy you yet." Damon's green eyes were hot and riveting. His mouth covered hers hungrily in an urgent and exploratory kiss while his hands curved around the soft mounds of her breasts. "I want you so much I can taste it. Better yet, I'll taste you, every gorgeous inch."

An edge of unease niggled at the back of her mind like a discordant note. Imani closed her eyes and let herself go with the sensual flow of Damon's words and the persuasive feel of his hands sliding down the length of her torso to dwell on her nylon-covered legs. With sure, circular motions his fingers traversed the length of her thighs.

All at once something within her froze. Imani tensed. She needed to be anywhere but here. With sudden clarity she realized that she couldn't sleep with Damon. Not yet. She wasn't ready to share herself with anyone.

She felt the heat of Damon's fingers cupping her through her pantyhose. Grasping his hands she sat up on the couch.

"What's the matter? Did I hurt you?" His voice was soft and urgent.

"Damon, I want to make love with you, but I can't."

Brows wrinkling, Damon stared at her in disbelief. "Why not?" he asked in a voice hoarse with frustration.

"I'm sorry but I-I'm not ready yet. I haven't slept with anyone since months before I lost the baby and I—"

"Is there anything I could do to make you more comfortable? To make you change your mind?"

Heat rushed to Imani's face. "No."

Breathing heavily, Damon doubled over with his eyes closed. Imani saw that his fisted hands shook. She put a hand to his hunched shoulders.

"Give me a minute!" he rasped, moving away from her.

Imani found herself trembling with nervous energy. Certain that Damon thought she'd simply been teasing him, guilt and anguish filled her. As several minutes passed, she stared at his back, certain that her behavior had caused his mind to fill with serious doubts. She'd surprised herself.

"We need to talk about this," she said.

The doorbell rang and Damon's head snapped up. "Who could that be at this time of night?" He stood, straightened his pants, and went to answer the door.

For the first few minutes Imani was glad for the chance to collect her thoughts and decide what she would say in her apology. After she'd practiced a couple of times, the rise and fall of barely audible conversation in the next room intrigued her. She got up from the couch, stepping over her shoes and padding out to the adjacent room.

The sight of DeAndra Blake standing in the foyer brought Imani up short. The blue halter-top she wore left her back bare and stopped short of her waist. Matching blue shorts hugged her bottom and displayed

148

her shapely legs.   DeAndra Blake was dressed for a night in Damon's bed.

Turning on clunky blue sandals DeAndra spotted Imani, her wide eyes taking in Imani's mussed hair and stocking-covered feet and then swiveling back to Damon's muscle-shirted chest.   "Oh, I hope I didn't interrupt anything," DeAndra said in a tone dripping with insincerity.

Rolling her eyes, Imani gritted her teeth.   "Nothing that can't be finished when you leave."

DeAndra's sharp eyes ripped Imani to shreds.
Imani's mouth spread into a slow smile.   "Is there something we can help you with?"

Perry gave Imani the wary look of a man who is caught between two women who don't like each other. He launched into an explanation, "DeAndra was visiting a friend in the area.   She must have hit a nail on the way home because she's got a flat tire."

"You didn't call your friend?"   Imani kept her tone light.

"My friend left her house when I did," DeAndra said defensively.   "I was hoping that Damon was home so that he could either help me fix the flat or give me a ride."
Imani kept her expression bland.   She was sure she knew exactly the sort of ride DeAndra was hoping for.   Poor Perry seemed oblivious.   "What are you going to do?" she asked Perry.

"I've already called a tow truck.   It should be here

149

within the next ten or fifteen minutes."

"Why don't you come have a seat in the living room while you're waiting?" Imani suggested.

DeAndra nodded and followed Imani and Perry into the next room. Her face colored at the sight of the bottle of wine and the two glasses on the coffee table.

Instead of taking his seat beside Imani on the couch, Damon hovered in the doorway as DeAndra took a seat in the plush cream chair. "Would you like some wine? I could get another glass."

"No, thanks." DeAndra seemed uncomfortable as she stared down at her fingers. Damon drew her attention as he passed to take a seat beside Imani on the couch.

Hero worship. Imani thought, watching the other woman's gaze follow Damon. The girl's got a crush a mile high.

"Did you just move in?" DeAndra asked Imani. Imani chuckled.

"No, Imani didn't just move in," Damon answered before Imani could, "not that it's any of your business."

DeAndra managed to look hurt. "I just thought…"

"Well, use your brain to think of something more productive, like the cases you're researching for the firm," Damon snapped.

DeAndra stood up in a huff. "I'm really sorry that I interrupted your evening. If it would make you guys feel any better, I could go outside and wait for the tow truck on the porch."

"That won't be necessary," Imani said.

"Cool your jets," Damon told her, "we're entitled to a reaction and we're having it."

DeAndra dropped back into her chair and crossed her legs.

Back to plan one, Imani thought, watching her swing the top leg in an effort to gain Damon's attention.

He gazed at DeAndra, his eyebrows rising a little. Then he walked to the couch and settled on a spot close to Imani.

"What street does your friend live on?" Imani asked, wondering how well DeAndra had prepared her lie.

"Ah, Shrewksbury." DeAndra's facial expression oozed innocence.

"That's about six blocks from here," Damon remarked, putting his arm around Imani.

DeAndra nodded. "Are you going to the Judicial Ball?"

"As one of the presenters, I don't have much of a choice," Damon said. "What about you?"

DeAndra hesitated. "I-I want to go, but I don't want to go alone. All my friends have made other plans."

That's hard to believe, Imani thought, biting her tongue. Sometimes it was better to let people hang themselves with their lies.

When Damon said nothing, DeAndra added, "I was hoping I could tag along with you."

Shifting on the couch, Damon cast a quick, doubtful glance at Imani. "I'll have to get back to you on that."

Imani lifted her glass and took a sip. She knew that the ball had been scheduled on a night that she had agreed to appear at a charitable function for Top Pro. This was not the time to tell Damon.

The doorbell chimed. All three of them rose and went to answer it.

Fifteen minutes later, DeAndra was on her way home. As Damon closed his front door, Imani went to him and faced him unflinchingly.

"Damon, I'm sorry. I can't describe how sorry I am."

"I'm sorry too, and seriously disappointed."

"I want you to know that I love you and I would never willingly tease you like that." Imani threw her arms around him and rested her head on his shoulder.

"I believe you. What made you think you were ready?"

Imani swallowed, not sure how to answer. "I—just thought it was time."

Damon flipped the length of her hair from its looped position on one shoulder so that it streamed down her back. "Imani, I haven't rushed you, so don't rush yourself. You hear?"

Imani inclined her head in agreement.

He gently kissed her lips. "I know you've been through a lot, so although I get a little frustrated sometimes, I think you're worth the wait."

She closed her eyes, relieved that Damon was being so understanding about the whole thing.

He pulled her closer. "If you want, I can take you home right now. It's not a problem, but I'd like you to stay. You could sleep alone in the guest room and we can have breakfast together in the morning. What do you say?"

Nuzzling his cheek, she answered, "I think I'll stay."

Lying in bed alone in Damon's guest room much later that evening, Imani thought back on how close she'd come to sleeping with Damon. She'd given him a plausible explanation for not going through with it, but she didn't know the real reason. How can you be engaged to a man you can't bear to sleep with? she asked herself and then quickly shifted her focus.

Damon Kessler was a wonderful man and she loved him. He was the sort of man she'd always dreamed of marrying: distinguished, kind, considerate, and handsome too! In time, she'd be able to share her love with him.

On Saturday morning Imani got up early and put together her shopping list. After a quick breakfast and shower, she dressed and headed for the supermarket. Enjoying the sound of "The Mix" radio station, she sped up and down the aisles filling her basket to the sound of golden oldies.

In the produce department she discovered Jimmy sitting in a basket mauling a banana. Her heart warmed at the sight of the little charmer. Perry was on the floor, picking up a bunch of bananas that the baby had obviously pulled down.

"Hello, Jimmy," she cooed, tickling the baby under his fat little chin, "are you keeping that uncle busy?"

Eyes sparkling, Jimmy threw back his head and infectious baby laughter rang out, drawing Imani into it. She chuckled, noting the two new teeth growing out of Jimmy's gums. When he dropped the banana and held up his chubby little arms, she leaned forward, grunting as she lifted the little heavyweight from the basket. This time he was dressed in a Detroit Lions football outfit with a number 20 on the front and the name Sanders on the back. A pair of the smallest tennis shoes she'd ever seen completed his outfit. All he needed was a helmet.

"I can see you've gained weight," she murmured, tossing her head so that Jimmy couldn't get his grasping fingers on her ponytail. She nuzzled her face against the infant's petal soft cheek.

Perry stood in Top Pro shorts and T-shirt, placing several bananas back on the display table. "No hello for the little runt's slave?"

"Hello, Perry. Looks like you're having fun."

"Looks like you're having more fun," he said. "You look good holding my nephew."

Imani worked at loosening one of the little fists holding a handful of her cotton knit top. "I love babies, even really busy ones like Jimmy."

"I'm surprised you showed up today. I really didn't expect to see you."

Shrugging her shoulders, she ran her fingertips across Jimmy's downy soft curls. "I didn't plan on coming. It just happened."

"I'm glad you did. It's nice to see you."

"Thanks." Kissing Jimmy's cheeks she asked, "How long are you baby-sitting today?"

"Till about seven this evening. I take a Saturday every month to give Ben and Sherry a break, let them forget they've got a little one."

"That's nice of you."

"It's good for me too. I get to feel like a dad for the better part of the day, then give him a kiss and take him home. What more could a man ask for?"

A baby of your own? Something in his eyes seemed to echo her thought, so she kept silent. She'd been down that road with Perry and wasn't planning to get stepped on twice. Shifting Jimmy onto her hip she said, "I bet you pick up a lot women who think you're this poor single dad."

"Yes, there are a lot of women who are attracted to babies and the single men with them."

Imani ignored the wise look Perry gave her. She checked her watch. "I should be going."

"Why don't you have lunch with us?"

"No." Imani shook her head. "No, I don't think

that's a good idea."

"I can't vouch for Jimmy, but I'd behave," Perry said. Imani laughed. "You haven't been behaving! Why should I believe you'd start now?"

"I guess you'll have to trust me."

"Yeah, right." Imani laughed again, deliberately ignoring the seriousness in his facial expression. "Some other time, Perry." She leaned over and put Jimmy back into the shopping cart. "Bye-bye Jimmy," she murmured, kissing his chubby cheeks and loving the sound of his answering gibberish.

When Perry cleared his throat and tilted his head up for a kiss, she shook her head vigorously and quipped, "Dream on, cookie."

She was still chuckling as she told him good-bye, bagged her produce, and headed for the checkout. Standing in line, she wondered how Perry could be so much fun to be around today when he'd been so difficult to work with all week long. Apparently Jimmy knew how to keep him in line.

Imani showered and dressed in the outfit that had arrived by Federal Express for her to wear to the charity dinner. In the mirror on the back of her closet door, she turned, admiring the Donna Karan bat wing jacket with its matching tube top and the cream colored miniskirt.

156

They'd even provided a pair of black and cream slings and earrings. She applied makeup and pinned her hair up into an elaborate style. After adding a little perfume, she left her room.

When she came downstairs and entered the living room, her mother was asleep in front of the television. Her eyes opened when Imani entered the room. "You look beautiful."

"Thanks, Mama." Imani took a seat on the couch.

"Are you going out with Damon?" She stifled a yawn.

"No, I've got to go to a charity dinner with Perry for Top Pro."

"I want to meet him."

Imani folded her arms defensively. "Why? He's not my boyfriend anymore."

"But I've wanted to meet him for a long time. Do I need another reason?"

"No," Imani said, realizing that Mama wasn't about to give up on this idea.

"So you'll ask him to come in for a minute when he arrives?"

"I guess so," Imani said in a resigned tone. She saw that her mother's head rested against the chair. She looked as if she would fall back asleep. "Mama, are you all right?"

"As all right as I'm going to be," she grumbled.

"You've been sleeping a lot lately and you still look

tired.

"Blame it on the fact that I am old and tired."

"You're not old."

"But I am sick, and I've got one foot in the grave."

"Don't talk like that. Please, Mama."

"Honey, I'm not leaving here until it's my time to go. It doesn't matter what those doctors say."

Imani walked over to hug her mother. "I need you here, Mama. We've got to get back to the way we were before—before…"

Mama patted her shoulder. "I know, honey. We're going to get there."

Sighing, Imani said wistfully, "If only I hadn't lost the baby."

"It wasn't meant to be. You've got to accept that."

"I…try, but when I see Perry in the grocery store with his nephew, I can't seem to let it go."

"Imani, faith, I named you right. You've got to have faith. You're going to have children someday, honey, whether it's with Damon or Perry."

"Not Perry, Mama. That's over with."

"That's what you keep trying to tell me, isn't it?"

"Yes, and you keep on refusing to listen."

Mama chuckled. "Isn't that a mother's prerogative?"

The doorbell chimed. Imani glanced at her mother.

"That's the chauffeur. Are you sure you want to do this now?"

At her mother's nod, Imani went to the door to talk

to the chauffeur. Minutes later she came back with Perry. He ducked a little as he entered the living room in his dark blue Armani suit.

"Hello, Mrs. Celeste. I've wanted to meet you for some time." Perry took her mother's hand and kissed her cheek. "Now I know where Imani gets her beauty."

"Thank you." Mrs. Celeste's eyes lit up. "Perry, I've wanted to meet you too. I've heard a lot about you."

"I hope Imani's been sticking to the positive things."

Mrs. Celeste lifted her eyebrows. "Imani has actually said very little. I've been reading about you in the newspapers and magazines and watching you on television."

Inclining his head with a painful facial expression, Perry said, "Then a lot of what you've seen and heard has been variations and inflations of the truth. Except for a little partying every now and then, I lead a quiet life."

Imani smothered a laugh.

Mrs. Celeste's expression was skeptical. "You know, Imani leads a quiet life too."

This time Imani burst out laughing and Perry joined her. "You asked for that!" Imani told him.

"Are your parents living in the area?" Mrs. Celeste asked.

"Yes, ma'am. They stay in West Bloomfield and they've met Imani. I also have a brother who lives in Southfield with his wife and son."

"I suppose his son is the baby Imani is so crazy about."

"Oh yes. Jimmy has wound your daughter around all his little fingers and his toes too."

"I wish you could see him, Mama," Imani said.

"I'd love to bring him by sometime," Perry offered.

"Please do." Mrs. Celeste smiled.

Imani could tell that her mother really liked Perry.

Perry checked his watch. "We've got to get going if we're going to make the dinner. Imani?"

Imani grabbed her purse and kissed her mother on the forehead, wondering at the oddly wistful expression on her mother's face. "The nurse is in the kitchen if you need anything. See you later, Mama."

Echoing her good bye, Perry led the way out.

Imani locked the front door and followed Perry down the steps. "Thanks for being so nice to Mama."

Perry stopped walking and turned to face her. "Don't thank me. Everything that just went on in that living room was real. I liked your mother and I meant what I said about coming back with Jimmy to visit."

At a loss for words, Imani stared at him, certain she didn't want to deal with Perry coming and going at her mother's house. She could almost see the two of them ganging up on her. "Let's go," she said finally, walking towards the driver standing by the open limousine door. As charity dinner guests courtesy of Top Pro, Imani and Perry circulated among the guests, talking to local automotive executives. At the long banquet table full of appetizers they got plates and selected several goodies.

"You're going to get fat," Imani warned as she watched Perry fill his plate with several deviled eggs, shrimp cocktail, egg rolls and hot wings."

"You're already boring with all that rabbit food," Perry countered, pointing at her plate full of carrot and celery sticks, pickle spears, and broccoli, and cauliflower with a bit of ranch dressing.

Imani rolled her eyes at him. "At least I'm eating to stay healthy."

"You mean skinny, don't you?"

Without a word Imani turned and walked to one of the little tables set up on the borders of the room. She couldn't believe the small arrow of hurt that shot through her when Perry implied she was skinny. He still had the power to hurt her and she didn't like it. She sat at her little table talking to Ron Randolph, one of the Compuware Inc. executives, about sports cars until Perry appeared at the table and introduced himself. The men discussed the Pistons and Perry's ankle injury before Randolph moved on to circulate.

"Nene, I'm sorry." Perry took a seat at the table.

"What for?" she asked calmly.

"Calling you skinny. I love your body. You're just right."

"Thank you," she said between carrot sticks, "but you didn't hurt my feelings."

"No?" His sharp eyes saw right through her defensive lie.

"No."

"Well, I didn't mean to put you down. I was trying to tease you. You used to have more of a sense of humor."

"I guess people change," Imani offered, feeling less injured now that he'd apologized.

"I guess so." Perry took her hand. "Wanna dance?"

"Yes." Imani stood, her body already bouncing to the beat of the song the live band was playing. As he led her to the dance floor and they began to dance, it was so much like old times that she gave herself a mental shake. Get real, girl. Perry is the past. Damon is your present and future.

They had so much fun they stayed on the dance floor for the next dance. Both of them cut up, laughing, dancing on each other and teasing each other so much that they drew a lot of attention. When the dance ended, Imani started back to the table, but Perry caught her hand and pulled her into his arms for a slow dance.

Floating around the dance floor in Perry's arms to the band's rendition of Luther Vandross's "Never Let Me Go" was like a dream of the past. She felt the hard-muscled length of his body beneath the Armani suit and the barely leashed essence of the man calling to her like a siren song. Where his fingers held hers, electric current flowed and spread throughout her body and throbbed where his hand held her waist. When she tilted her head up to look at him, his lips were so close that they brushed the side of her forehead, leaving a tingling sensation.

For a moment they stared into each other's eyes, the naked emotion there too raw to acknowledge. Then each of them carefully glanced away. When the song ended, they quietly walked back to their table. Shortly thereafter, the master of ceremonies announced dinner seating in the next room and Imani and Perry followed the crowd out of the ballroom.

Top Pro provided prime seats for the two of them at the head table where they sat with General Motors, Ford, and Compuware executives. They listened to a couple of speeches in which the sponsors were thanked for providing funds for charity and sending representatives to the event, and then another speech where they were informed how the funds would be utilized.

As the staff started serving the salads, Imani noticed that Perry was unusually quiet. A very faint sheen of sweat shone on his forehead as he stared down at the tablecloth.

"Are you all right?" she asked.

"Yes. I've just got a few stomach cramps," he said.

"Do you want to leave?" she asked. Knowing Perry's high tolerance for pain, if he was admitting to a few stomach cramps, he was in serious pain.

"No," Perry said calmly, "it'll go away."

Imani ate her salad and watched Perry pick through

his and talk sports with the Ford Motor Company executive seated on the other side of him. She couldn't rid herself of the nagging worry that never strayed far from her thoughts.

The main dish was prime rib with green beans almondine and roasted potatoes. Imani dined on the alternate, Hawaiian chicken, and discussed the new play at the Fisher Theatre with the General Motors executive seated next to her. Her gaze never strayed long from Perry, who ate very little of one of his favorite dishes, prime rib. He was really sick. He had to be.

As the wait staff started serving desserts, Perry stood, excused himself, and left the room in an easygoing gait.

It took all the self-control she possessed to stay in her chair and continue the current discussion on places to vacation. Still, she worried. Except for a few basketball injuries, she'd never seen Perry sick. He's a grown man, she told herself, he can take care of himself. Imani was so preoccupied with worry for Perry that she ate half of a slice of cheesecake without wistfully staring at the other half.

When Perry came back, the faint sheen of sweat was gone from his forehead, but he looked worse than he had before. The laugh lines around his mouth looked more like grooves and his eyes looked glassy. He sat around laughing and talking with the other men, acting as if there was nothing wrong. When he leaned forward and folded one arm across his stomach, the hand curving around his side, Imani decided to take control of the situation.

In the background the band started up again and people started crowding around the dance floor. At the resultant lull in the conversation, one of the guys asked her to dance.

"No, thanks," Imani said, standing with both arms crossed over her stomach, "I'm not feeling well." She turned to Perry, who had heard her comment and was scanning her features. "Perry, I'm going to leave now. I'm not feeling well."

"I'm coming with you," Perry said, concern ruling his facial expression.

Chapter 8

Imani and Perry said their good-byes to other guests at their table. As they left the banquet room, Imani felt the barely concealed tension in Perry's hand holding her arm and noticed an uncharacteristic stiffness in the way he held his body. Attempting to affect his normally smooth, athletic grace was taking a toll.

Imani mentally braced herself for the coming battle. Her stomach was quivering in sympathy with Perry's. She gently held it as they went down the escalator and out the glass doors to the waiting limousine.

When they were seated in the limousine, he pressed the intercom and told the driver to take them to the nearest emergency room. Turning to Imani, he explained, "If your stomach cramps are half as bad as mine, you need to see a doctor."

Imani squeezed his hand nervously. "What about you? Don't you need to see a doctor?"

He shook his head. "I'll be fine. Unless I'm losing my touch, I recognize the signs of food poisoning and my stomach is built like a tank. I could also have the flu, but I don't think so. I wouldn't want you to risk your stomach cramps being something serious."

Imani took a deep breath and gave him a heavy dose of the truth. "Perry, people die of food poisoning. Don't just shrug this off. I'm worried about you and I don't want you to risk your life. That's why I told you I was sick."

"You mean you're not?" Exasperation and disgust filled his tone.

"No," she admitted in a low voice, "I suspected that you'd be unreasonable, so I let you think I was sick too.

Perry hit the button on the intercom. "Driver, we're not going to the emergency room."

Imani shot him a look filled with alarm. She wasn't physically sick, but she was sick of worrying about him.

"Why not?"

"Because I'm not. I'm not up to being poked and prodded by a doctor or having my stomach pumped. I'm doing just fine on my own, thanks!"

"But why can't you just—"

Suddenly Perry gulped, a mortified expression on his face. He hit the intercom once more. "Driver, pull over!

Pull over!"

Cutting across two lanes with quick, efficient maneuvering, the car zipped over to the side of the road. Perry was out of the limousine in a flash, running up the grassy embankment, and heading for a nearby tree. Imani nearly followed, but halted when she saw him double over to forcibly eject the contents of his stomach.

In the car, Imani's stomach fluttered nervously. She hit the intercom button. "We'll take him home first," she told the driver.

Perry came back to the car patting his mouth with his handkerchief.

"We're taking you home," Imani told him, wishing he would agree to go to the emergency room. How could she have forgotten how hardheaded he was? She'd never been able to convince him do anything he didn't want to do, even if it was something he should do.

Merely nodding, he leaned back against the seat to close his eyes. Imani stared at his classic profile, wanting to help him and failing. She could hear him breathing shallowly through his mouth. Reaching out, she grasped his hot hand, not certain whether she was reassuring him or herself. She was surprised when he returned the pressure.

The limousine finally pulled up in the circular drive of Perry's West Bloomfield home and the driver helped him out. Imani followed, fishing the keys from Perry's pocket, opening the front door, and punching her code into the alarm keypad in the hall. She was surprised to find that her personal code still worked. He hadn't cancelled the code!

"I'll be back!" Perry called, running to his bathroom.

Imani turned to the driver, knowing she could not leave Perry like this. "Come back for me in an hour, please."

The man gave her a white business card. "Why don't you just beep me when you're ready? I won't go far."

With that settled, she walked across the glorious oak floor, past the great room to the west wing, and into Perry's plush carpeted bedroom. It felt strange to be in his bedroom again after all the months they'd been apart. She drew back the black and white satin coverlet on his bed. As she went to the third drawer of his dresser and retrieved a pair of gray cotton pajamas, she couldn't help checking the black lacquer nightstand to see if the picture of her and Perry still graced the surface. As she'd expected, it was gone.

She heard the shower running in the bathroom. She knocked lightly on the door. When there was no response, she cracked open the door and placed the pajamas on the vanity table. Barely visible behind the frosted glass, Perry moved beneath the hot, steamy, spray. A warm shiver of awareness rippled through her. The clean, masculine scent of his body wash filled the bathroom. Not wanting to get caught looking, Imani turned away, closing the bathroom door.

Searching the cabinets in the spacious kitchen, she found a lot of the tea she'd purchased when they were together, still wrapped in cellophane. Opening a box of peppermint tea, she put water in the kettle to boil and placed two mugs on the counter.

She heard a noise and looked up to see him standing in the doorway, dressed in the pajamas. He looked a little better, but Imani's sharp eyes took in the way his fingers gripped the doorway.

"It's strange to see you here like this," he said. "I didn't think you made 'house calls' anymore."

She shrugged, determined not to let him shake her. He needed her, whether he wanted to or not. "I-I just couldn't ride off and leave you like this."

"It would have been all right. I've been taking care of myself for a while now." He stared at her for several moments, as if he wanted to say more. Then he shifted on his big, bare feet. "Thanks for the pjs. I'm going to go lie down before I fall down."

"I'll bring you some tea in a minute," she called after him, "and a bucket, in case you get pukey again and don't want to get up."

"Okay." He trudged back towards his bedroom.

Imani found the bucket on the first landing of the stairs to the basement. Things were pretty much the way she'd left them. She'd helped Perry design the house and he'd had it built. If things had gone as planned, they would have been married and living together in the

170

house with the baby. Refusing to allow herself to examine the pain that overwhelmed her at that thought, she ran back up the stairs.

He was lying on his stomach, breathing harshly with his eyes closed when she brought the bucket. His eyes opened to view her with a hint of wonder. "This is weird. I keep thinking this is a dream."

"It's probably because you're so sick," she told him as she placed the bucket on the floor by the bed. "Here's the bucket."

"Thanks." He sighed. "Hope I don't have to use it."

"Me too." She scanned him sympathetically. "I'll get the tea."

Back in the kitchen, she found a tray table and loaded it with sugar and the mugs of hot tea. When she brought the load to his room, Perry sat up in bed to drink the hot tea. She drank hers from the cushy white recliner near his bed.

"I've read somewhere that mint is soothing to the stomach," she said conversationally.

He took another sip. "I think it's helping."

She touched her fingers to his forehead and realized that although he wasn't sweating anymore, he still had a fever. "You've still got a fever. Do you want me to call anyone? Your mother? Cynthia? Your brother?"

He swallowed more of his tea. "No, don't call anyone. They'll ask fifty million questions and they'll never let me sleep. Just stay until I fall asleep, okay?"

"Okay," Imani said, crossing her fingers behind her back and wondering why she'd bothered to ask him. Perry didn't like people making a fuss over him. She'd call his mother as soon as he fell asleep.

"Good thing we don't have anything scheduled for the next few days," he remarked, swallowing the last of his tea. "It gives me a little time to recover from this."

His reference to time reminded Imani to check her watch. It was a quarter to twelve.

Perry missed nothing. His expression was guarded when he asked, "Got a late night date?"

"No, but I'm going to have to call Mama's nurse if I'm not going to be back by one."

"Maybe you should go now," Perry said, scooting down into the bed.

"I'll wait until you've fallen asleep."

"Won't this cause problems with Damon?"

She chuckled. "He's my fiancé, not my keeper. He trusts me."

"Yes, but does he trust me?"

"Let me worry about that." She sighed. "How's your stomach?"

"Not so bad. I've probably gotten rid of whatever it was."

"Go to sleep, Perry," she ordered.

Surprisingly, he obediently settled back against the pillows and closed his eyes. Ten minutes later, he was asleep. Imani stood by the bed and brushed her fingers across his smooth forehead and back onto his soft hair. Then she leaned forward and dropped a kiss on his forehead.

In the kitchen, she used the phone to beep the driver. Then she found the number for Perry's mother in the Rolodex and dialed. The sleepy voice on the other end of the phone grew more alert as she talked.

"Imani? Is that you?"

"Yes, I'm at Perry's and he's been sick."

"Is he all right now?"

"I'm not sure, but he's better than he was. We were at a charity dinner at Cobo Hall and he started having severe stomach cramps. Then he started barfing and he had a fever."

"I hope you guys went to the emergency room."

"He wouldn't go. The only way I got him to leave the dinner was to tell him I was sick."

Anna Bonds voice rose. "That boy is stubborn as a mule! Put him on the phone."

"Well, he's asleep now and he seems to be better, but I think someone should check on him in the morning."

"We'll do that, hon. I'll be over there myself by 8:00 a.m. sharp. Are you sure he's okay for now?"

Imani spoke from the heart. "I couldn't leave if he wasn't."

"Are you two back together?"

Imani's head came up at the question. "No. We were at the charity dinner at Cobo Hall as representatives of TopPro."

"Oh." Anna Bonds' voice rang with disappointment. "Take care of yourself Imani, and thanks for calling."

"You're welcome." Imani hung up the phone and gathered her purse. She'd heard the limousine pull up a few minutes ago. As she left, she turned off the lights.

On the way home, she thought about the evening she'd spent with Perry for Top Pro. Although she was still worried about Perry, she knew that she needed to keep her distance. She decided that she would avoid his house at all costs and keep their time together on a professional level.

It was close to one o'clock when Imani got home. The nurse left immediately. Passing by the living room on her way to her room, she was surprised to find her mother in the recliner in front of the television. Scanning the still figure while she turned on the lamp, a flicker of fear caught Imani and grew. Her mother had started looking frail and tired again. Did that mean death could take her at any time? She wasn't ready for Mama to go. One thing Imani had finally figured out was that the doctors didn't know enough. No one knew how long her mother had to live. "Mama?" she called, lightly touching her shoulder.

"Mmmph?" Her mother stirred, blinking in the light.

The butterflies in Imani's stomach settled down and

her thoughts went back to the evening's events.

"Did you have a good time?"

"Yes," Imani said, realizing for the first time that she had enjoyed herself, "but Perry got sick."

Mama yawned. "Is he okay now?"

"I think so." Imani stifled a yawn. "He's so bull-headed that I couldn't get him to go to the hospital."

"He seemed like a real nice young man."

"He is, most of the time," Imani replied, thinking that her problems with Perry had revolved around his traveling and partying with the team with a constant stream of women throwing themselves at him, his reaction to the news of her pregnancy, and his walking away from her when she'd offered him a way out of their relationship after she'd lost the baby. As far as she was concerned, he'd abandoned her and she'd fallen deep into depression. She'd always loved him, but had he really loved her at all?

"Your daddy was a nice man, but he died young and left me with a young child to raise. I never really got over his death. And Louis...Louis is dead as far as I'm concerned." Her mother's face fell as she tugged her sweater over her shoulders. "You just don't know how lucky you are to have two good men in love with you," she said in a strangled tone.

Imani counted to five and said, "Mama, I'm engaged to Damon. When I'm with Perry, it's strictly business."

Mama gave her a hard look. "Keep telling yourself that,

you hear? That Perry looks like he could drink fifty gallons of your bath water. If I were you, I'd let him."

Imani grinned, a warmth enveloping her at the picture her mind conjured up of Perry drinking her bath water, or better yet, drinking her. "And Damon?"

"He's okay. I like his looks and I like the idea of you marrying a judge, but the way he follows you around makes him seem more like your pet than your fiancé."

Imani's grin died and she found herself defending Damon. "I disagree. Damon is good for me." She touched her mother's arm again. "I'm heading up to bed. Are you coming?"

Her mother grumbled, but accepted the hand Imani offered. "Here I was, waiting up to hear the details, and ..."

"I'm tired, Mama, and I've got to call Damon and let him know I'm home."

Mama stood and let Imani lead her towards the bedroom down the hall. "I guess I'll have to settle for hearing everything in the morning."

"If you're still awake after I talk to Damon, I'll come and talk to you."

"I guess that'll have to do." Mama walked slowly into her room.

Imani got her mother settled into bed. Then she went to her room and dialed Damon's phone number to let him know that she was home. The phone rang several times before the answering machine switched on. For someone who'd been so worried about her staying out late with Perry, he had his nerve staying out late with Miss DeAndra. More than a little annoyed, Imani took a shower and got ready for bed.

As she sat in the middle of her bed after her prayers, the phone rang. Damon's voice sounded in her ear. "Are you just getting home?" she asked.

His voice rang with exhaustion. "Yes. I had to drag DeAndra away from the ball. That girl loves to party."

"Sounds like you had a good time," she said cautiously, as she rolled a corner of the cotton sheet between her fingers.

"I did, but it would have been a lot better if you'd been there. How long have you been home?"

"Since about one o'clock."

"Did you have a good time?"

"Yes, but Perry got sick. I think he had food poisoning."

"So you took him to the emergency room?"

"He refused to go!" Imani fumed, "The man had severe stomach cramps, a fever, and he was barfing like crazy, but he was still too macho to go to the emergency room."

"So what did you do?" Damon asked softly.

"We took him home and I made him some tea."

"We?"

"Yes, we had a limousine driver, Damon."

"I can't believe you went to his house. What were

you thinking?" he asked in a holier-than-thou tone.

Imani could almost visualize him looking down his nose at her. "He was sick, Damon. He needed my help," she explained, gritting her teeth.

"So, how long were you there?"

She took a deep breath and let it out slowly. "Less than an hour."

"Did you go into his bedroom?"

Imani fought to keep her voice down. "Damon, he was sick. I brought him some tea!"

"Tea and sympathy. Sounds pretty cozy to me."

"I don't appreciate your tone and I don't like what you're implying," she said explosively. "Perry was too sick to try anything and he wouldn't anyway. I couldn't just leave him sick like that. I had to make sure he was getting better."

"Having you in my bedroom would certainly make me feel better, especially since I'm still waiting for that wondrous occasion. So was he asleep when you left?"

"Yes, and I don't like what you're implying. Nothing the least bit intimate happened. You've got your nerve grilling me about Perry when you've been hanging out with DeAndra Blake!"

"Really? I never went into her bedroom."

"Well, she wasn't sick," Imani huffed.

"And she's not my old girlfriend either," Damon shot back. "You almost married Perry and you slept with him. I have a right to be concerned. You've never slept with me."

"That's what this is really about, isn't it? You're jealous because we haven't made love. Well, this isn't the way to get there, Damon. I hate pressure and jealousy."

"I noticed, except when you're the one expressing it. You're jealous of DeAndra Blake and she's just someone I mentor.

"Keep telling yourself that and one day you'll believe it."

"I already believe it."

"Oh yeah? She's got a big crush on you."

"What's the matter, Imani, afraid that someone else wants something you don't?"

Imani gasped, she didn't like this new Damon. "How can you say that? I love you and I do want you."

"Do you? It's really hard to believe right now."

"Believe this," she said angrily. "I'm so mad at you right now that I can hardly stand to talk to you. You obviously don't trust me."

"Are you dumping me?"

"I—I…no, but stay away from me for a while." Imani slammed the phone down and drummed her fingers on the nightstand. What was Damon's problem? She hadn't done anything wrong! In fact, she'd let him put her on the defensive instead of discussing his evening with DeAndra Blake. Maybe she should have dumped him.

Fuming, she went back downstairs to talk to her

mother. "Mama?" she called softly from the doorway.

Her only answer was soft, even breathing. Realizing that her mother was asleep, she ran back upstairs to her room.

When she calmed enough to turn off the lights and lie down, she stared into the darkness, twisting his ring on her finger. In her deepest thoughts she wondered whether she really knew and loved Damon Kessler enough to marry him.

Something awakened Perry and he wasn't sure what. Eyes closed, he rolled over in his king-sized bed, reaching out to touch the cold, empty space beside him. In his dream he hadn't been alone. He opened his eyes, blinking against the bright morning sunshine filtering past the edges of his blinds and checked Imani's white recliner. He caught a hint of her perfume in the air, but she was gone. When he closed his eyes, he could see her sitting in the chair she'd selected for their house, her exotic eyes filled with worry and love for him.

The stomach cramps had ceased, but he felt weak and sore inside. Fleetingly he wondered if he should have gone to the hospital and immediately deleted the thought. He'd hated hospitals since he'd lost his grandma in one, when he was ten. His hatred of hospitals had intensified when the baby died there a year ago and

180

Imani turned away from him forever.

He heard a faint bump and a muffled clang. Perry sat up in bed, wondering if Imani was still in the house, or if a thief had found his safe and was busy helping himself to all the valuables. Glancing at the drawer in the nightstand, he wished he hadn't let Imani talk him out of keeping a loaded gun there. As the sound of footsteps grew louder, he decided to face the intruder from his bed. He gasped in surprise when the footsteps ended and he saw the familiar figure in the doorway of his gray and mauve bedroom. "Mom?"

"Yes, it's me, checking up on my baby."

"Mom, your baby is twenty-seven years old."

"I don't care how old you get, you'll still be my baby," she huffed, entering the room to give him a fierce hug and a kiss on the cheek.

"It's good to see you, Mom. I can't remember the last time you used your key."

"It's good to see you too, baby. Now, what's keeping you in bed at eight-thirty in the morning?"

"I'd like to say it's that sexy girl who's in the hot tub, but I ate something that made me sick last night. I'm feeling better now, but my stomach's sore and I feel weak."

She smoothed his hair with her fingers. "I don't suppose you'd run down to the doctor's office with me?"

"No. I'm feeling better now."

"Then I'm calling Dr. Randall and asking him to

come and take a look at you."

"Mom!"

"I'm not asking you, I'm telling you. So go take a shower and change those pajamas."

"Don't you have something important to do at home?" Perry grumbled, swinging his legs over the side of the bed. He felt a little dizzy.

"Of course I do!" She steadied him, waiting for him to stand. "I just happen to think that family is more important. Do you need me to help you to the shower?"

"No, I'm okay." He rose slowly and made his way into the bathroom.

"I'm going to change your sheets and call the doctor. Then I'll make you some oatmeal," his mother called.

Taking a shower helped Perry feel better. He found the fresh cotton pajamas his mother had placed on the vanity and remembered Imani doing the same thing last night. Imani still cared for him. That was obvious. He simply hoped that she loved him enough to confront her fear and overcome the pain of the past enough to come back to him.

He was climbing back into bed when the phone rang. When he answered, Imani's sensual voice set his pulse racing.

"Perry? Are you feeling better this morning? I hated leaving you like that last night."

"Then maybe you should have stayed," he teased, his fingers adjusting the cordless phone over his ear, "I'd have been glad to have you."

"Behave Perry," she ordered. "You're obviously feeling better. Tell me about it."

He told her and added, "You know Mom's here."

"How would I know that?" she asked innocently.

"Because you called her," he answered in a voice ringing with certainty.

"Why would you think that?"

"Because I can't remember the last time she's been here at eight-thirty in the morning."

"Are you going to see the doctor?"

"That's why you called her, isn't it?"

"Are you going to see the doctor or not?" Imani's voice took on an edge.

"Mom's asked him to drop by and take a look at me. Satisfied?"

"For now. Perry, I was worried."

"I know. I'm okay. Thanks for taking care of me."

"You're welcome. Anytime."

"You probably should check with Damon on that."

"You know what I mean, so stop taking everything I say out of context."

"Yes, Imani, I know what you mean. Are you going to admit that you called my mom?"

"No," she said, a hint of amusement in her tone. "I've got to go, Perry. Feel better, okay?"

"Okay. Take care."

She agreed and quickly severed the connection, leaving Perry with the sound of the dial tone and the powerful urge to call her back.

Damon's mother entered the room with a bowl of oatmeal, a cup of tea, and a cup of coffee on a tray. "The doctor will be here in about an hour and a half. Were you talking to Imani?"

"Yes."

She set the tray in front of him. "I like her, Damon, and she's good for you. Are you two getting back together?"

"I've done everything I could think of, Mom, and it hasn't worked. I know she cares, but I can't seem to get through to her."

"Just be yourself. I think you're pretty loveable," she said, making herself comfortable in the recliner with a cup of coffee.

"Did you know that she's engaged to Judge Kessler?"

"Yeah, yeah, yeah. I know Damon Kessler and he's a nice guy, but have you ever heard the saying that it's not over until the fat lady sings?"

Swallowing a mouthful of oatmeal, he answered, "Yeah, but Imani's made up her mind and the more I try to convince her to change it, the more she'll cling to her decision. That's how she is."

"Then don't tell her she's making the wrong decision, show her."

"How?"

"You know her. You love her. Find a way to remind

her without telling her that she still loves you. Just think on it."

"I will," he promised as he swallowed the last of the oatmeal. He'd tried replacing Imani and failed miserably. Cynthia was nice, but Imani had been special and as beautiful inside as she was on the outside. It was time he focused on getting Imani back again.

"Heard from your dad?" his mother asked innocently.

"Isn't he at home?" Perry asked, coming out of his private thoughts.

"He's on a fishing trip." Something in her tone made Perry give his mother a hard look. She was trying to look normal, but he detected sadness and anger in her facial expression and the way she fidgeted with her mug and spoon.

"What's the matter, Mom?"

"He's been out of sorts lately, real distracted. I've had a hard time talking to him. Last week he just up and decided to go on a two-week fishing trip in Cancun and made a point of not inviting me." Her eyes glistened with unshed tears. "Perry, you know that we almost always take our vacations together."

"Maybe he needed a break."

"Maybe he's out there catching something besides fish."

"Mom! Dad's not like that."

"You mean he never was before. His young and

beautiful secretary is also on vacation somewhere. What would you think?"

"You could be jumping to conclusions."

"You don't know how much I want to believe that." She placed the mug and spoon on his nightstand. "Maybe the truth is that I've gotten old and boring."

He took an objective look at his mother's shoulder-length chestnut curls, her still youthful-looking face, and her slim, girlish figure. She looked a lot younger than the mothers of his friends. "No, Mom. You're wrong. You look good enough to be my date."

Smiling briefly, she thanked him. "Your dad has only called twice since he left and he hasn't had much to say. I know that I'm the one who usually does most of the talking, but right now, I really need to know what he's thinking. I've been so angry and upset that I've even thought of hiring a private detective…"

Perry shook his head furiously. "Don't do that! Things could get out of hand."

"I don't know about that," she said, biting her lip. "If things take a turn for the worse, I could always have the detective serve the divorce papers."

He gripped her hand. "Mom, don't even talk like that! I'll get to the bottom of this, I promise. Will you give me till next week?"

She nodded. "He should be back by then."

"I'm not going to wait for that, I promise. Give me the number he's been calling from and I'll do the rest."

He wasn't surprised to see his mother take a pad of paper from the nightstand and jot the number down. "I wasn't going to say anything," she mumbled, placing the paper in his hand. "I didn't come here to talk about me."

"I'm glad you did." Perry pulled his mother into a hug.

Chapter 9

Imani tried to keep up the pace as she and another model, Marsha, jogged through the park on the tree-lined dirt trail.

"Girl, you should have seen the way DeAndra Blake held onto your man at that Judicial Ball. Looked like she thought he was Santa Claus and she'd gotten everything she'd ever wanted," Marsha said.

Imani patted her wet face with the end of her towel and flipped the wet tip of her ponytail behind her. "Damon took her with him because I couldn't go and none of her friends were going."

"Really? You should have seen the way she shook her butt in his face. Now she had on a 'real' dress this time, and I mean it actually fell more than an inch below her butt, but it was this close to being tight!" Marsha pinched her thumb and forefinger together so that a small fraction of the tip of her forefinger remained.

Imani smiled. She really couldn't talk about anyone when it came to wearing clothes that were short, tight, or low cut. As a model, she'd worn them all without an ounce of shame. Even now, she knew that the rounded cheeks of her own butt were hanging beneath the short, black Top Pro shorts she was jogging in. No, she had no shame, worry or concern, unless Perry Bonds was running behind her, watching her butt and making sexy little comments.

"You're not worried about DeAndra, huh?" Marsha's facial expression left no doubt that she thought Imani was a fool.

"No, I'm not worried. If he wanted her, he's had several years to give it a try. He hasn't. She's got a crush on him and the man is totally oblivious!"

"Well, I think she managed to get his attention the other night. She dragged him to the dance floor for every slow dance and then she lay all over him."

"Can we talk about something else?" Imani stopped to sit on a park bench. She'd pulled out her water bottle and had taken a drink when she saw a familiar figure rounding a curve through the trees. Excitement rippled through her. It was Perry. She watched the smooth, rolling symmetry of his milk chocolate limbs in motion as he ran, and decided that he'd recovered from his stomach ailment.

"This looks like a good time to do another lap," Marsha said, taking off with a slow jog.

When it looked as if Perry might run past her, Imani called out to him. He stopped to run in place, apparently spotting her for the first time.

"So how are you doing?" she asked.

"I'm fine. The doctor made me rest, drink a lot of fluids, and he changed my diet for a while. I spent a lot of time trying to figure out what made me sick. My guess was the deviled eggs."

Imani nodded. "Mine too.

Perry shook his head negatively. "The doctor said it was probably the grilled chicken sandwich I had for lunch."

"Oh." Imani gave him a sympathetic look. "I guess you never know what you're getting when you eat out."

Perry agreed.

"How's your mom?"

He chuckled. "As feisty as ever. She's talking about hiring a private detective to find my dad and serve him with the divorce papers."

"What's going on?" she asked curiously.

"My dad jumped up on a whim and took off on a two week fishing trip without Mom. His secretary just happens to be out of town too."

"Do you really think he's on that fishing trip with his secretary?"

Shaking his head, he shrugged. "I don't know what to think. I hope not. He's not usually so impulsive. But sometimes you think you know people, what they will and will not do, and then they go and surprise you. Sometimes you discover that you really don't know people at all."

Imani couldn't help thinking he was talking about her. The hint of wariness in his eyes emphasized his point. She shifted uncomfortably on the wooden bench, glad that her friend had run on when she recognized Perry.

She lifted her chin. "I know what you mean," she said, looking straight into his leaf brown eyes. "I've had some devastating disappointments."

"So have I." Perry picked up the pace with his feet. "Maybe we'll both do better next time."

Imani lifted her water bottle. "I'm counting on it. I think Damon will make an excellent father. He's loving and generous—"

"I'm sure he is," Perry cut her off abruptly. "I've got to go. See you later!"

As she uttered her good-bye, he turned and sped off into the distance. Damon will make a good father, she told herself as she watched Perry's rounded rear and athletically sexy legs grow smaller and smaller.

Marsha ran back, panting. "Is that your ex?"

Imani nodded. "Yes, that's Perry."

"Mmm-hmm good! Can I have your leftovers?"

"If you can get him, you can have him," Imani laughed. "Just beware of the fact that he's not one for the long haul. I need a man who will stick with me through thick and thin."

"Me too," Marsha said, dropping down on the bench beside Imani, "but other than the fact that he is your ex, he would do nicely until Mr. Right comes along."

Turning to stare at an attractive male figure in the distance, Imani said, "This could be Mr. Right."

Marsha turned to look. "Oh my, yes!"

That afternoon when Imani walked into the studio with Damon, she wondered at the wisdom of bringing him on this particular day. She wished she hadn't set it up weeks ago, when they were getting along better. They'd only had one strained date since the blowup over her helping Perry when he was sick, and her nerves and thoughts were scrambled. She wasn't in a mood to be tolerant with either man.

As the studio door closed behind them, she looked around for Cynthia Williams. The filming would be much more pleasant if she were there too. No such luck, Imani decided, when she spotted Perry at the reception desk, alone, and still dressed in casual attire.

She saw the wry twist of Damon's lips as he sat in the chair she indicated, his attention on Perry.

"I'm going to have to go through hair, makeup, and wardrobe," she told him as she handed him a stack of magazines, "but I shouldn't be long because we're going to be working out."

When she looked up, Perry appeared at her side, greeting them, and making polite conversation with both of them. Then he proceeded to show Damon the break area and the hidden stash of pop and snacks. He was so pleasant that she didn't know how to take it. Baffled, she disappeared into her dressing area to let the crew work their magic.

Imani came out of the dressing area about an hour and a half later, dressed in a sleeveless, flesh-toned body-suit with contoured white racing stripes along the sides. The staff had pulled her hair into a thick ponytail with braids mixed in and tendrils of her hair framing her face. She wore her Top Pro workout shoes with white sport socks.

Perry, already in the workout area adjusting some of the equipment, did a silent double take, his hungry eyes devouring her. He seemed oblivious to the hostile glance Damon gave him.

Damon whistled under his breath. "Imani, you're beautiful," he said, when she stopped to speak with him before beginning the shoot. "I can't wait till we're one with each other."

Imani touched his hand, gave him a tentative smile, and shoved the pressured feeling to the back of her thoughts.

The producer/director, a young, preppie-looking guy with red hair, took Imani and Perry aside and described the concept. "As you know, the major theme of this campaign is Top Pro basketball star on the court, Top Pro star off the court. Today we're filming the two of you as the successful couple who have it all, working out in your private gym. We want happening, sexy and provocative. We want people to look at this commercial and want the life you're demonstrating or as much of it as they can get, mainly, the Top Pro look."

"Exactly what do you want us to do?" Imani asked.

"Let's keep it simple. Work out with each other and flirt like crazy. You two are very attractive people with a lot of sex appeal. Let's make it work for Top Pro." The producer inclined his head towards Damon. Is he going to be a problem?"

Imani glanced at Damon and saw that his arms were folded and his lips formed a straight, stubborn line. Unhappy already. She turned back to the producer. "No, he's not going to be a problem."

Perry scanned the equipment, looked at Imani, and then asked their producer, "Will you be recording our words?"

"Nah. We just want the setup, the look, and the two of you interacting. There'll be a voice-over saying everything we want the audience to know."

"Where do you want to start?" Imani asked Perry.

Perry pointed to the treadmills and they headed for them. Holding the handlebars, they stretched their bodies. Then they started jogging. At one point Imani was jogging so fast that Perry tugged on her ponytail and told her to wait for him. She laughed. Shortly thereafter they moved to the weight bench and Perry spotted Imani as she lay on her back and lifted a seventy-pound weight overhead.

Arms shaking, Imani gazed up past the barbell, staring into Perry's eyes. She wet her lips and watched his eyes simmer in response. He helped her replace the barbell and then his hands slid down her arms to rest on her shoulders as he leaned down to touch his lips to hers in a gentle kiss. Imani trembled in response, wanting more and knowing there was no way she could have it. Perry had always known just how to excite and please her.

Near the end of the session the producer stepped in and made suggestions. He made both of them work up a sweat, and then he positioned Perry on the universal machine, to work his shoulders by pulling down on the bar. As directed, Imani walked over, towel hanging around her neck. When she leaned forward, her cleavage was close to Perry's face as he continued working his shoulders.

"Perry," she called, bending down so that her damp hair touched his face. She felt the steamy heat from his body along the sensitive surface of her bare skin. Her fingers traced the curve of his bicep as she planted a kiss on his sexy mouth.

"Cut!" The producer/director's voice brought Imani back into the present and the prospect of a jealous fiancé. "I think we've got exactly what we need."

Imani moved away from Perry, her body still throbbing with excitement. As she approached Damon, she lowered her lids, attempting to school her features and convince her yearning body that Perry was not the solution.

"Did you have to kiss him?" Damon asked when she took a seat next to him on the loveseat.

"Yes," she said evenly, meeting his glare head-on. "What do you do when you flirt outrageously with someone you know well? It was not an intimate kiss. You know that we were performing for the cameras."

"Were you? It looked pretty real to me."

She was silent as Perry walked past on his way to his dressing area. He didn't look at them and he seemed deep in thought. Once the dressing room door closed behind him she told Damon in a low voice, "Damon, it's not as if you don't know what this campaign is all about. If there wasn't an interplay or tangible attraction on film between me and Perry for people see, I wouldn't be here."

"I wish you could get out of the contract. This campaign is going to do nothing but cause problems between the two of us."

Imani scanned the area, glad to see that the producer director had gone into the back with most of the crew to watch the film. She and Damon were the only people in the room. "Damon, in case you've forgotten, I'm not independently wealthy. I need to see a paycheck on a regular basis."

He cupped her face in his hands. "That wouldn't be so important if you were my wife."

She swallowed uneasily. "This job is also important for my career. Do you know how many models would give their eyeteeth to be in my shoes right now? I'm at the peak of my career."

"Is that career going to touch you in the morning or keep you warm on those cold winter nights?"

Eyes narrowing, she stiffened. "You're threatening me."

"No." He stroked the sides of her face, "I wouldn't do that, but I know you, Imani. All you've ever really wanted was a loving husband and a couple of kids. Lifestyle is important, but the career has always been secondary." He pressed his lips to hers.

The truth in Damon's words shook Imani on a profound level because he'd so accurately summed up the mix of feelings and emotions that had been thwarting and confusing her for more than a year.

"I'm fighting for us," Damon said, pulling her close. "So am I." Imani pushed away from him and stood. "I've got to shower and change. I'll be right back."

Imani showered and removed the Gucci outfit from her bag. She donned the almost-see-through gold and beige print shirt with black pants and high heels. Brushing her hair, she was glad she'd decided to leave it down and wash it when she got home.

She wished she'd followed her intuition and asked Damon to come to another session. The atmosphere on the set before and after the shoot had been negative because of his presence. She decided that she would not let Damon attend any other filming sessions or events associated with the ad campaign. Placing the still damp workout suit in the bag, she headed for the waiting area. Freshly showered, Perry was standing outside one of the rooms, watching her with an intense look in his eyes. "You look beautiful."

"Thanks." She took in his handsome face. The muscle shirt emphasized the rise of his chest, his powerful shoulders, and the rope-like muscles in his arms. Warm up pants covered his trim waist and powerful thighs. She swallowed, a hungry ache drawing her to him like a parched desert reaching for a summer storm.

"I hope I didn't do anything to cause a problem for you…"

"For you and me, it was pretty tame," she admitted honestly, her mind replaying highlights of the many erotic ways they'd used to end their workout sessions.

"I remember." His voice was low and husky. Naked desire flamed in Perry's eyes, scorching Imani. His body tensed and his hand clenched into a fist.

The almost tangible attraction between them sizzled. Feeling hot and vulnerable, Imani forced herself to look away. "I-I've got to go. Bye, Perry."

"See you in the Bahamas," he called as she walked out of the dressing area.

In the car on the way home, Imani and Damon were unusually silent. She tried to ignore the heavy silence but found herself waiting for Damon to start fussing about the shoot. Finally, when traffic slowed considerably, Damon turned to Imani and said, "You still have feelings for him, don't you?"

"I have feelings for everyone I've been close to, Damon. You can't just turn them off because things don't work out."

"Then how can you stay objective and unaffected when the two of you are flirting and carrying on for the camera?"

A momentary wave of guilt hit her because she knew she had enjoyed the flirting with Perry more than she should, but when she reminded herself that she hadn't actually done anything wrong, the familiar, frustrated feeling grew. Imani snapped. "It's a job, Damon! How can you stay objective and unaffected with DeAndra Blake throwing herself at you all the time?"

Damon pulled over to the side of the road immediately. "Don't even think about comparing my mentoring DeAndra and helping her get over her grandmother's death to your flirting around with your ex-lover."

"This engagement is not going to work!" Imani shouted furiously. She twisted the diamond engagement ring off her finger and tossed it at Damon. "I don't know why I ever thought we could actually get married and be happy. I don't recognize you anymore. And I definitely don't like you right now." Grabbing her purse, she opened her car door and climbed out onto the sidewalk.

"I'll get home on my own. Good-bye, Damon."

"Imani! Imani, wait," he called after her. "Don't do anything stupid."

She started walking away from the car. A few steps down the block she turned, coolly waving her hand at the taxi she'd spotted before she left Damon's car. As she settled into the back seat of the taxi, she saw Damon drive off.

Folding her arms in front of her, she breathed a sigh of relief. She knew she could get pretty emotional at times, but when it came to her safety, she rarely did anything stupid. *Too bad you're stupid when it comes to men*, a voice chuckled at the back of her mind. *Damon was a major mistake.*

Imani covered her face with her hands. She was going to be by herself for a while and for a change, the thought brought her nothing but relief.

Perry sat on the plane reading the Detroit Free Press. He was in route to the resort in Cancun where his father was staying, and he was afraid of what he would find when he got there. It had been all he could do to keep his mother from accompanying him.

The flight attendant stopped by his seat. "Would you like another drink, Mr. Bonds?"

Perry declined the offer and thanked her, noting that she still hovered nearby.

"I saw you get injured last season and worried about you. How's the injury?" she asked.

"Not quite back to where it should be, but I'm making a lot of progress. I'll be fine by the time the season starts."

"I'm glad," she continued. "I just wanted you to know that my family and my entire neighborhood are rooting for you."

Perry thanked her and went back to reading the paper. Once the plane landed, it didn't take long to get processed at the airport in Cancun because he'd let the team's travel agent make all the arrangements. He stepped out into the hot, brilliant sunshine and caught a cab to his father's resort.

The resort was like an oasis in the desert with picturesque one and two bedroom villas near the beach and larger, townhouse-like structures further back. The beach was loaded with amenities that included a full bar, scuba gear, jet skis, boats, wind sails, and surfboards. Perry left his suitcases to be delivered to his villa, but he stopped in briefly to look around the luxurious surroundings.

Sparkling sunshine lit the air-conditioned villa from

large panoramic windows that spanned entire walls. The furniture was light and airy. The bedroom was private, with a large, pillow-filled bed that called out to Perry's jet-lagged body. A large bath, complete with Jacuzzi and shower, opened off the bedroom, and a tiny kitchen hid behind the open space of the breakfast table and chairs in the great room. Perry couldn't help thinking that this was an ideal place to be alone with a woman.

After washing his face and drinking a glass of bottled water, Perry headed for his father's villa. He'd purposely picked accommodations that were next door to his father's. As he knocked at the door and waited for an answer, he glanced into the panoramic windows of the great room and saw no one. When he was just about to give up, the door opened and his father, looking older and more tired than Perry could ever remembering see-ing him, filled the frame. There was more gray in his thick black hair, and his eyes drooped as though all the sadness and trouble in the world were dragging him down.

At the sight of his son, he stared in surprise. "Perry! What are you doing here?"

The fresh scent of lemon air freshener with a slight undertone of something unpleasant filled Perry's nostrils as he stepped close, hoping his father would take the hint and invite him in. "I came to see you because we're all worried about you, dad."

A secretive look flickered in his father's eyes and

quickly disappeared. "I'm fine. Can't a man get away by himself to think?"

"Not if he's never done it before." Perry took in his father's old white shorts and T-shirt, and bare feet. "Can I come in?"

"I guess so." The older man stepped back to let Perry in. "You came all this way just to check on me?"

"Actually, I have a Bahamas shoot for Top Pro in a few days, so I thought I'd come this way first and see you. Dad, we're worried about you." Perry hugged his father hard, struck by the fact that his father had lost a lot of weight. The old man actually seemed fragile. "Are you sick? You've lost weight."

"That's what happens when you don't eat."

"So you're not sick?"

His father shrugged.

"Why aren't you eating?"

"I haven't been thinking about food."

"What have you been thinking about?"

"Life," his father answered cryptically.

Perry scanned the area, looking for signs that his father was staying with another person and finding none.

"Are you here alone?"

Preston Bonds leaned heavily on a cane as he limped over to the windows and settled into one of the chairs. He carefully propped his bandaged foot up on another. "You know, I'm getting a little tired of this game of twenty questions. If you want to look around, go ahead."

The Love We Had

Perry took a little tour of the villa and quickly discovered that his father was alone and had been alone. He felt a little ashamed of himself when he returned to the great room and took a seat beside his father.

"Satisfied?" the older man asked.

Perry nodded sheepishly.

"Who were you looking for?"

"I wasn't sure, but isn't your secretary on vacation right now too?"

The old man grinned. "Thank you, son. Didn't know you thought I still had it, but you know that I've always been faithful to your mother."

"As far as I could tell. I didn't want to think—but I didn't know what to believe." Perry got up to check to refrigerator in the kitchen. He came back with two beers. "What's going on, Dad? Why are you here all alone?"

His father made a strangled noise deep in his throat.

"The last time I checked, I was the parent and you were the child. I'll ask the questions."

Perry opened his beer and took a swig. "What do you want to know?"

"For starters, your mother sent you, didn't she?"

Perry nodded. "It was me or the divorce lawyer."

"Divorce lawyer? In all the years we've been married I've never had a vacation by myself. What's wrong with that?"

"It's not you, Dad. You don't like to be alone. When we heard that your secretary was on vacation too and nobody knew where, some people jumped to conclusions."

Preston Bonds sighed and rubbed his stubbled cheek. "I'm going to have a talk with your mother."

"Are you going to tell her what's bothering you?"

"If I have to."

"Will you tell me too?"

Instead of answering, his father stared out the window at the point where the golden sun floated on the bright blue ocean.

"Dad?"

"I heard you. I'm still thinking about it." Preston Bonds took another draught of beer and continued to stare out of the window.

When the sun started sinking into the ocean and Perry had just about given up, the older man began to talk. "You know I've been having a problem with my foot for a long time."

Perry nodded, his heart in his throat. "Dad, it's not cancer, is it?"

"Hell no!"

Perry breathed an audible sigh of relief.

"They're talking about gangrene."

A picture of rotting flesh formed in Perry's mind. Now he could identify the odor beneath the lemon scent permeating the room. He grabbed his father's arm, certain this news wasn't much better. "No, Dad! When did this happen?"

"You know I hurt my foot in that freak accident with the fishing boat. I took a lot of different antibiotics, but it's hard to heal when you're a diabetic. It's got steadily worse. Well, now they're saying that they're probably going to have to take my whole damned foot."

"Dad, did you get a second opinion?" Perry choked out, his heart aching for him. He knew that his dad had been so proud, that for months after the accident he'd limped along without a cane. After losing his balance and falling a few times, he'd been forced to use a cane.

"Of course I went and got a second opinion! I've still got all my senses. The other doctor said pretty much the same thing. I've got to have surgery and fast."

"So when are you going to have it done?"

"I'm not sure I will." His father's voice seemed to come from far away. "Once they start cutting on you, they don't never stop."

"Dad, this should be a no-brainer!"

Preston Bonds shrugged. "I don't know about that. This is my body. When you get older, the way you live your life can have a lot of impact on whether you want to live or die. I've been trying to make up my mind. It took me a long time to get used to this cane. If I let them take my foot, I'll never get rid of the cane."

"If you don't let them take care of it, you won't be around to worry about it!" Perry snapped, heated frustration burning in his eyes. "You might have to use a prosthesis, but we'll love you just the same."

His father glared at him. "I want my own damned foot.

You know as well as I do that some things define the way a man feels about himself. I can't see me living my life as a cripple."

Staring into his eyes, Perry gripped his father's shoulders. "I wouldn't care if you had to go around in a wheelchair, Dad. I love you and I want you to live." He hugged his father hard.

Preston Bonds returned his son's hug. "I've lived my life as a man and I want to die as a man."

"Dad, this has nothing to do with pride or being a man!" Perry's voice rose as he pushed back to anxiously scan his father's face. "You're going to have that operation because we're not going to lose you."

"I'm going to—to think about it," his father said stubbornly and went back to staring out the window.

Perry clenched his fists impotently. He could see that he was getting nowhere with his father.

After a few minutes, Preston Bonds leaned back on the pillow-covered couch.

"Dad? Are you in pain? Can I get you anything?"

His father closed his eyes. "I've already had a pain pill."

"Do you want me to leave?" Perry asked.

"Nah, stay and keep me company."

Perry sat with his father until he fell asleep, then he walked around the villa and worried. His dad had always been a good, supportive father, the best. Was he about to lose his dad because of pride and stubbornness? How was he going to tell his mother? Should he tell his mother? The questions cycled uselessly through his mind.

Wiping tears from his eyes, Perry went into the kitchen with his cell phone and dialed his mother's number. When the answering machine clicked on he froze, not sure what to say. At the sound of the beep, he shook himself mentally, and left a message for his mother to call.

He needed to talk to someone close, someone who'd understand. As he sipped bottled water, he gave in to compulsion and dialed Imani's number. When she answered, he listened to the sweet sound of her voice, suddenly unable to speak.

"Hello? Hello?" There was a long silence. "Perry, is this you?"

Hearing his name, he placed the phone back on the receiver.

For want of something to do, Perry read the room service menu and ordered a meal for his father and himself. By the time the food arrived, his father was stirring on the couch. Because of the expensive resort's policy, the waiter refused Perry's tip and went on his way.

As the flavorful aroma of steak and potatoes wafted through the room, Preston Bonds sat up on the couch. "I can't believe how hungry I am."

"Why don't you wash your hands while I put the food on the table?" Perry suggested. He watched his father leave the couch and carefully make his way towards the bathroom.

A knock sounded on the door. Perry and his father stared at each other.

"I'll get it." Preston Bonds changed direction and headed for the door. When it opened, his wife Anna stood there in a rumpled red suit, her eyes wild and defiant, her hands shaking. "Anna," he said softly, his voice almost a whisper.

"I'm here to see for myself," she said, reaching past him to drop her suitcase on the floor of the cabin. "I love you. I need you to tell me what's going on. If you don't want me here, you're just going to have to kick me out!"

"I want you here," Preston said, "I love you." Suddenly they were in each other's arms, hugging and kissing.

Perry saw that his mother was crying. "I-I thought you were trying to get rid of me," she moaned, rubbing her face into the shoulder of his worn T-shirt.

Preston Bonds stroked the back of his wife's head, smoothing the shoulder-length brown hair and soothing himself. "You're my best girl, my only girl. Why did you think that?"

She wound her arms around his waist. "You left me…you wouldn't talk to me. You've never done that before."

"I've never had such bad news before."

"Bad news?" Anna Bonds allowed her husband to draw her into the cabin.

Deciding it was time to give his parents some privacy, Perry moved into their line of sight. "Mom, Dad, I'll be next door if you need me."

"Perry." Anna Bonds threw her son a sheepish look. "I followed you, Perry. I couldn't stand to wait another minute."

Perry walked over and kissed her cheek. "I don't care about that, Mom."

"But you both look so upset." Her eyes darted back and forth between her husband and her son.

Perry lifted her suitcase and placed near the sofa. "Dad's got something to tell you. If you guys need me, I'll be next door."

Anna Bonds gripped her husband's shoulders, her eyes widening in fear.

As he stepped out into the hot evening air and closed the door he heard his mother say, "All right, let me have it…"

Instead of going back to his quarters, Perry took a walk on the beach. His heart and his thoughts were with his parents. He knew that if anyone could convince his father to have the operation, it was his mother. Would she? Sometimes his mother was unpredictable. Would she choose to enjoy the time his father had left without the surgery or push him to take a chance on the long haul?

Oblivious to the effects of the heat and water on his shirt and slacks, he waded into the warm water. He thought of Imani and himself. They weren't together now, but she'd always had his heart and always would. If he were facing the choice his father faced, he had no doubt that he'd choose the long haul with Imani and their child.

He walked the beach until late in the night, and then stumbled back to his villa to lie on the bed.

In the morning, Perry had breakfast with his parents. His mother's eyes were red from crying, but she said nothing about the decision to be made. His father seemed more reflective than ever.

They went on a boat ride and explored the resort. The day progressed to noon without a word on the decision. Unable to bear the suspense, Perry asked his father about his plans. Preston Bonds drew his wife close and told Perry that they hadn't decided. When Perry again tried to convince his father to have the operation, his father thanked him and politely asked him to butt out. Then his father revealed that he'd given Perry's brother the facts and asked him to do the same.

Perry felt defeated when he left both his parents in Cancun two days later. They hadn't made a decision, but Perry knew that no decision was in itself a decision to die. His father was literally rotting away.

Chapter 10

Imani checked into the Caribbean Princess Hotel before noon and followed the bellman back to the luxury villas. After tipping him, she toured her spacious villa, admiring the professionally decorated great room, kitchen, and half bath on the first floor. Climbing the winding carpeted stairs to the bedroom suite, she admired the contemporary furniture, the large bed fit for a queen, the private bath complete with Jacuzzi and shower, and the luxurious attention to detail.

Making her way back down the stairs, she threw open the door to the beach, and took in a view of sandy beach, endless blue sky with white fluffy clouds and miles of rippling blue water. She breathed in the glorious smell of the ocean. "I love working for Top Pro!" she sang.

This was surely a dream assignment and a first rate chance to pretend everything was right in her life.

A movement on the patio in front of the villa next door captured her attention. Turning, she saw that a privacy screen hid most of the person on the adjacent patio. From her vantage point, nothing was visible except a large, white, Top Pro athletic shoe. "Perry?"

"Yeah, I've got the room next to yours."

The low-key reply piqued Imani's curiosity, especially since he continued to sit behind his side of the partition. She crossed the patio and skirted the barrier to face him. One look at his face, frozen in a reflective mask, and she was slipping into the chair at his side. "Perry, what's wrong?"

His eyes were red and glassy, his fingers clenched at his side. "I've had some bad news."

Imani scooted her chair closer. "Your dad?" she asked. At his nod, she continued, "He wasn't vacationing with his secretary, was he?"

"No." Perry swallowed and continued in a hollow voice. "He was trying to decide whether he should have his foot amputated. He's got gangrene."

"Oh, Perry." Imani shuddered, biting her lip in anguish and sympathy. She knew how active Perry's father was. Quick tears stung her eyes. She bent forward in her chair and gathered him into her arms, massaging his back and shoulders. "I'm so sorry. I think I know how you feel because I've been through so much with my mother. I wouldn't wish that on anyone." She kissed his smooth chocolate cheek and simply held him for several minutes. "Did he decide on the operation?"

"Not yet." Perry clung to her, his body tense. "I tried to convince him to go for the operation, but he's more concerned about walking with a cane forever. If he does nothing, he'll die for sure."

"Then you've got to pray that he makes the right decision," she told him.

Leaning his head against her, he rubbed the area between the bridge of his nose and his forehead with his fingertips. "That's about all I can do, 'cause he's not taking any input. I feel helpless!"

"Do you think Mama listens to me?" Imani expelled her breath in a rush. "Sometimes it seems as if I'm begging for the privilege of taking her to the doctor and paying the bill. I don't mind helping her. In fact, I want to help her. I just wish…"

"She'd consider your feelings more?" Perry caught her hand and slowly moved out of her embrace.

"Yes." Imani brushed the moisture from her eyes with the tips of her fingers. "If the doctors are right, she might not be here in the fall. Perry, what am I going to do?"

"Exactly what you've been doing." He reached up and stroked her cheek.

She shook her head, feeling utterly selfish. "I'm sorry. I didn't mean to talk about Mama and me. I just wanted to make you feel better."

Perry squeezed her hand. "You have. You always do. It's one of the things I like most about you."

Looking into his eyes, Imani saw deep into the heart of the man. She smiled, appreciating that he could find it within himself to comfort her while he was under considerable strain. Seeing Perry, talking with him like this made it seem as if they were still together. It also made her aware of how much she missed him. In a sudden burst of inspiration she stood and slipped behind his chair to knead the tightly knotted muscles in his neck and shoulders.

"Awowwl!" Perry winced in pain, but didn't move away.

"You're pretty tense," she remarked, not letting up on the pressure of her fingers.

Gradually his eyes closed and he moaned softly.

She allowed her fingers to drift down his sides, manipulating the firm flesh, and then advance up towards his neck with her thumbs trekking against his spine.

Perry's deep sigh resonated within her. She felt some of the tension leave his body. She continued to massage him, her thoughts wandering on to admire the rope-like muscles in his arms, the breadth and shape of his shoulders, and the sexy way his chest extended outward. His male nipples were hard and rubbery as she swirled the tips of her fingers around them.

What are you doing? Imani froze, suddenly aware of just what she was doing. Not only had she been playing with Perry's chest, her fingers had started dipping lower to his washboard stomach and what lay beneath. She felt hot, her short, travel-worn suit sticking to her skin. Her body throbbed with excitement.

Perry tilted his chin up and slowly opened his eyes. The irises darkened and he grasped her hands and drew her around the chair to face him. Then his heated gaze slowly covered every inch of her body, burning right through her clothes to scorch the sensitive skin beneath.

"Imani..." His voice was so low that it fairly rumbled in his chest. Like rays of sunshine, he radiated sexual magnetism.

She struggled to catch her breath. Liquid sensation ebbed within her and oozed down her insides to pool at her very center. She stepped back, shaking all over. "I —didn't mean to do that."

He reached out and captured one of her wrists. "I enjoyed it. I like it when you touch me."

Her fingers itched to do it again. Imani clenched her fingers and tried to rein in the part of herself that had been stirred by his words and was aching to hear more. Current flowed through her from the spot where Perry lightly held her wrist.

"Imani...," he called again, tugging her close. "Baby." His big hands cupped the fullness of her hips, holding her in place as he rubbed his face into her

216

abdomen.

Hot whorls of sensation radiated out, enticing her into a sensual prison. Imani gasped softly. She tottered, her knees weakening when she felt his warm breath penetrate her clothing to stimulate the damp place between her legs.

Tightening his hold on her buttocks, Perry steadied her and inhaled her scent. "You smell so damned good," he murmured, nuzzling her, "just like you do in my dreams."

Gripping his shoulders, she said his name. A bead of sweat trickled down her neck and slid down between her breasts.

"I want to feel you, to touch you all over," he continued in an aching voice. "Let me love you, baby."

"I--I want to, but I can't," she answered miserably. She couldn't forget how miserable she'd been when she'd lost the baby and he'd abandoned her. No one had ever hurt her the way Perry had. She'd never given anyone else the power.

"Kiss me," he demanded, looking up at her with dark and compelling eyes.

Imani hesitated, knowing that if she did she'd probably lose herself in his passionate kiss and let him carry her inside to make love in the shower. Would they even make it that far?

A nearby door on the patio slammed shut and they both jumped. Despite the privacy screen, both knew that they were still partially visible. His eyes strong and demanding, Perry held her tightly, refusing to let her move away. They heard footsteps echo across the pavement and disappear.

"I've tried so hard to forget about you, but I can't," Perry told her. He stood and took her in his arms. "I love you, Imani, and I'll never feel the same about anyone else." He brought his lips down on hers in a hot passionate kiss that had Imani drowning in a sea of sensation. His tongue whirled and danced in her mouth, sliding against hers.

Imani's hands slid up his back and shoulders, rubbing, gripping, and massaging. Moaning, she drank from his mouth, as thirsty for the man as a parched desert reaching out for the refreshing spring rain. She felt his big hands kneading her butt and then they restlessly wandered up to part her jacket and palm her aching breasts and tease her nipples through the thin silk of her blouse. The hardened length of his sex pressed against her center. Electric currents of desire rippled through her.

She was shaking with need when he wrenched himself away from her, a question in his eyes.

"I've been holding this love inside for so long that I'm about to burst!" he said hoarsely.

Deep inside her head, the voice of reason screamed for her to move away from Perry. She took a shaky step backwards, certain that was what she should do, but a potent combination of need and want and love decimated her will. She couldn't think beyond this moment. Helplessly she nodded. "I want you too, Perry. I've got to have you."

Perry pulled her close once more to sear her lips with a burning kiss, and then taking her hand, he drew her into the cool interior of his villa. Imani kicked off her shoes. As the door slammed behind him, he lifted her into his arms and headed for the steps. "I can't make it up all those steps!" he growled in frustration.

Standing at the bottom of the stairs, he lifted Imani and placed her on the carpeted square of the landing, his hands already sliding up the sides of her skirt to hook his fingers in her pantyhose and tug them down and off her long legs. Then he was lifting her skirt to her waist and cupping and caressing her through her damp lace panties. Panting, she spread her legs, fire arcing through her as she reached out for him.

Bending forward, he dropped a quick kiss on the inside of each thigh and mouthed the damp treasure between. She moaned softly and tilted her hips forward, offering herself to him. When his hot hands traced the curve of her hips and slid the peach scrap down her legs and off.

When Perry stepped between her legs, she tugged his shorts and briefs down his muscular legs. The heavy length of his engorged sex sprung out at her and she stared, mesmerized. "Now, Perry! I want you now!"

"Just one more thing, baby," he mumbled as he

removed a small packet from the pocket of his pants and tore it open with his teeth. He presented the contents to her. "It's all yours."

"All mine." Imani smiled and gently eased the protection down the length of him.

Positioning himself with his hands on the carpet to each side of her, he entered her gently with two deep thrusts. They both gasped as liquid heat spiraled through them into pure explosive pleasure. Perry thrust into her with a wild and crazy tempo like a prize bull in heat. With her legs locked around his hips, Imani rocked back in a passionate frenzy that mimicked the pounding of her heart. As her body arced in a sharp peak of erotic pleasure, she felt Perry throbbing and exploding within her and they both cried out their surrender in a volcanic shower of sensation.

Afterward they lay panting on the carpet, holding each other, their bodies still vibrating with emotion. Imani cradled Perry's head against her still heaving breasts.

Perry lifted his head and she felt his warm, wet tongue tracing the valley between her breasts, just above the plunging vee of her blouse. He gently kissed a path to her lips. His mouth opened on hers in a slow, drugging kiss. Tangling his fingers in her hair, he told her, "That just took the edge off. I want and need a whole lot more, Imani."

Her voice thickened and she felt herself trembling

again in excitement. "Me too."

His eyes darkened with emotion. "I want to be in you and on you until I can't move anymore," he whispered.

"That's good because I want you inside me," she whispered back. "I want everything you've got to give because I've got this empty void inside of me that's gotten bigger and bigger since we've been apart. I really missed you and I still can't believe we're together now."

"Believe it." Perry stood and helped her to her feet. "We'll go upstairs and take a shower and then I'm going to make love to you until you can't take anymore."

Pressing herself against him, she felt vulnerable as she nuzzled his cheek. "It's going take a lot. I—I haven't been with anyone since we broke up."

Perry pushed back and cupped her face, staring into her eyes with wonder and love. "I couldn't bring myself to do it either. I thought I was a fool, especially with you engaged to Kessler."

"That—that's over with," she said as he lifted her into his arms and started up the steps. Troubled thoughts associated with Damon, Perry, and herself circled the edges of her mind, but she was simply too happy to entertain them.

"You never belonged to him," Perry whispered with conviction, "But you will always belong to me."

Imani acknowledged that truth to herself as he continued up the stairs, and tears stung the back of her eyelids.

He stopped and covered her mouth with a tantalizingly hungry kiss. "Let's do it in the shower."

Upstairs Perry removed her silk blouse and her lacey peach bra. He sent tingles radiating throughout her body when he stopped to suckle the taut nipples of each of her breasts as he unzipped her skirt and allowed it to drop to the floor. He stared at her nude body, his gaze hot enough to raise goose pimples on her flesh. "You're still the most beautiful woman I've ever seen."

She shivered with desire. She ran her hands across his milk chocolate chest and then lower to fondle him. Then she took his hand and they stepped into the steamy shower.

Imani took the musk-scented soap and carefully washed every inch of his sexy body. Dropping to her knees, she took him into her mouth and lovingly pleasured him until he gripped her shoulders and cried out in ecstasy.

Soaping a washcloth, Perry washed Imani's body, lingering on her breasts and buttocks and the sensitive area between her legs. He covered her flesh with warm kisses and stinging little love bites. When he urged her down on the shower bench and placed her legs over his shoulders she protested.

"I want to taste you," he told her, smoothing his hands up and down her thighs, "I've been thinking about it for months. I'm going to pleasure you till I can taste you in my sleep." Bending forward he covered her sex with his warm mouth. Waves of ecstasy throbbed through her. Sighing, she tilted her hips up and held on to the safety bar. She felt his moist tongue swirling around her flesh and darting in and out of her in an intimate imitation of the act of love. When he sucked her gently, she lost her hold on reality and her love flowed like warm honey as she dissolved into a quivering mass.

Perry held her tenderly and whispered sexy words of love until she calmed. Then he urged her to stand and bend at the waist with her hands on the safety bar. He paused and she heard the sounds of him opening another packet. His hands and fingers roamed freely between her legs and all over her aching flesh, till he gripped her buttocks and filled her from behind with his engorged flesh. Imani gasped and held on to the bar for dear life. Her legs trembled as Perry ground and rotated into her with long, lusty strokes. She could hear him panting and feel the warmth of his body behind her. Sensual heat rippled through her. Twice, her body convulsed around him before he cried out hoarsely as he climaxed. Afterwards they took another quick shower and slipped into the bedroom to lie together in his king-sized bed.

They lay spooned together in companionable silence until Imani's stomach began growling in earnest. "Have you had lunch?" she asked, a little embarrassed when it wouldn't stop.

"It's dinner time now, but I wasn't hungry." Perry

played in her hair, combing his fingers through the long, silky strands and gathering the length of it in one of his hands.

"That must be a record for you," she teased, "It's the first time I've heard you say that."

"Maybe you should write it down," he said, his free hand massaging hers.

Imani lifted an eyebrow. "I'd rather get something to eat. The fruit plate on the plane wasn't enough to feed a rabbit."

"That's what you get for passing on the real food. Imani, you don't eat enough."

"Perry, you know why. I can't afford to gain any weight. Now are we going to order room service or go explore this place until we find a good restaurant?"

"I'd rather have you and room service," he said provocatively. "What's it going to be?"

"I've still got some tension to work off," she giggled as she retrieved the room service menu from the night-stand.

Perry's fingers skimmed the curves of her body. "We've got the rest of the evening and all night long."

Imani opened her mouth, wanting to say something, but at a loss for words. She knew how hard she'd fought herself to be here with Perry. Despite the fact that she loved him, their relationship was not set in stone. Was it wrong to snatch this bit of happiness? She didn't think so. Imani kissed him and then began to read the menu choices out loud. She was determined to enjoy this bit of happiness for as long as it lasted.

Imani awakened very early the next morning, her body tingling, aching, and throbbing from all the loving erotic attention she'd received from the insatiable Perry Bonds. Carefully easing out of the bed, she tiptoed to the bathroom. Fleetingly, she thought of making a very early spa appointment, but she knew that Perry would never forgive her.

Catching sight of her face in the bathroom mirror, she smiled at the vision of a woman who'd spent all evening and a good portion of the night making love with her man. Her eyes were clear, and though the whites weren't as bright as usual, her face looked calm and relaxed. Except for a few tender spots on her body, she couldn't remember feeling this good. She filled the Jacuzzi with jasmine scented bath salts and stepped in to luxuriate for half an hour.

The touch of warm lips on her neck and shoulder awakened Imani. She'd fallen asleep in the Jacuzzi. Gazing up, she saw Perry kneeling behind her on the tile. "Good morning." Imani imagined that she still heard his rumbling morning voice as he kissed a shivery pathway across the other shoulder to the other side of her neck.

"Good morning." She sighed. "You're spoiling me

with all this attention."

His mouth covered hers in a gentle kiss. "No, I'm spoiling me by immersing myself in you. I missed you."

He scanned her face and his eyes narrowed slightly. "Are you okay with us being together like this?"

"I—I don't know. Whenever I start thinking about the past and all the negativity, the only way I can go on is to tell myself to enjoy the present and what we're sharing now."

Perry shucked off his briefs and climbed into the Jacuzzi with her. He sat down in the hot, bubbling water and urged her down into the spot between his legs. "I can't forget the love we had." He gathered her into his arms. "We can make it work again. Give us a chance." Imani clung to him and enjoyed the warm, affectionate kisses he pressed to her temple and the side of her face. She reclined back into the cradle of his body until her back met the curving planes of his chest.

Perry's hands were touching her breasts and rolling the tips with his fingers. His big hands roamed freely, tracing her curves, stroking her thighs, squeezing her buttocks and dipping inside her to move in and out of the slick moisture there.

She could only cry out and hold on to the sides of the tub. The flowery scent of jasmine sharpened as Imani tensed, her body arcing in sudden quivering pleasure that seemed to go on forever.

Perry held her gently and pressed a series of little

kisses to her temple and the side of her face. "I just want to touch you, to feel you," he murmured. "We don't have to do anything."

Maintaining her hold on the bars on the sides of the Jacuzzi, Imani turned around in the water until she was straddling Perry. "Oh, I do so disagree…," she cooed softly as she retrieved one of the packets on the side of the tub, removed the contents, and smoothed it down the heavy thickness of him. They stared into each other's eyes. Moving closer, she slowly eased herself onto him. "Perry…"

In the early morning hours Imani sat on the beach with Perry while the photographer loaded his camera. She gazed out at the reddish-orange ball of the sun rising from the glassy blue surface of the water and took its beauty as a positive sign of things to come in her life. She was back with Perry and despite the nagging questions and worries that she'd always had when it came to Perry, her heart was filled with happiness and love.

Eyeing Perry in his brief black and gold swim trunks, she felt the throb of excitement reverberating through her body. The man had her in a sensual haze.

Turning, Perry caught her looking at him and responded with a sexy grin. His simmering eyes lingered on the cleavage revealed by her skimpy gold Top Pro swimsuit, her thighs, shiny with baby oil and sunscreen, and the area between her legs.

Imani didn't need to ask what he was thinking because her mind had gone to the same sensual place. As soon as the photo shoot was over, she knew that they'd race back to Perry's villa to make love. She couldn't stop thinking about Perry, his sexy body, and the wonderful way he threw himself into loving her. How had she ever let him walk away?

The question started the negative voice at the back of her mind to reciting the litany of his supposed sins. Ignoring the voice, she concentrated on the rushing sound of the water and leaned back, stretching out her legs in the sun. She glanced up, surprised when the photographer snapped the first picture.

The next day was beautiful with more sparkling sunshine and balmy Caribbean breezes. Imani felt happy and relaxed. They'd finished the photo shoot yesterday and then attended a black tie fundraising dinner for the Tom Joyner Foundation on behalf of Top Pro. Tomorrow they were scheduled to board a plane to head back to Detroit.

Too bad this can't last, Imani thought as she sat at the breakfast table in a dark red halter dress that barely covered her bottom, reading *USA Today* with Perry. Every now and then she would lean forward to distract him with a tantalizing view of her cleavage or draw one leg up into her chair to offer an alternate view of her matching red underwear. She loved teasing Perry.

He watched over the top of the financial section as she dropped the entertainment section on the floor. Throwing him a hot glance, she lifted one long leg and rested it on the lengthwise edge of the table so that her three-inch slide hung over the edge.

Perry's burning brown eyes centered on the shapely length of her leg, egging her on. "Keep it up and you're going to get what you're asking for!"

Imani laughed. "Is that a promise?"

He lowered the paper and one warm hand caressed her leg from the fullness of her thigh to the curve of her calf, ending with the sensitive arch of her foot. "If I didn't know better, I'd think you kept me around for my ability to perform stud service."

Flicking a fingernail at him, she lifted the other leg and crossed it over the one on the table. "It is high on the list of your personal qualifications!"

"All right." Perry stood with his hands on her legs and hovered over her. Then his hands slid up the sides of her body to tickle her sides and tummy until she dissolved into a fit of laughter.

Grabbing her out of the chair, Perry rolled with her on the carpeted floor. "You're going to learn not to mess with me!"

"Oh yeah?" she challenged as his mouth came down on hers in a deep, soulful kiss.

"Yeah." He tugged her ponytail playfully and rolled

so that she came out on top.

Imani lay on top of him with her head on his warm, T-shirted chest. She could feel his heart beating beneath her cheek. "I wish we could stay longer."

"Maybe we can."

"No, I've got to get home to see about Mama. When I called this morning, I heard that she refused to go to the dialysis appointment yesterday."

"Do you think she's getting sick again?"

"She's been sick all along, Perry. She just gets stubborn sometimes. That's why I've got to see her in person."

When the phone rang and Perry got up to answer it, she watched him with an odd sense of foreboding.

"Hello? Mom! Dad? It's good to hear from you." Perry's long fingers fiddled nervously with the phone cord. "Yeah, we've been here for a few days shooting a commercial and some stills for Top Pro. You did? His voice shot up several octaves.

Anxiously watching and listening, Imani felt her stomach quivering nervously.

"Oh." His voice fell dramatically and his brows furrowed. "So—so when?" He began pacing up and down the length of the kitchen as he listened intently to the voices on the other end of the line. "I'll be there."

Imani reached his side just as he hung up the phone. He looked shell-shocked. "What's happened, Perry?" she asked as she gathered him into her arms. The heaviness in her chest made it hard to breathe.

"Dad's going for the operation," he answered in a shocked voice.

Extending her hands, she ran her fingers through his hair in a combing, caressing motion. "That's a good thing, isn't it?"

"Yes, but I won't breathe easy until he shows up for surgery and wakes up without his foot. Hopefully they won't have to take more than that. My dad has always been so physically active that losing a limb will practically kill him."

Framing his face in her palms, she pressed a kiss to his cheek and pushed him down into a chair. "Baby, all you can do is hope and pray," she said softly.

Perry spoke in a choked voice. "I'm not ready to lose my Dad, especially over something that can be taken care of. I can't imagine not being able to talk to him."

Imani stroked his head. "Stop thinking so negatively. It'll work out. It has to." She nuzzled his cheek. "When is he having the operation?"

"First thing in the morning, the day after tomorrow." He took her hand; naked fear and a pleading look in his eyes. "You're coming with me, aren't you?"

Imani gripped his hand, her eyes watering. "I've got to take Mama to her dialysis appointment. When she's in her stubborn mood, no one else can do it."

Perry's lids dropped, covering the expression in his eyes. His jaw clenched. "I know you have to take care of your mother."

She cringed miserably at his obvious disappointment. "I'll come as soon as I get her back home and settled," she promised. "How long will the surgery take?"

Perry lifted a shoulder and let it drop. "Three hours at least, probably several hours more."

"Which hospital?"

"Beaumont in Royal Oak."

Imani bent down and kissed his lips. "I'll be there. I want to help you through this, Perry."

"Then I'll be waiting for you."

Much later, Perry sat in a chair by the bed rubbing his forehead. He could hear the washing sound of the waves outside the villa. Two o'clock in the morning and he couldn't sleep. Instead of spending half the night making love to Imani, he'd spent the time worrying about his Dad. Although he'd been distracted, he had managed to rise to the occasion and make love to Imani when she came out of the bathroom in black silk baby doll pajamas that looked like something out of a Victoria's Secret Catalog. The sizzling sexual excitement between them had fizzled after that.

Hope grew within him as he gazed at Imani sleeping in his bed with one hand beneath her rosy walnut cheek. Still as beautiful as ever, he thought, mentally caressing the dark brows and long lashes that accented her exotic eyes, the silky length of black hair fanned out on the pillow, and the natural pout of her sensual lips. He was glad that early in their relationship he'd been able to see past that beautiful body to the glorious woman within.

In his heart he truly believed she was his other half, but convincing her long enough to get down the aisle... Maybe they would make it this time.

The sounds of people talking as they walked on the beach awakened Perry. The room was dark. He reached for Imani and touched empty space. Sitting up in bed, he rubbed his eyes and checked the clock. Eight o'clock already! Where was Imani? Had she gone back to her villa to pack?

Dragging himself out of bed, he padded into bathroom, opened the shower, and turned the water on. Then he stripped and stepped into the warm spray with the bar of deodorant soap. When he'd showered and dressed, he went downstairs.

"Good morning!" Imani met him at the bottom of the steps with a juicy kiss and a hug.

He returned her greeting. "Wanna go back upstairs?"

She winked at him. "There's no time. I ordered coffee, bagels and fruit. Want some?"

"Sure." Perry sat down and helped himself to a banana. "No bacon?"

"Perry, you know I can't eat that every day. That's why I didn't order any. We can get you some."

"That's okay." He poured himself a cup of coffee. "Why'd you let me sleep so long?"

She took a seat across from him, nibbling at a chunk of fresh pineapple. "Because you stayed up all night worrying. I'm glad you finally fell asleep," she said in a casual tone that didn't sound quite right.

He scanned her face, trying to determine what had changed in her manner. "I guess I ruined our last night together here."

"Don't say that." She touched his hand lightly and sipped her coffee. "You don't have to entertain me, remember? When you really care for someone you want to be with them, no matter what."

"I didn't forget." He took one of her soft hands and drew her up and around the table to sit on his lap. "Are we back together or what?" he asked, laying his head on her full breasts, his arms locked around her waist.

"I guess so," she murmured, fingering his hair.

"Don't sound so excited." he said irritably. He wondered if she was getting ready to kiss him off again.

"I'm kind of exhausted, Perry. It's been an emotional roller coaster weekend. First I heard about your Dad and then we made love after all this time, and now we're worried about the operation. I know what it feels like to face losing a parent." She pressed a kiss to his forehead. "With all that's happened, I can't think straight."

"Am I losing you too?"

"I don't know what you mean."

"The hell you don't," Perry snapped. "Be honest. Do you love me or not?"

"I love you, Perry," she said without hesitation.

"Baby!" He drew her into a tight embrace. "I love you too."

He hugged her tightly, feeling as if she was already slipping away from him. "Will you marry me?"

Imani tried to rise from his lap. "I don't think I'm ready."

"Why not?"

"Because last week I was engaged to Damon and this week I've been in bed with you. I'm not a fickle person so there's something's wrong with that picture."

"You fixed the picture when you dumped Damon Kessler."

Shaking her head, she slid off his lap to kneel on the floor at his feet. "Perry, I don't think I'm ready to be a basketball wife."

Perry massaged the silky skin on her arms, wishing he could alleviate some of the worry in her eyes. "You would be my wife. What's bothering you?"

"The travel, the women, the press, and the parties. That's a lot of temptation to throw at any man."

He tilted her chin up with a finger. "I'm not just any

man. I'm your man. Imani, do you think I cheated on you?"

"I didn't say that."

"But you still think it, don't you? You don't trust me because you believed all the press about me and Rasheeda, despite everything I said."

"I apologized for that and I believe you now," she tossed back.

"Maybe, but you still don't trust me, do you?" He stared at her, knowing that despite her words, there was still a problem. Frustrated, he wished he could pull the information from her mind.

Imani looked straight into his eyes. "I lost my faith in you when you left me after I lost the baby. You really hurt me, Perry."

Perry's nostrils flared and his words tumbled out in a rush. "With no faith and no trust there can't be any love. Imani, you sent me away! I hung in there with you for weeks with you constantly telling me to go away. You acted as if you hated me."

Hands clenched into fists, Imani rounded on him angrily, pain shining in her eyes. "You didn't want the baby, so when—the baby died, I kept thinking that you didn't want me either!"

Stunned, Perry reached out to pull her into his arms, but she held herself so rigidly that he could only grasp her shoulders. "I did want the baby! At first I was sure I wasn't ready to be a father, but you brought me around,

Imani. You made me see the baby as a product of our love and a person with the right to live. I love you, Imani, and I've always wanted you. How could you ever doubt it?"

"You left me, Perry!" She wiped away a tear with her fingers. "What kind of love is that? I didn't even know myself after that. Sometimes I didn't want to live, especially when all the stories came out about you and that starlet-harlot, Rasheeda. I was all alone. I'd never let myself love any man so much that I couldn't live without him, and I'm not sure I want to go there again."

Perry moved closer and gathered her stiff form into his arms. "Imani, I want to marry you. We could be together. You wouldn't be alone. We could put the past mistakes behind us."

Not allowing herself to be comforted, Imani stepped away, wiping away another tear. "No, Perry!"

That hurt. Perry felt as if she'd slammed him against the wall. He found himself straightening his shoulders and stiffening in defense. "Are you saying that you don't love me? Because that's not what I heard a few minutes ago."

"I love you, Perry, but I don't want to. I've been fighting it for a while now. I don't like being jealous, suspicious, bitchy, and miserable. I don't like who I am or the way I feel when we're together."

"You seemed to like the past few days we spent together. You were all over me and you couldn't get enough," he said angrily.

Imani slung back a long strand of black hair, her peachy skin darkening as she blushed. "I haven't been with anyone since we broke up last year, so I was vulnerable. You know as well as I do that sex has always been good between us and I'm not going to apologize for that. Sex has always been one of the best things going in this relationship."

Furious, Perry swore viciously. He felt as if he were in a sauna and the pressure release valve was in the red zone blowing superheated steam into the room. "Well, I hope you enjoyed it because I'm not going to play this game anymore. Providing stud service is not something I'm willing to do for you."

Gasping, Imani turned and headed for the door.

"Where are you going?" he called after her.

She opened the door. "I'll wait for the limo in my villa."

As the door slammed behind her, Perry paced the room in a nervous rage. He couldn't believe he'd allowed himself to experience the pointy end of Imani Celeste's foot again. When was he going to learn? She had no faith in him and she definitely didn't trust him. She'd never really loved and appreciated him and she probably never would.

The ride to the airport was quiet since neither spoke. On the plane he found himself sitting next to a brutish-looking older woman who acted like a drill sergeant.

Imani had changed her seat assignment. Scanning the various rows, Perry saw that she'd taken a seat in the last row of first class.

His nerves stretched as tight as a vibrating wire. He wasn't up to making a scene with her. He wasn't ready to deal with his father's operation. Sipping bottled water, Perry stared out the windows at the fluffy white clouds and tried to imagine a future that still included two of the people he loved most. *If she shows up tomorrow, maybe we can straighten things out.*

Chapter 11

Bright morning sunshine from the flower garden filtered in kitchen blinds and spilled across the white table tiles and matching ceramic floor, making a day that was sure to be emotionally exhausting look like an advertisement on a picture postcard. Imani sat with her chin in one hand and the handle of her black coffee mug in the other, trying to think of another way of getting her mother to go for her dialysis appointment.

"Just because you made an appointment for me does not mean I have to go," Mrs. Celeste said stubbornly as she sat at the table in the kitchen, drinking decaffeinated coffee in her old blue bathrobe.

"Mama, you're sick and you're getting worse. You know that you need to go," Imani said, her eyes discreetly checking the clock. She had an hour and a half to get her mother dressed and over to the dialysis center.

Shaking her head Mrs. Celeste poked her lip out. "I don't want to go. I'm tired and I don't feel good. Quit pushing me, Imani."

Imani scooted her chair closer. "Mama, what is this really about?"

"I'm just tired of doctors and hospitals and being sick," Mama said, her fingers curving around her coffee cup. "Somehow, leaving here for good doesn't seem like such a bad thing anymore."

At her words Imani felt a sharp pain behind her eyes. Fighting back tears and covering her mother's hands with her own she said, "Mama, please. I'm not ready for you to go. I don't think I'll ever be. Couldn't you hold on a little longer and do what you can to stay?"

Mrs. Celeste looked at her and smiled gently, sadness in her eyes. "You don't need me, Imani. I know I'm a tremendous burden for you to bear. I've lived my life and had my fun. It's your turn."

Blinking, Imani squeezed her mother's hands. "You're not a burden on me. You raised me and took care of me, Mama. Why shouldn't I take care of you?"

"Because you need to live your life, get married and have babies."

"If you really feel that way about it, shouldn't you at least wait until I have a baby?" she asked, changing tactics with a little humor.

241

Her mother laughed. "If Perry is half the man I think he is, I don't have long to wait."

"We're not together," Imani said quietly.

"Why not?"

"Because I'm not ready to be a basketball wife. I don't know if I ever will be, and just being with Perry makes me this jealous, needy, and bitchy person who is forever on an emotional roller coaster. I can't take it."

"You love that man so much it scares you," Mama said astutely.

"You think so?" Imani asked, ignoring the cackling voice inside her head declaring the truth in Mama's words. "We can't seem to stay together."

"How much of a chance did you give him, hmmmh? You were on that assignment for three days, barely time for anything more than some good sex."

Imani blushed, remembering her days and nights in the Caribbean with Perry. It surprised her that her mother could read her so well.

"You're not happy now, but you're more relaxed and you've lost that stressed look."

"There has to be more to the relationship than good sex, Mama."

"I agree. Tell me you don't love that man and I'll drop the subject."

"Sometimes love isn't enough to keep people together," Imani said, picking up her cup and staring at her reflection in the shiny, dark liquid that filled it.

"Tell me about it," her mother said smartly. "Your father was the only love that really worked out for me."

Imani waited, almost holding her breath for Mama to broach the subject of Louis, her second husband. It didn't happen. She stared at Imani, her facial expression troubled. Then she lowered her lashes and checked her watch. "I need to get dressed if we going to make that appointment."

"Do you need any help?" Imani asked, relieved that her mother had decided to go for the dialysis appointment but disappointed that she had once again avoided talking about her second husband.

"You've already picked an outfit for me to wear. I think I'm old enough to dress myself," her mother said tartly. "Why don't you clean up the kitchen while you're waiting?"

Imani helped her mother to her room and then went back to the kitchen to rinse the dishes and put them in the dishwasher. As she cleaned off the table she thought about Perry and his father's surgery. They were probably arriving at the hospital about now. She could almost see Perry and his brother bringing up the rear as their parents entered the patient intake area.

Yesterday she'd promised Perry that she would come to sit with him at the hospital while he awaited the results of his father's surgery. She dreaded it because sometimes she felt as if it could be her sitting at the hospital awaiting the results of an incident with her mother. Perry tended to be pretty easygoing, but his dad's sudden need for surgery had thrown his equilibrium off. Imani knew that when most people looked at their parents and loved ones, they wanted and expected them to live forever, but she'd learned that the reality is that everyone's time on earth is much too short.

At William Beaumont Hospital, the sounds of doctors being paged on the loudspeaker system in the hall penetrated the chilly room. Perry checked his watch, stood, and resumed pacing the bright blue carpet in the windowless waiting room. He couldn't think straight and an air of unreality enveloped him.

"If you keep that up, we're going to have to supply this hospital with new carpet," his mother cracked nervously. He glanced at her, his mind too numb to try to formulate a response. Just looking at the dingy whites of her brown eyes, the dark circles underneath, and the worn grooves around her mouth, Perry knew that she hadn't slept a bit the night before. None of them had been able to sleep. They'd all gone out with his dad to an expensive lunch at a fancy restaurant where no one managed to eat, and then they'd all gone to a silly movie where no one laughed.

Perry stopped at the little stand where they'd set up coffee service for the families of the patients in surgery. "Want more coffee?" he asked his brother Brent.

Brent glanced up from his computer magazine, obviously struggling to focus. Perry saw that he'd been on the same page for the last forty-five minutes. "No, I'm all right. Any more coffee for me and I'll be following you up and down the carpet."

"I just can't sit still," Perry admitted, clenching his fist and turning around to pace in the other direction. "I feel like I should be doing something to help Dad."

"Pray," his mother said in a rusty voice, "that's what I've been doing."

Perry nodded. "I've been doing that ever since he told me about the gangrene."

"Me too," Brent chimed in.

Stopping momentarily, Perry shifted his feet and rotated his stiff shoulder. His body was a little stiff from his lack of exercise in the Caribbean. Instead of using the health club and catching a few games as he'd planned, he'd spent the time with Imani. Stretching the muscles and then rotating his shoulder again he thought back to his last few moments with his dad. "I just can't get over the way he talked to me before they wheeled him off to surgery. It was as if he knew he'd never see me again. I hope he's wrong."

Ginetta Bonds wiped her eyes with a tissue and blew her nose. "He was terrified and there was no way I could help him. I've never seen him like this. I kept wishing it had been me losing a limb instead of him. I'd have been able to handle it better."

"No, Mom!" Perry and Brent cried out in shocked unison.

Perry went to his mother and put his arms around her. "Don't wish that on yourself. He's going to be all right, I just know it."

"Dear lord, I hope so," his mother cried, " 'cause I can't imagine being here and going back to that house with a man who's lost the will to live!"

"Think positive, Mom." Brent moved over to hug his his mother too. The three of them huddled together, hugging and drawing strength from one another for several minutes. Slowly, they eased apart to sit separately on the pillowed wooden chairs.

"How long has it been?" his mother asked in a wavery voice.

Again, Perry checked his watch. "Just half an hour."

"It'll be at least another hour," Brent said. "Anybody want anything to eat?"

His mother shook her head. "I'm not hungry."

Perry piped up, his stomach fluttering at the thought of food, "Me either. My stomach is a jumbled mess." Although he knew the room was cool, he felt hot as he wiped moisture off his forehead with the back of his sleeve. Resisting the urge to check his watch again, Perry resumed his pacing.

When he glanced towards the entrance to the room, he saw Imani in the doorway, looking like a fairy-tale princess in a white cotton sundress with the liquid silk of her hair streaming down her back. His heart swelled with love. Something eased within him at the sight of her and he realized that he'd needed to see her. Her light perfume with the hint of musk floated on the air as she stepped into the room on white, strappy sandals to hug his mother and whisper soft words of encouragement. He waited, unconsciously holding his breath as she stopped to speak to his brother and hug him too.

When it was Perry's turn, she simply called his name and pulled him into her arms and hugged him tightly. "It's going to be all right," she whispered soothingly.

Rocking her from side to side, he anchored himself, holding on to the warm, solid, softness of her. It took a minute for him to realize that he was shaking with uncontrolled emotion.

Imani made soothing sounds in a husky voice and smoothed her hands up and down his arms.

He focused on Imani, her scent, her fingers on his arms, and the sound of her voice. Slowly the shaking stopped.

Imani reached up and framed his face in her hands, her golden brown eyes filled with concern. She kissed his lips affectionately and then his stubbled cheek, gently wiping away the lipstick. "How much longer until they're done?"

"At least another hour."

She grasped his hand firmly. "Let's go get you something to eat," she suggested.

"I-I can't eat right now. I'm too nervous about my dad."

"Then walk me down to the cafeteria for some hot chocolate."

Torn, he scanned his stressed-out mother, who had her head bowed and her eyes closed, her lips moving silently, and his brother, who'd gone back to staring at the same page in his computer book. He knew that he had added to the stress with his pacing the room, but he couldn't help himself. Perry came to a decision. "I'm walking Imani to the cafeteria. Anybody want anything?"

Perry strode down telescoped hospital corridors that seemed to go on forever. Deep blue carpet muffled the sound of his and Imani's footsteps. He barely noticed the other people in the corridor, Imani's soft, warm hand anchoring him.

Bright sunlight filled the cafeteria where Imani bought two cups of hot chocolate and harassed him until he drank one. The warm sun tingling on his skin and the hot, soothing drink lifted his spirits and calmed his stomach. Sitting shoulder-to-shoulder in a booth with Imani, he talked about his father, how his dad helped him decide to take the basketball scholarship at Michigan, how his dad enrolled him in numerous basketball camps and events once he realized that Perry's interest in basketball was serious, and how special their relationship was. Imani didn't say much, but she encouraged him to talk, and little by little he felt better.

Not long after they returned to the waiting room, the

doctor came out to speak to the family. Removing his surgical mask, he smiled. "We've successfully removed Mr. Bonds' gangrene infected foot and the surrounding tissue."

"How's he doing?" Mrs. Bonds asked, her voice choked with emotion.

"His condition is fair. He's doing as well as can be expected for a person his age.

"Thank-you, Jesus!" Ginetta Bonds cried out. Perry, Brent, and Imani breathed sighs of relief and hugged each other.

The doctor added, "He'll be in recovery in about ten minutes, but because of the anesthetic, he'll be out of it and unable to talk to you for at least another hour or so."

"Can we see him now?" Perry's eyes brimmed with tears of joy.

Inclining his head, the doctor considered it for a moment. "I don't think they'll let you into the recovery room, but you can ask the nurse. He'll be in his room in about an hour."

Ginetta Bonds blew her nose. "We'll wait."

Perry saw Brent stride over to his chair and fumble until he found his cell phone. When the nurse informed him that the cell phone could not be used in the hospital, he headed for the pay phones.

Imani squeezed Perry's hand and he turned to face her, not missing the tears sparkling on her eyelashes. "Do you want me to wait with you?"

"Yes, please." Perry pulled Imani into another hug, his fingers tangling in the silk of her hair. "I never knew how much I needed your support until when you walked into the waiting room this morning. I was going crazy and you made everything better for me. Thank you for being here."

"You're welcome," Imani whispered, "you always will be."

Staring at her, grateful that she had been with him during the morning's strain and was still with him to share the triumph, he reminded himself that Imani had turned down his marriage proposal and gone out of her way to avoid committing herself to him. She was here because she was a loving and loyal person, but when the dust settled and his father was on the way to recovery, she was likely to cut Perry out her life completely.

He caught her hand, reluctant to give up the contact.

"Let's wait over there," he said, pointing to the group of chairs they'd occupied earlier.

Perry's mom was the first to go into his father's hospital room. Perry found himself gripping the sides of his chair when she entered tentatively, obviously afraid of what she might find. Fifteen minutes later she came out beaming. "It's going to be all right!" she cried happily. "Go on in and see him. I'm going to run down to the chapel for a minute. I'll be back in a little while."

Despite his mother's words, Perry swallowed hard at the sight of his father. Preston Bonds lay still in his hospital bed, his face pale beneath his pecan coloring. The bottom of his right leg was covered in bandages. As each of his sons took one of his hands, he gripped both of their hands tightly, opening his eyes. "Okay boys, I'm still here and if I could, I'd be dancing around the room celebrating right now. I was feeling so good that I had to check and make sure they actually did take the foot." His eyes grew shiny. "I guess I'm going to have to learn how to do other things."

"Dad!" Both men sat on their respective edges of the bed and leaned in to hug their father.

"You scared me this morning with all that talk of taking care of Mom and the copy of your will," Perry told him. "I thought there was something you hadn't told us about and I worried about you making it through the operation."

"That was family business, son. A man's got to make sure he takes care of his family, no matter what. Haven't you heard that people die all the time during operations just from the anesthetic? Anything could have happened. I was sure I wasn't going to wake up from that surgery because I haven't done all that I could have with this life."

"You did a good job of raising us with Mom," Brent told him. "I hope I do half as well with Jimmy."

His father drew in a deep breath and coughed. "You'll do fine," he assured Brent. "Is Sylvia home with Jimmy?" When Brent answered with a nod, Preston Bonds turned to Perry. "Perry? Is that Imani standing

251

behind you?"

Perry nodded. He felt Imani's hands on his shoulder and sensed her nearness as she leaned around him to speak to his father. "Hello, how are you feeling, Mr. Bonds?"

"Like I'm stuffed in cotton and talking to you all through a hole in the wall," he cracked. "You can call me Dad."

Imani smiled. "Okay, Dad."

"So are you going to marry my son?"

"I-I don't know, Dad."

Perry's father cleared his throat. "Well, a blind man could see that you two love each other."

Perry patted his father's hand gently. "That's not the problem, Dad."

"If you've got love, there ain't no problem you can't solve."

Imani's hands curved around Perry's shoulders. "We're working on it."

"That's all anyone could ask." Preston Bonds fell silent, his chest rising and falling slowly. Just when they were certain he'd fallen asleep, he spoke again. "Sorry about that. I didn't mean to fall asleep, but that anesthetic is doing a job on me. I'm still groggy and sleepy."

"It's okay, Dad," Perry assured him. "We expected you to be out of things. We just wanted to make sure you were all right."

Preston Bonds took a sip of the water Brent offered

him. "When your mother comes back from the chapel I want you all to go home. It's been a long day at the hospital for all of us."

Brent snorted. "You know Mom isn't going to leave you like this."

"Then you boys are going to help me convince her."

Perry and Brent exchanged knowing looks and then promptly changed the subject. Later, Perry walked Imani to her car and they hugged each other close for several moments. Then as he accepted her kiss on the cheek and helped her into her car, he was more determined than ever to fix his relationship with Imani. "I'm going to call you," he told her when she drove off in her red Mustang convertible.

Once home, Imani discovered that her mother was already asleep. The nurse informed her that her mother had barely eaten and that she'd had a slight fever. Concerned, Imani had the nurse recheck her mother's temperature. This time her body temperature was normal. Imani's breath came out in a heartfelt sigh. She was going to have a talk with her mother's doctor.

The next morning when Imani called the doctor, he simply reminded her that her mother had high blood pressure, a heart condition, and bad kidneys and that a terminal diagnosis had been made several months ago. As far as he was concerned, Mrs. Celeste had been doing much better than expected. Disgusted, Imani hung up, determined to manage her mother's care for the long haul.

Two days later, Imani arrived at the McCleary Modeling Agency to pick up a check and talk with Mariah about assignments to follow the work on Perry's endorsement contract with Top Pro Sportswear and Apparel. Lynn Ware, Mariah's assistant, was waiting for her in her office with a check and a cup of cappuccino.

"Your hair is gorgeous, Lynn," Imani remarked, taking in Lynn's loose, caramel-brown curls that were cut into a swirling pattern that emphasized her pretty face.

Lynn flashed a mouthful of pearly whites, her cheeks dimpling. "Thanks. Anthony got inspired the other night when he came up with this."

"I wish I could get someone to get inspired enough to do something uniquely different with my hair." Imani sighed, knowing that Anthony's greatest talent lay in the clothes he designed and that he only did Lynn's hair because she was his girlfriend and he couldn't bear to let anyone else do her hair.

"You'll find someone to do it," Lynn assured her. "Anthony gave me the name of a friend you might want to go to."

"Great!" Imani thanked her. "Where's our expectant mother this morning?"

Lynn glanced towards the door with a grin.

"Mariah's sorry she's not available to meet with you this morning. She's in marathon negotiations with Tyler cosmetics for Mia Myron and it's going good."

Imani raised her eyebrows. "You guys are really doing well!"

"Yes, I think you started it with the contract with Top Pro." Lynn tapped the envelope with Imani's check in it. "You might check the amount to make sure that it's what you were expecting."

Imani tore open the envelope to examine the sum printed on the right hand side of the check. "Ohh," she exclaimed in surprise, "did someone add a bonus?"

"Yeah, Top Pro. They're talking about extending the period of your contract."

Imani's pulse sped up at the thought of extending her period of working with Perry, but she wondered whether it was really good for her personal peace of mind. She was definitely weak when it came to Perry and she was determined not to let him push her into getting married anytime soon.

Lynn considered Imani intently, her eyes narrowing. "You don't look very happy about it," she remarked.

"Don't you want to work with Perry? You guys look good together."

"Sometimes it intrudes on my personal life," Imani said carefully, "but that won't be a problem. I'm sure we can still work together."

Again Lynn smiled warmly. "I hope so. Mariah's

going to be getting back with you to talk terms, okay?"

"Fine." Imani drank her coffee.

The intercom on Lynn's desk chimed and then a male voice sounded in the room. "Lynn, Imani, have you ladies concluded your business?"

Lynn looked at Imani. When she inclined her head, Lynn spoke into the intercom, "Sure, Ramón, come on in."

The door opened and the handsome Ramón Richards burst in oozing charm. "Good morning, ladies!" He kissed each of them warmly on the cheek. "You're both looking well. Since my wife is still in nego-tiations, I'm being stood up for lunch, and since I have reservations at the Whitney, I was wondering if you two would like to join me?"

"I've got a lunch date with Anthony," Lynn answered, "but I'd love to go another time."

"Imani?" Ramón asked hopefully.

"Sure." Imani smiled at her friend. She hadn't had a chance to really talk to him in quite a while. "We can catch up on what's been going on."

Minutes later she climbed into his gray Mercedes and fastened her seatbelt. "How's Mariah doing?"

Ramón took off with a burst of speed. "She's gotten over the morning sickness, thank God."

"I'm glad," Imani said, "So when do you expect the baby to come?"

"About the fifteenth of November."

"A Scorpio, huh?"

"Yeah," Ramón chuckled, his eyes still on the road, "we've been decorating his room with a Teddy bear and balloons theme."

"You're sure it's a boy?"

"That's what everyone says." He shrugged. "If they're wrong, we'll simply redecorate. Nothing about being a father is going to bring my spirits down."

"That's the spirit." Imani reclined against the seat. "I don't suppose you guys have picked a name, have you?"

"That's a no brainer," Ramón chuckled. "What man wouldn't want a son named after him? He'll be Ramón Richards, Jr."

"I like the sound of that," Imani sighed, her thoughts slipping back to the baby boy she'd carried and lost. He would have been named after Perry.

Soon they were on Woodward Avenue and pulling up to the Whitney valet parking to exit the car. Inside the elegant restaurant they went through the Great Hall which was full of crystal chandeliers and a spectacular grand stairway with the rich woods and gold and silver washed plaster work featured all over the restaurant. They were seated in the Music Room, which boasted authentic Tiffany stained glass windows and a ceiling mural featuring cupids dancing on clouds.

When the waiter arrived, Imani ordered lobster-lentil soup and ginger and tamari- seared salmon with stir-fry vegetables and a coconut citrus broth. Ramón ordered calamari with garlic, lemon grass, tomato and fresh basil and the Whitney bouillabaisse with halibut, shrimp, oysters, and salmon in a tomato lobster broth.

"What's up with you and Perry?" Ramón asked as they sat drinking white wine.

"I don't know," Imani said honestly. "I don't think I'm cut out to be a basketball wife and I can't forget how he left me after I lost the baby."

Perry extended a hand across the table to tap hers lightly. "Imani, I love you dearly, but that's not the way I remember things and I was there too."

"What are you trying to say?" she asked, gleaning from the pitying expression on his face that she wasn't going to like what he had to say.

"I'm trying to say that you drove the man away. You flogged the man in public with that lethal tongue of yours for at least a couple of months before he slunk off to lick his wounds. It must have taken a superhuman effort for him put up with you as long as he did."

Her friend's words hit her like a volley of sharp needles. Imani folded her arms in front in her, massaging the chill bumps on her arms. The back of her eyelids stung as she took a sip of wine and thought about the days before and after her miscarriage. She couldn't think about it without tears threatening to fall. "I was miserable because I knew he wanted to leave me all along. He never wanted the baby and afterwards, things were never the same. He jumped at the first chance he had to leave me."

"Ha!" Ramón cursed under his breath. "Because I'm your friend, I'm going to tell you flat out. You were a bitch. I'd have left you too. A man can only take so much."

Holding back tears, Imani bit the insides of her lip and threw Ramón a reproachful look. "I haven't been able to talk to you for so long. Did you invite me to lunch just to beat me up?"

"No," he said calmly, "I'm taking the opportunity to try and talk some sense into you. Perry's a good man and I personally think you love him. I know he loves you. The man's not going to keep bashing his head up against a brick wall. Imani, you need to cut the crap. Take the man or leave him alone."

"He won't leave me alone," she said petulantly, her eyes on the fancy white tablecloth.

"Do you really want him to?" Ramón asked in disgust. "That's why he's in the doghouse now, isn't it?"

"Get off my back, Ramón!" she demanded angrily. "I can't explain it to you and really shouldn't try."

"Let me guess," Ramón said brutally. "It's about trust. Either you trust someone or you don't. Either you love someone or you don't. Do you love Perry?"

"Yes." Imani found a tissue and blew her nose.

"What about this Kessler guy you were engaged to? Do you love him too?"

"Yes." Imani fiddled with her fork. "Just not as much."

"Then I guess you do have a problem," Ramón said as the waiter brought their first course. When the waiter walked away, Ramón turned to her. "I can't understand how a woman as beautiful as you are can be so insecure." Imani moved the food on her plate from one side to the other. "Just because a person is what other people consider beautiful does not mean they feel beautiful inside. And all that attention is nothing if it's not coming from the right person."

Ramón raised an eyebrow and inclined his head in agreement. "I guess that's true."

They ate the first course in companionable silence, relishing the delicious food.

"I'm sorry, I didn't mean to spoil your meal," Ramón said apologetically when the waiter took the plates away and brought the main course.

"You didn't," she assured him calmly. "I just forgot how hard you push sometimes, and you don't hold back on your words."

"I thought you were going to cry."

Imani laughed, her eyes stinging as she remembered his hurtful comments. 'I came close."

"Bottom line, Imani, if you really want him, get things straight as soon as possible."

Imani broke off a piece of salmon with her fork. "I'm going to try."

Chapter 12

On Friday evening Damon Kessler dropped by and insisted that Imani accompany him to dinner. She argued against it, but between Kessler and her mother, she really didn't have much choice. Imani quickly changed into a yellow tube dress and matching sandals.

Damon's green eyes lit appreciatively when she appeared. "You look beautiful, Imani," he said reverently, folding her into his embrace. "I can't tell you how much I've missed you."

Embracing him briefly, she murmured, "It's good to see you, Damon."

"I wanted to apologize for my behavior the last time we were together. It was inexcusable. My only excuse is that I was incredibly jealous of you and Perry."

"It's all right, Damon. I know how you feel. I've felt that way too, and I don't like it."

Damon stroked her cheek. "I thought you might still be in love with Perry."

"I do love Perry," Imani confessed, "but I love you too."

Damon's brows furrowed and his stare turned penetrating. He looked as if he were trying to read her mind.

"Do I even have a chance?"

"Do you want a chance?"

"I wouldn't be here if I didn't." Damon kissed her on the lips.

"Then you have a chance," she answered smartly.

Damon placed a hand at her waist. "Let's go."

At the restaurant Damon sat across from her, holding her hand. "I went a little nuts when you climbed out of my car and into that taxi. I knew I was being unreasonable."

"I'm not angry with you, Damon. I just couldn't take any more. There's no way I'm going to get out of the contract with Top Pro. I don't want to. It's the best assignment I ever had and I'm not going to mess it up."

"So that's how it is…"

"That's how it is," she said confidently. "I'm a professional and I'm good at my job. I can't let you limit my career."

"I guess I could learn to live with that," Damon said slowly. "Would you consider wearing my engagement ring again?"

"There's something else you should know." Imani's voice dropped, as she looked straight into his eyes.

"This is bad," Damon muttered under his breath, "I can tell from the expression on your face."

Imani inclined her head. "I, uh, had a few weak moments while we were shooting in the Caribbean. Perry was upset and I...while I was trying to comfort him, things got out of hand."

Damon's eyes widened. "You slept with him?"

"Yeah." Imani's face was hot as she stared down at her fuchsia-colored fingernails. She couldn't explain her behavior with Perry in terms that Damon would understand.

"More than once?"

"Yeah, and I really don't want to talk about it." Imani's tone of voice grew stronger. "It's not as if I cheated on you because we weren't together then. I just thought you should know."

"I see." Damon nervously rubbed his temple. "I've also got something to confess."

"You do?" Imani straightened in her chair.

"Yes." Damon forced the air from his lungs. "I was upset over the way we broke up, so when DeAndra asked me to take her to a law school function, I saw no reason not to. Afterward, when she came on strong to me, I couldn't seem to help myself, so we ended up in bed together."

"You slept with DeAndra Blake?" Imani asked incredulously. She couldn't believe he'd fallen into DeAndra Blake's carefully laid trap.

"Yes," Damon answered in a low tone, his eyes not quite meeting hers.

"More than once?"

"Yes." Damon grasped her hand. "I'm not so stupid that I didn't realize that she's been maneuvering me into this position for some time, but I was weak enough to take her up on it."

"I see," Imani said slowly as she scanned his features in amazement. Despite his explanation, she was beginning to think he cared more for DeAndra than he was willing to admit. Suddenly the distance between them seemed insurmountable. "Maybe we should leave the engagement where it is."

"Wouldn't that be like throwing the baby out with the bathwater? You're the one I love."

"What about Perry and DeAndra?"

"What about them?"

Imani threw him a quizzical look. "Damon, I slept with Perry and you slept with DeAndra. That puts them between us. Yes, we both made mistakes. That's why I don't think we're ready to even talk about marriage. Whatever happens before I get married, happens, but once I get married, there will be no one between me and my husband. I feel that vows are sacred and if I make them, I mean to keep them. I don't believe in sharing my man with anyone and I wouldn't ask my husband to share me with another man."

"I wouldn't ask you to share." Damon moved closer. "You're all the woman I'll ever need. Believe that. If we'd shared our hearts and our bodies, then I wouldn't have been so vulnerable."

She didn't like the words he used. Steel crept into her tone. "You're not trying to blame me for your—"

"No. No I'm not." He stroked her arm and leaned forward to kiss her cheek. "I'm trying to make sure you don't talk yourself out of being with me."

Imani's lips fanned out into a smile. "I like you, Damon."

"Enough to wear my ring again?" Opening his palm, he flipped open a small velvet box and his big diamond ring flashed at her.

She chuckled as she closed the box for him and stuffed it into the pocket of his suit jacket. "I'll think about it, but don't hold your breath. My judgment seems to be off these days."

"Mine too." He lifted a hand and smoothed her hair back from her face. "We could still have a long engagement."

Shrugging, Imani reached past him to retrieve her coffee. "You know that DeAndra's not going to give up without a fight."

"With you in my corner, she doesn't stand a chance. What about Perry?"

Imani tried to think of something smart to say and failed. The truth was that Perry scared her. In her secret heart of hearts she suspected that she didn't have a chance of being happy without Perry, but she'd been trying as hard as she could to prove herself wrong.

"I don't know about Perry," Imani said honestly. "I haven't seen or talked to him since his dad had surgery."

"Well, I'm not going to give up on you unless you tell me that's it over because you're going to marry Perry."

"I don't see that happening," Imani told him. "And it's more likely that you and I will fall back to our old friendship."

"I doubt that," Damon said with a smile. "I can almost see our home, our children, our life together. Imani, I could really make you happy if you'd let me."

"I'm really going to think about it. I promise."

"Well that's all I can ask for now, but do you think we can discuss this again in a couple of weeks?"

"Of course we can." Imani hugged him affectionately.

"I want you to know that I really appreciate your friendship."

Damon kissed her lips. "Ditto." He opened the desert menu. "Now how about some desert?"

When Imani arrived home, her mother was already asleep. Thanking her mother's friend for sitting with her, Imani headed up to her room. She was amazed that despite her confession about sleeping with Perry in the

Caribbean, Damon still wanted to marry her, and she was still getting used to the fact that he had ended up in bed with DeAndra Blake. It all sounded like something out of a messy soap opera. She couldn't really imagine herself marrying Damon as long as she had a weakness for Perry and she'd turned down Perry's marriage proposal. According to Ramón, she'd driven Perry away. Ramón's words still hurt. She wondered if she'd done the right thing.

Get your head straight, girl! She sighed as she got ready for bed. Decide what you want and go for it.

Two days later, Imani spent most of her morning strolling in and out of the shops at the Somerset Mall.

When her stomach started growling, she checked her watch. It was eleven o'clock. With several bags from Gucci, Coach, Liz Claiborne, and Hudson's, she wandered over to the food court for some Bourbon Street Grill Jack Daniels chicken and a diet drink. As she arranged things on the table, she was surprised to see DeAndra Blake striding towards her in a short black, pinstripped suit that caressed her curvy little figure.

Narrowing her eyes, Imani tried to imagine Damon in bed with DeAndra Blake and failed. She hated sneaky women. Several nasty, well-deserved names came to mind.

"Hi, can we talk?" DeAndra's voice sounded deceptively sweet and innocent.

Imani worked at exuding an air of calm. "Sure, have a seat," she answered, thinking that the two of them had little to discuss besides Damon Kessler.

Imani watched DeAndra pull out a chair and gracefully settle into it, her short hair gleaming in a chic style.

"Did Damon tell you what happened?"

Imani felt her hackles rising. "I'm not sure what you're referring to," she said politely, determined not to make things easy for DeAndra.

"We made love." DeAndra boldly met her glance.

"Yes, he told me you slept together." Maintaining a bland expression, Imani peeled the paper off her straw and poked it through the hole in the lid. "If you're looking for apologies or excuses, you'd better talk to him."

"I don't expect apologies or excuses," DeAndra gushed. "It was the best thing that's ever happened to me. I just thought you should know."

At her words, Imani wanted to puke. She threw DeAndra a wise look. "What did you do, DeAndra? Get him drunk and then climb into bed with him?"

"That's not what happened and we made love more than once."

"Are you saying that he hadn't had a lot to drink?"

I'm saying that he wasn't drunk. He was hurt and depressed because you dumped him. I love Damon. I simply let him know how I felt about him, how I've always felt about him. Then I kissed him and one thing led to another. It was beautiful. He's a wonderful lover."

Imani could barely bring herself to listen to the poison spewing from the girl's lips. She had had enough. She put down her fork and pinned DeAndra with a glance.

"Just what did you hope to gain by getting in my face and telling me all this? Did you think he wouldn't?"

Startled, DeAndra blinked and sat up in the chair, twisting her hands in the leather handle on her purse. "I was hoping you'd leave him alone. You don't love him. Not the way you should when you're going to marry someone."

"Excuse me?" Imani's tone was cold and cutting. "You don't know me and you certainly don't know how I feel about anything. I'm not engaged to Damon, but he's begged me to reconsider. Let's get something straight: He is my friend and I love him. If you think you're going to trap him by coming up pregnant…"

"No! I'd never do that to Damon," DeAndra gasped, her eyes filling with tears. "I love him. I've loved him for years. In the past, I was too young, but now, all he thinks about is you."

Against her better judgment, Imani felt a wave of sympathy for DeAndra. She searched for something to say. "Well, I can't help you," she said finally. "You can't tell someone who to love. You can't even tell yourself who to love. You're going to have to find your own way to his heart."

DeAndra patted her eyes with a tissue and blew her nose. "So, you're not going to marry Damon?"

Imani swallowed a bite of chicken. "I'm not planning to marry anyone."

After DeAndra left, Imani sat at the table shaking her head. She didn't feel any closer to straightening out her love life. She'd had a fiancé that she couldn't bring herself to sleep with and she'd had an ex-fiancé that she couldn't stop herself from sleeping with. There was a message in her actions. Too bad she didn't want to hear it.

On Friday morning Imani got up and had breakfast with Mama. The jaundiced appearance to her mother's skin, the dullness in her eyes, and her cantankerous mood worried Imani. Despite her mother's protests she called the doctor and secured his promise to come by and take a look at her mother.

Hours later the doctor left after putting Mrs. Celeste back on bed rest and changing her medication. When Imani mentioned canceling her planned trip to California on behalf of Top Pro for the filming of the Soulful Image Awards, her mother insisted that she go. "Give me something new to brag to my friends about," she insisted. "You know I'm going to have my VCR running. I'll play the clip over and over until everyone gets sick of it!"

Perry was not on the flight to California. This surprised Imani, who knew he was scheduled to be her escort and fellow presenter at the award show. Jet-lagged and tired, Imani checked into the small luxurious hotel and immediately disappeared into the luxurious bedroom for a nap.

Three hours later the phone awakened her. It was the front desk announcing a special delivery package and offering to bring it to her room. After tipping the bellman, Imani closed the door and excitedly opened the package. In the first bundle she found white evening sandals with a matching purse. The second bundle obviously held a dress. It took forever to uncover the white material that would serve as her dress for the Soul Image Awards. Staring at the material, she seriously wondered how she could wear the soft, silky strips of material and still manage to cover the bare essentials?

Award show outfits for movie stars and models had been getting pretty racy, but Imani had noticed that most maintained a certain basic level of decency. Although the coverings over breasts and buns might be sheer, no one totally bared more than a bikini would reveal. Considering the soft white panels, she wondered how she would keep them together and what underwear, if any, would fit underneath without showing through the sheer material.

After a determined search, she found a scrap of materiel that might serve as the crotch to a pair of panties, but where was the rest of the panty? When she noticed the Velcro and snaps on both ends, she groaned. She was definitely going to get a lot of attention in the dress tonight, and that was good, but she worried about the dress falling apart on her in public. It didn't appear to be very sturdy.

The phone rang again. This time it was the dress designer and Imani was glad to hear from her. Within minutes, they'd arranged for the designer to show up at the hotel an hour and a half before the award show to help Imani with the dress. Checking her messages, she discovered that Top Pro had scheduled a hair appointment with an exclusive stylist in the hotel's beauty salon. She began to relax. They'd thought of everything.

Back from the hairstylist with an inch trimmed from her freshly washed and set hair, Imani sprawled on the couch, careful not to muss her hair. It was time to call her mother. When she lifted the receiver, there was no dial tone. "Hello?" she said tentatively, knowing that she didn't hear the phone ring.

"I dialed your room, but I didn't hear the phone ring." Perry's deep voice vibrated in her ears.

"I was about to make a call, so I guess I got to it

beforehand."

"So you made it."

"Yes, where are you? I didn't see you on the plane."

"In the suite next to yours. Something came up and I had to take a later flight. You weren't worried, were you?"

"Just a little. Anything could have happened."

"A publicity event for the team went into overtime. You know the season's starting and we've got some exhibition games scheduled."

"Yes, I know you're happy about that."

Perry's voice rose with enthusiasm. "I'm ready to play. It's going to be a good season."

"Perry, I've been thinking about your dad. How is he?"

"Still recovering. I think he's doing fine. Mom's pushing him. You know how that is."

Chuckling, Imani swung her feet up onto the large white pillows. "I think I can relate."

"How's your mother?"

Imani took a deep breath. "I'm worried. She's barely eating, she looks haggard, and the dialysis appointments take a lot of the little bit of strength she has left. Perry, I didn't believe those doctors months ago when they said she didn't have long to live. Now I'm afraid it's true. I thought about canceling for this event, but she and the doctor insisted I go."

"Want me to come over?"

Perry's voice caressed her eardrums. Flexing her bare legs, Imani shivered as she realized just how much she wanted him to see him. "It's probably not a good idea."

"Why not?"

"I just had my hair done and I'm going to have to start getting ready for the award show in a little while."

Perry's laughter was low and sexy. "I didn't offer to come over to jump your bones, Imani. I was offering to come lend you a little moral support."

She felt her face getting hot. "Don't go reading extra meanings into the things I say," she said smartly. "If you could see the dress Top Pro sent over, you'd know what I really mean."

"Sounds like my kind of dress. Let me guess: Something on the order of the award show dresses worn by Jennifer Lopez and Toni Braxton?"

"You've got it. I have a box filled with strips of material and no idea how it all fits together to make a dress or how I'm supposed to wear underwear and stockings underneath without them showing. The designer is due to come over to help me in about fifteen minutes."

"Mmmmh, I can hardly wait. I was going to pick you up early anyway, but now I'm going to put a rush on it."

"What are you wearing?" she asked.

"A white Armani suit."

"Just what the doctor ordered," she said, feeling a little jealous. You get to wear what you probably would have worn anyway."

"They let me pick it out."

"And nobody asked me what I wanted to wear?"

"They'd already decided to have you wear something unique and memorable."

"Okay." Imani yawned and stretched. "What time are you picking me up?"

"An hour before the show starts. That way we can go over the presentation and find our seats."

"I'll see you then. I'm going to call Mama." She exchanged good-byes with Perry and replaced the phone. When Imani called home, her mother was asleep, but the nurse informed her that her mother had eaten most of her dinner and that she had asked to be awakened to watch the award show. Feeling hopeful, Imani opened her makeup kit and threw herself into getting ready for the show.

The dress designer, Arena Sarducci, arrived promptly with a small carrying case full of her supplies. In no time at all, she assembled the dress on Imani. Two wide, curving strips formed a sheer halter top that crisscrossed below Imani's breasts and attached to the bottom with a fancy gold ring. The bottom of the dress resembled a bikini bottom with vertical strips of fabric forming a skirt. Arena joined the top of the dress to the bottom. Then she showed Imani how to use the Velcro and snaps on the detached crotch to form a panty.

In mere minutes Arena had woven her magic by using Velcro strips, hooks, and snaps to draw the strips of fabric into a sexy dress that barely covered the essentials. Imani wore a sheer half body stocking underneath. Shaking her hair out, Imani stepped into the evening shoes and added gold earrings that matched the ring above her navel.

"Beautiful!" Arena said, swinging open the closet door to reveal Imani's reflection in the full-length mirror. She used body glue around the edges of the halter to insure that Imani's breasts would stay covered.

As Imani turned in the mirror, strips of silky white fabric floated on air to reveal tantalizing views of her legs and thighs. The top of the dress adorned her body like a piece of fine jewelry.

Arena opened the garment bag she'd brought along and drew out an elegant, white silk coatdress. "Use this to keep your dress hidden until you make your presentation on the stage. I'm expecting to see you and this dress on the news tonight."

Imani executed a few graceful, hip-swinging steps. "Piece of cake."

When Perry arrived to take her to the show, he stood tall and handsome in his white designer suit. It emphasized his wide shoulders, trim waist, and long legs and draped his body like a lover's caress. His hair was freshly cut, the sides low and the top waving. Imani's fingers itched to touch that square jaw and clean-shaven cheek.

She looked her fill and tried to be satisfied with that.

Perry threw her a teasing look. "Do I pass inspection?"

She forced the hand she'd lifted to trace the length of his black and white silk tie to the curve of his shoulder, relishing the texture of the expensive material beneath her fingertips. "With flying colors."

"Well?" His voice deepened.

"Well?" she answered, mockingly.

"Don't I get a private preview of the dress?"

She walked to the other end of the room and slid the coatdress off. Then she stalked towards Perry like a huntress seeking her prey. Energy coiled within her, tighter than a spring. Stopping just short of him, her facial expression turned seductive and daring.

"Mmmmmh-hmmmh." Perry stared hard, his penetrating stare making her tingle all over. "Oh baby! I'm going to call this the delectable yum-yum dress." With a finger he traced the bare curve of her slim waist, continuing along the line of the dress just below her belly button. "You look good enough to eat."

At his touch, a current of heat ran through her. Imani jumped, her skin burning. She took a small step backwards, wetting her lips.

"Something tells me that you're going to need help getting out of that dress," Perry murmured. "Let me be the first to volunteer."

Imani's lips spread into a smile. She gently grasped

his finger and moved it away from her body. "I'll call if I need you."

"I'll be right here, ready for duty," he chuckled, retrieving the coatdress and slipping it over her shoulders. She lifted her white evening bag from the coffee table. "Is there a limo downstairs?"

"Yes, I've already spoken to the driver and there are a couple of bodyguards in the hall. Top Pro's a great one for details. Let's go." Perry opened the door for her.

She glided out, her fingers naturally locking with his as they headed for the elevator. When she realized they were holding hands, she slowly relaxed her fingers until both their hands dropped.

At the studio where the show was being taped, Imani and Perry waited in a quiet room backstage, watching the show on closed circuit television until the time for their presentation drew near. Then a production assistant came to get them and install them in their places on either side of the curtain.

Imani heard the band strike up a soul tune as Halle Berry walked off the stage with an award.

The master of ceremonies told a joke that caused the audience to laugh. "And now, sponsored by Top Pro Clothing and Apparel and here to present the Soulful Image Award for modeling are Detroit Pistons forward, Perry Bonds, and rising supermodel, Imani Celeste."

Imani and Perry walked out on the stage to oohs, aahs, thunderous applause, and rousing music. Bulbs flashed in their faces like a million small flashing suns. Imani faced the crowd smiling, determined not to mess up.   As the audience quieted she spoke her lines. "Tonight's award winner in the modeling category was one of the first African Americans to solo on the cover of *Sports Illustrated Swimsuit Edition*. She 's been featured in a number of films and the fabulous show *Soul Food*, and is also well known for her work in the *Victoria's Secret* catalog."

Perry lifted his microphone.   "And the recipient of this prestigious award is... Tyra Banks!"

The crowd went wild as Tyra strolled to the stage in a stunning gold Dior gown that hugged every curve. Perry gave her the award and kissed her cheek and Imani hugged her.   Both faded into the background as Tyra began her acceptance speech.

Perry and Imani met backstage to collect their belongings and then made their way to their seats out front.   They sat at the table nibbling appetizers, drinking champagne, and watching the show for the next hour and a half.

"Do you want to get something to eat?" Perry asked as they climbed back into the limousine afterward.

Imani patted her stomach, which felt as if it were beginning to swell. "I'm full from the appetizers and champagne.   There might be something to eat in that little refrigerator in the bar."

Releasing his seatbelt, Perry maneuvered across the

seat to open the little box and rummage through the contents. "Ah-ha!" he cried, pulling out a tray loaded with jumbo shrimp and cocktail sauce surrounded by fresh pineapple chunks. He settled into the seat beside Imani to eat the shrimp cocktail and feed her tidbits of fresh pineapple. They were both stuffed by the time they made it back to the hotel.

Perry checked his watch. "Want to hit some of the local clubs? One of my partners is from L.A. and he gave me a list of clubs to check out."

Imani checked her outfit. It was still as white and pristine-looking as when Arena Sarducci had arranged the strips to form the dress. "I don't know," she replied honestly. "But if I go anywhere, I'm changing clothes. I don't know if this dress could stand up to some dancing and I'm tired of trying to keep it clean."

They told the driver they would check with him in an hour and entered the hotel with one of the bodyguards in front and one behind them. Perry slipped into the room with Imani. "I'll help you with the dress if you want," he offered, "no strings attached."

"Thanks," she said gratefully as she kicked off her shoes. She'd been wondering how she would get out of the dress without ripping her skin or destroying the dress. "Let me get something to put on and the Q-tips and alcohol."

When she came back, Perry was sitting on the couch. He'd already taken off his shoes and tie. "I had to get rid of those shoes and that tie was choking me," he explained. "Come here and let me help you."

Imani walked over to him and gave him a Q-tip soaked with alcohol. "This is supposed to take the glue off," she explained.

Perry turned her around and unhooked the strips behind her neck. The soft material covering her breasts remained in place. With the saturated Q-tip in one hand and the edge of the material in the other, he began working at separating the material from her skin.

Closing her eyes, Imani tried not to think about the warmth of Perry's fingers on her skin, or the cool, tickling sensation of the damp swab.

"Halfway there," Perry murmured as soon as he freed the golden mound of one breast. The dark, apricot colored tip was a hardened nub. For a moment, they simply stared at one another, the temperature of the room rising rapidly. Then he took another saturated Q-tip and began to work on the other side of the dress.

This is silly! Imani told herself as she concentrated on keeping still. It's not as if he hasn't seen your breasts before. He's done a whole lot more than look at them. Finally, he finished that part of his task and the entire top of the dress fell forward, completely baring her breasts. Perry didn't look at her as he lifted the lace cover-up she'd brought and helped her into it. "Can you do the rest by yourself?"

"Yes, sure," she answered quickly, turning her back to

him and trying to work the hidden hooks and snaps.

After letting her try for a few frantic moments, Perry gently turned her around and kneeling in front of her, went to work on the bottom portion of the dress. "Do you have anything on under this thing?"

"Not much," Imani grinned, feeling better now that she was partially covered, "But you've seen it all before."

"I could spend my life happily viewing this scenery," he cracked. "And if I can't get this thing off, I'll rip it off you."

Imani covered his hands with hers. "Please be careful with this. It's one of a kind."

"I can believe that." He tugged sharply and the bottom of the dress gave.

Soon Imani was stepping out of the bottom, clad only in her half-body suit. She pulled the edges of her cover up together and tied it. "Thanks a lot, Perry. I don't know what I would have done without you."

"Hopefully you wouldn't have had to ask one of the bodyguards to help."

Imani shook her head. "Oh no. I'd have slept in it first."

"Good thing I was around to help."

"Yes it is." Before she knew what she was doing, she'd stepped forward and pressed herself against him in a deep, heartfelt hug that joined them together from breasts to thighs. Relaxing her hold, she pressed a soft kiss to his cheek and then his lips. In her heart she knew that she would always love Perry.

Perry tangled the fingers of one hand in her hair and cupped her face in the other. "Did I tell you how beautiful you looked tonight? How beautiful you are?"

"Yes," she whispered just before his mouth came down on hers with the soft, sensual, swirling of his tongue. She savored his kiss, hot sensation melting her insides and oozing to the very core of her. Between several silky kisses she whispered, "You look like every woman's dream. Did I tell how handsome and virile and sexy you looked tonight?"

"No, you didn't." Perry rubbed his cheek against hers, his fingers tracing an aching path down the edges of her robe to her breasts.

"Then I'm telling you now," she declared boldly as she tugged his head down for a wild, wet kiss that signaled her surrender.

The warmth of his hands penetrated the thin material covering her breasts. She felt his fingers flex, then tug open her robe. Imani gasped when he covered one breast with his open mouth and lovingly sucked. Her knees buckled.

Perry held her up, one hand teasing her other nipple. "I want you in bed."

"Yes," she moaned, her fingers fumbling with the buttons on his shirt.

He gazed into her eyes, his expression a mixture of love and lust that made her shiver all over. Then he lifted her and carried her into the bedroom. Together they threw back the sheets.

With her heart full of love, she finished undressing him, not knowing if she would ever experience this particular pleasure again. Desire rippled through her at the sight of his male beauty. She caressed his body, covering the milk chocolate expanse of it with hungry kisses until he growled in protest.

Perry slipped the lace from her shoulders and licked a path from her neck to her navel. She writhed beneath him, his name on her lips. He laved her nipple, sucking hungrily as he hooked his fingers into the wet, half-body suit and tugged it off her. She cried out as his fingers found and worked her center, moving in and out of the moisture until her body contracted in helpless spasms of ecstasy.

They rolled on the bed until he settled in the cradle of her thighs.

"I really love you," he said as he entered her, the thick hardness of him reaching so deep within her that she struggled to catch her breath. Imani gripped his tight buns with both hands, her head spinning and her body rocking.

He thrust slow and steadily, his brown gaze holding hers as he pleasured them both. Suddenly he arched his back, his eyes glazing over with erotic pleasure and they both tumbled off the face of the earth into a hot passionate storm.

Chapter 13

Perry sat in first class on the early flight to Detroit, waiting for takeoff and wondering where he'd gone wrong. This morning he'd awakened in her room alone. Imani had left a note explaining that she needed some time alone and was therefore taking the red eye back to Detroit.

He hadn't gone to Imani's room after the award show with the intention of spending the night with her, but when he'd helped her with the dress, things had quickly gotten out of hand. When they'd made love, there'd been an air of finality and he'd seen tears in her eyes. He'd been extra tender with her, hoping she would come to the right conclusions on her own. Now he was afraid she was going to do something they would both regret.

Outside his window on the sun-splashed tarmac, airline employees loaded luggage. Perry watched and thought about Imani. He knew she could be flighty, tempestuous, and bitchy, but she could also be generous, loving, and exciting; and it was all good to him. Do you really want to marry a woman who has kicked you to the curb time and time again? A woman who says she loves you in one breath and that she doesn't trust you in the next? In his heart he didn't hesitate. The answer was yes. He loved Imani and wanted her any way he could get her. No other woman mattered.

He played basketball for a living and it was an integral part of his life. He couldn't change that right now, but he couldn't and wouldn't play forever. He planned to work as a photographer when his playing days were over and had already started generating income with his photography. If he could only convince her to take a chance, to go with her heart the way she had before, everything would work out. Perry shifted in his seat, his spirits low. Every time he saw Imani, hope soared within him, but she managed to kill it. He couldn't keep this up much longer. He'd run out of ideas a long time ago.

In the middle of the busy and crowded hubbub in the luggage claim area at Detroit Metropolitan Airport,

Imani dragged her bag off the luggage carousel. A man in a blue uniform and cap approached her.

"Ms. Celeste?"

"Yes."

"I'm Steven Williams from Best VIP Limousine Services." He flashed his identification. "Top Pro has secured our services for pick up and transport to your home."

Imani nodded, allowing him to take charge of her bag. She was surprised that Top Pro had been able to accommodate her last minute change. As she followed the driver to the area outside, she stopped only to buy the *Detroit Free Press* to read in the limousine.

As the limo took off, she fastened her seatbelt and began to read the newspaper. Inside, on the top left-hand side she found a picture of herself in the white designer dress. "Yes!" Imani broke out into a smile. It was a good shot of her and the dress. She knew that Arena and Top Pro would be happy. There was even a shot of Perry giving the award to Tyra Banks.

She folded back the section of the paper and read the few sentences describing the event over and over again. Then she stared at the pictures, lingering on the one with Perry. Perry and Imani? Damon and Imani? Or Imani by herself? The words repeated inside her head, over and over again. She couldn't go on like this.

Forcing herself to concentrate on the paper, she turned page after page, not really digesting the words or the pictures. In the section before the classified ads she stopped, her attention caught by a picture in the section featuring local events. Again, she read the caption: "Local judge cuts a rug at charity benefit for Focus Hope".

The picture looks innocent enough, she told herself, examining Damon's stylish suit and DeAndra's short and sexy little dress. But there was something in their rapt facial expressions that didn't seem quite right, something that made her think there was more to the picture than the obvious. She wanted to talk to Damon.

Imani got a pad from her purse and scribbled down Damon's West Bloomfield address. "Driver? Could we go to this address instead?"

"Yes ma'am. Can you give me the nearest cross streets?"

Imani told him and then leaned back to watch the green grass, trees and shrubbery go by. She hadn't forgotten about seeing DeAndra in the mall or forgotten what she'd said. If she'd been weak enough to fall back into bed with Perry, would it be so surprising if Damon fell back into bed with DeAndra?"

As the limousine turned and advanced down Damon's street, she wondered if she would be better off alone. The limousine stopped in front of Damon's house and Imani prepared to get out. She'd already released her seatbelt when she saw DeAndra Blake's little Geo Storm pulled deep into the driveway. Stunned,

Imani could only look at the house's dark windows and imagine Damon and DeAndra in bed together and smile.

The driver opened her door. "Ma'am?"

Briefly, she thought of ringing his doorbell to see for herself. What would it prove? she asked herself, except what you've known for a while. You and Damon shouldn't even be thinking of getting married to each other. He couldn't trust you to stay away from Perry and it looks as if he can't stay away from DeAndra Blake.

"Ma'am?" the driver repeated.

Imani gave him her attention. "I'm sorry. I've changed my mind. I'd like to go home now."

The driver scanned the house, pausing on the white Geo Storm at the rear of the driveway. "No problem, ma'am." He shut the passenger door carefully and got back into the car.

At her mother's home, restlessness engulfed Imani as she tipped the driver generously and closed the front door. The house was quiet because it was only seven o'clock in the morning. The nurse was on the couch in the living room reading a book. Checking her mother's room, she saw her mother sleeping peacefully.

Too wound up to sleep, Imani dragged her bag to her room as quietly as she could and changed into a running outfit. Then she took off for a run in the park.

The Love We Had

It was warm and sunny and nearly eleven in the morning when Perry pulled up at the home of Imani's mother. He hoped the family was up because he had only a short amount of time before he had to go home and catch at least a quick nap before the exhibition game scheduled for the evening.

He opened the back door of his Mercedes and Jimmy gurgled at him. "Hey man, you were so quiet on the ride over here that I almost forgot you were back here."

Jimmy grinned and gave him a reply in gibberish that included something sounding close to Perry's name.

Perry released the lock on the car seat and lifted his heavy little nephew into his arms. "Did you say my name, huh? Have you learned to do that already?" He felt Jimmy's legs lock around his waist and saw that the baby already had his chubby fist full of his white shirt-sleeve. Slamming the car door shut, he strode up the cement walkway and climbed the stone steps. Shifting the baby in his arms and straightening the gray and white Detroit Pistons outfit, he rang the bell.

A dark-haired woman in a nurse uniform answered the door. "Hello. Oh, what a beautiful baby!"

Perry thanked her. As Jimmy wiggled and tried to go to the nurse, Perry told her who he was and asked to see Imani and her mother.

"I haven't seen Imani today," the nurse replied, "but Mrs. Celeste is having coffee in the kitchen. Let me see if she wants company. I'll only be a minute." She closed the door.

A few moments later, the nurse opened the door and gestured them in. Perry went through the hall and made his way to the kitchen.

"Perry!" Imani's mother set her coffee cup on the center of the table and pushed her chair back a little. "What a wonderful surprise! Is this Jimmy?" When Perry nodded, she held out her arms. "Can I hold him?" Perry came closer and placed Jimmy onto her lap. "Is he too heavy for you?"

"Oh no, he's perfect." Mrs. Celeste's face was wreathed in smiles. She ran a gentle hand across Jimmy's soft little curls. Always the charmer, Jimmy looked her in the eye and launched into a string of sincere conversational gibberish. "I think he's trying to tell me something," she chuckled.

Perry grabbed one of the wooden kitchen chairs and sat down. "This little fellow always has plenty to say."

She caressed a dimpled, caramel cheek. "He's gorgeous."

"Thank you."

"And he looks just like you."

"Thanks again. Did Imani tell you how she saw me in the supermarket with him?"

"A little."

"She was sure he was mine."

Mrs. Celeste turned to look at him. "I can see how

she might think that. You know, I look at Jimmy and I can't help thinking about the baby Imani lost. She's still hurting over that. I'm thinking that the only way she'll be able to let it go is to try again."

"With Damon Kessler?" The words were out of his mouth before he realized it.

"No, with you. Imani loves you and I think you know that."

Perry shrugged helplessly. "It didn't stop her from getting herself engaged to Kessler. I'm glad that's over with."

"Oh, I don't think Damon's given up yet." She smiled, her eyes sparkling with amusement. "He's handsome, charming, well-fixed financially, a pillar in the community, a good friend, and he loves her to death. Personally, I think his biggest qualification is that he's not you. I think she's afraid of you."

Perry gripped the arm of his chair. "I never wanted to hurt her, but I made some mistakes. I love her."

"It's never easy when you love someone," she said sympathetically. "The two of you will work it out. I'm sure of it."

Jimmy used his hold on Mrs. Celeste to pull himself up to a standing position. "Bah, bah, bah!" he sang and then pressed his wet lips to her cheek.

"Thank you, Jimmy." Mrs. Celeste patted his back, her other hand just below his diapered bottom. When her eyes met Perry's, he could have sworn they were shiny with tears. "What are you going to name your son?" she asked.

"If I get another chance, I'm going to name him Perry. He'll be called Perry Bonds Jr."

"I like the sound of that." She sighed.

Jimmy began pumping his legs up and down.

Mrs. Celeste gave him her attention. "Oh, you want to be bounced, huh?"

"Let me do it." Perry jumped up to retrieve the baby. "He's no lightweight."

"No, he isn't," she chuckled. She watched Perry catch hold of Jimmy's waist and move him up and down. The room rang with baby laughter.

Mrs. Celeste laughed too. "I can't remember when I've had this much fun. Thank you so much for bringing Jimmy by."

"You're welcome. I hope to get to do it again."

"You'd better, or I'll never forgive you," she threatened. "So what do you have planned for today?"

"I'm in an exhibition game at The Palace this evening. You know the season's starting." At her nod, he checked his watch. "I've got to go. I have to take Jimmy back and get some sleep or my timing will be off."

"I really enjoyed this visit," she said as Perry leaned forward and kissed her cheek. Then he offered Jimmy's soft, dimpled cheek for her kiss. "Bye, Jimmy." She caught the little hand that shot out to grab the edge of her hairnet and gently disengaged it.

Outside the house, Perry had just opened the rear passenger door of his Mercedes when Imani walked up the driveway. "Perry!" she called as she approached. A fine sheen of sweat covered her face, neck, and arms, and the tip of her ponytail was wet. She dabbed at her face and neck with a little towel. "How long have you been here?"

"Half an hour, forty minutes."

She stared at him, regret and something he couldn't define in her eyes. "I was so wound up that I knew I wouldn't be able to sleep, so I went to the park."

"Did you have a good run?"

"Yes." She extended her hand to touch his arm. "I-I'm sorry I ran off like that last night. It was silly and childish and…"

"Do you know what you want now?"

"Yes, I think so."

"Well, give me a call when you know that you really want me." Perry lifted the bar on the car seat and placed the baby inside.

"Wait," Imani's voice wavered. "Let me give Jimmy a kiss."

He stepped aside and watched Imani coo at Jimmy. Then catching his busy little hands in hers, she placed a soft kiss to his cheek. When she'd finished, Perry stepped forward and locked the car seat.

"Can I kiss you, too?" Imani asked.

He turned to face her and saw sadness and confusion

in her facial expression. He didn't understand himself, didn't understand why something inside of him refused to let him put her at ease this one last time. When he'd seen her walking up the driveway, a wave of hopelessness had hit him with bruising force. Maybe it's better if you aren't with the person you love, he thought. It wouldn't hurt so much. He was tired of hurting.

She curved her fingers around his shoulders and leaned towards him, careful not to get him wet. Then she gently pressed her soft lips to his in a caressing motion that made him ache. "Bye, Perry," she said softly, her eyes large and luminous.

"Bye." He forced himself away from her and walked around to the driver's side of the Mercedes and got in. As he drove off, he risked a glance in the rearview mirror out of the corner of his eye. She stood in the driveway, watching until he turned the corner.

Closing the front door, Imani went into the kitchen and poured herself a large glass of water."

"That Jimmy is a beautiful baby," Mama said from her chair at the kitchen table.

"Yes, he is." Imani drank the water in a short series of gulps.

"Are you going to marry Perry?"

"I don't know, Mama. Maybe. I know that I'm not

going to marry Damon."

"Did something happen?"

Imani dropped down into a kitchen chair. "I went by his house early this morning on my way home from the airport. DeAndra Blake's car was at the back of his driveway. It looks like she spent the night."

Her mother shook her head. "I never really thought you would marry Damon anyway."

Imani shrugged. "Maybe he cares about her more than he thinks. I was a little sad because it seems like I've never been able to trust the men I love, but when I thought about it, I realized that I wasn't as upset as I should have been. I was seriously crushed when I thought Perry was screwing around with that starlet-harlot Rasheeda." She patted her face with the end of the towel. "Anyway, I know that I can't point a righteous finger at Damon when I've ended up in bed with Perry a couple of times since the breakup."

Standing, Imani tugged at her damp running shorts and top. "I've got to get out of these wet clothes and into the shower. I can't stand the way these wet things feel against my skin."

"Are you sleepy?" her mother asked. "I want you to come back down and talk to me for a while."

Imani yawned and stretched. "Not really. I'll shower and come right back."

"I'll wait for you in the living room."

Imani helped her mother up from the chair and into

the living room. "I won't be long," she called as she bounded up the steps. In the shower, she stood under the hot spray for several minutes, thinking about Perry. She'd never doubted that she loved him, but she'd taken their problems to a new level by getting engaged to Damon. Would Perry forgive her for being so insecure? She knew it wouldn't be easy.

As she filled her hands with Vitabath Spring Green shower gel and lathered her body, the unique scent with a hint of musk teased her nostrils. The scent never failed to refresh her. She wondered at Mama's mood, glad that she seemed to be feeling better. Imani smiled. Could one sweet-talking little cherub named Jimmy have anything to do with that?

Descending the steps in a white terry shortall after her shower, Imani entered the living room and stretched out on the couch. She dangled her bare feet over the arm of the sofa. "What did you want to talk about, Mama?"

"I thought it was time we talked about Louis."

Imani's pulse sped up and a black cloud descended on her. She sat up immediately, her gaze riveted to her mother's anxious face. "What about Louis?"

"I couldn't bring myself to talk about him for the longest time, but I don't know how much longer I'll be around and you deserve to hear the truth and my apology." Her voice shook with emotion. "He was one of the biggest mistakes I ever made. I was young and dumb." Her mother's fingers twisted in her lap. "After you left, I discovered what a skirt chaser he was. He propositioned all my friends and they were afraid to tell me. I actually came into the room one time to hear Thelma tell him that if he didn't stop trying to put his hands on her, she was going to tell me everything." She lifted her head to meet Imani's stare. "And then I heard him say, "If she didn't believe her own child, what makes you think she'd believe anything you have to say about me?"

Imani sat on the couch with the hands of her crossed arms massaging her skin against the cold she suddenly felt despite the warmth of the day.

Tears flowed down her mother's face as she grabbed a tissue and blew her nose loudly. "I went and got your daddy's gun and I told him to get out of my house and never come back. He laughed at me, but he didn't come back. I went to see a lawyer the very next day and filed for divorce. I wanted nothing from that man."

Imani took a deep breath. "Mama, I never did anything with Louis. He followed me around all the time, trying to touch me, and when I tried to tell you, you wouldn't listen," she cried.

Her mother let out a long shivery sigh, full of remorse. "I'll regret that till the day I die. Kicking you out of the house was the biggest mistake of my life and there's no excuse for what I did. When I came into your room and saw you in those skimpy shorts and top on the bed with him, I went crazy. I blamed you because you were seventeen, beautiful, and always running around half-dressed, flaunting yourself. He'd already told me that you'd been coming on to him."

"Mama, I didn't!" Imani cried. All the hurt and pain of being unjustly accused and convicted came back. "He wouldn't get out of my room, so when I tried to leave, he grabbed me and pulled me down on the bed. I was trying to get away when you opened the door."

"I know that, baby. He was a dirty dog and a low-down SOB. I was so hurt and ashamed when I realized the truth, that I couldn't lift my head for years and I wasn't woman enough to come and get you from that home for runaway girls. I kept seeing that shell-shocked look on your face. Can you ever forgive me?"

"You— -you thought I was bad and that I-I did things with men," Imani stammered shakily. "He lied, Mama."

"I know that, baby. I was angry and upset and so wrong that I'll never forgive myself." She broke down and sobbed. "Once you were gone, I had a hard time believing that you'd done all those things. Come here. Come here, Imani." She opened her arms and Imani crossed the room to fall into them. Both women cried hard until they had nothing left.

"When I found out how sick I was, I just figured it was God's punishment for being a terrible mother to you." Mama gently stroked Imani's head. "And then when you came back to take care of me, I didn't know what to do. Imani, I don't deserve a daughter like you."
Imani got to her knees and hugged her frail mother tight-

ly. "I love you, Mama."

"I love you too, baby."

For a long time they simply sat silently holding each other, their minds finally at peace about the past. Then they talked about the future and her mother told her that she hoped Imani would marry Perry.

Mama's voice softened. "He's a good man and I know you love him. I can almost see the grandbabies, looking a lot like Jimmy."

"We've got strong genes in our family too," Imani reminded her. Then Imani stared hard. "Mama, are you all right? You look as though you might be in pain."

"I'm just a little tired, child. I've been up since early this morning and I haven't had a nap."

"Then let me take you to your room," Imani urged, taking her arm. "We can talk more later."

"I'm feeling fine," her mother said, walking smoothly, a peaceful smile on her face. "If I die tomorrow, everything will be all right because you and I have finally made our peace with the past and you've forgiven me." Turning, Imani helped her into her room. "Yes, Mama, I forgive you, but I wish you would quit all this talk about dying. I want you to hang around a while longer."

"When it's your time to go, you go whether you're ready or not." She sat on the bed. Imani helped her take her shoes off.

"I guess so." She watched her mother stretch out on the bed, and then she unfurled the flowered comforter and covered her with it. Straightening the coverlet, she felt the effects of the flight from L.A., her morning run, and the excitement of the past few days dragging her down. "You know, I'm sleepy now. I'm going to go upstairs and take a nap too." She kissed her mother's cheek.

"Sweet dreams," her mother called as Imani left the room.

"You too, Mama."

Imani climbed the stairs and entered her room. Then she slipped between the fresh white linen sheets and was asleep before her head reached the pillows.

It was late afternoon when Imani awakened and sat up in bed. Someone had called her name from far away. She couldn't quite tell who it was. The house was awfully quiet. Climbing out of bed, Imani took the carpeted stairs barefoot. Now she remembered telling the nurse she wouldn't be needed after one o'clock. No wonder the house was so quiet.

She walked into her mother's room and saw that she still slept peacefully. It was a shame she had to wake her up to take her medicine. Approaching the bed, Imani shook her gently. "Mama?" When she didn't answer, Imani shook her again. "Mama, you've got to take your medicine now." Still, there was no answer.

Suddenly all she could think about was her mother's talk about dying. In growing alarm, she felt for a pulse and found none. "Oh God, please help me!" she cried as she turned on the speakerphone, dialed the emergency number, and climbed onto the bed. In a flurry of desperate activity, she tried all the CPR techniques she could remember. When the emergency staff came on line, she asked for an ambulance and gave them the details of her mother's condition.

At the sound of the sirens, she rushed to open the door, her chest pounding painfully. Was Mama going to die? Was she dead already? Imani was running as she led the way to her mother's room. Biting her lips, she hugged herself and held her breath as the emergency technicians checked her mother's vital signs.

"She's still alive," the short, stocky one with the kind face shouted as he put an oxygen mask over her nose and mouth.

Imani released her breath, quick tears filling her eyes. "Please, please, please," she prayed as they lifted her mother onto a stretcher and hurried to the door.

"You need to come along and give the hospital all her medical information," the heavyset one told her.

Imani suppressed a nervous giggle. Of course she would come along! Imani grabbed her mother's Coach purse and ran into the hall to get her own. She looked down at her skimpy little shortall and decided it was enough that the essentials were covered. Stuffing her feet into a pair of navy sandals she found in the hall closet, she locked the front door and ran down the steps. In the yard, they were putting her mother into the back of the ambulance.

It was half time. Perry had taken a quick shower and put on a clean uniform when one of his buddies nudged his shoulder. "Hey man, isn't that Imani on the tube?"

Perry turned to see a pale-looking Imani dressed in next to nothing, climbing out of an ambulance behind a woman on a stretcher. He felt his heart hitch in his chest. Several of the team members gathered around the television monitor as someone turned up the volume.

The station switched to the news anchor. "Local celebrity supermodel Imani Celeste was spotted at Detroit Receiving Hospital's emergency room about an hour ago with her mother, Detroit native Ginetta Celeste. Mrs. Celeste has been admitted and is reported to be in serious condition. The nature of her illness is undisclosed. Imani Celeste is most recently remembered for the provocative dress she wore to the Soul Image Awards Program." The camera switched to a shot of Imani looking like a goddess in the Arena Sarducci dress. Then the anchor went on to the next story.

Perry left the television monitor and went looking for the team coach because he didn't want Imani to be alone at the hospital. Forty minutes later, he strode into one of the private waiting areas at the hospital. Imani sat in a chair shivering, with her face in her hands. Taking off his jacket, he took the seat beside her, slipping his jacket over her shoulders.

She turned to look at him, fear shadowing her exotic eyes. "Perry? Perry, Mama's had a heart attack and they don't think she's going to make it. She's in surgery now." He gathered her into his arms, tugging the ends of the jacket closed as he pressed a kiss to her temple. "I figured as much. What happened? She seemed fine when I saw her this morning."

"I don't know. I don't understand. She walked and laughed and enjoyed this day in ways I haven't seen in months. She said she felt better and she talked about Louis..."

"Your stepfather?"

"Yes. She discovered the truth about him a long time ago and divorced him, but she was too ashamed to try to make up with me. I think she was afraid that I would never forgive her."

"Did you?" he asked, knowing the answer. Imani had a kind, loving disposition that a lot of people never got close enough to see.

"Yes, I forgave her." Imani leaned her head on his shoulder. "I just had to know that she knew the truth about what really happened. Then she started talking about making her peace and dying."

Perry rubbed her arms through the fabric of the jacket. "I'm glad the two of you talked about Louis. I know that what he did has bothered you for years. Imani, it wasn't your fault. He was a sick man."

"I know that," she whispered, her eyes glazing with tears. "I just want Mama to live."

Perry pressed another tissue into her hands. In the doorway of the waiting room a doctor removed his surgical mask and gestured for them to approach. Supporting Imani, Perry approached him.

"Miss Celeste?" The doctor took Imani's hand. "I'm sorry to have to tell you this but your mother did not survive the operation. She passed away at 8: 23 p. m."

"No! No, no, no, no!" Imani sobbed, breaking down. "She can't be gone. I want to see her!"

"Can we see her?" Perry asked the doctor.

"I don't advise it, but if you must, come this way." He led them down the corridor to a cold, almost empty operating room where people were busy cleaning up. A hospital staffer starting wheeling the gurney away.

"Hold on a minute," the doctor told the staffer. He lifted the sheet to reveal Mrs. Celeste's face.

"Mama?" Imani stepped closer with eyes only for the body on the gurney. "Oh, Mama." She dissolved into tears.

Perry curved his arms around her, his heart breaking for her. He couldn't forget that he'd almost been in the same position little more than a week ago when his father had gone through surgery.

She lifted a hand and touched her mother's forehead. "She's cold, Perry."

He swallowed, overcome with emotion and unable to speak. He could barely believe that someone so vital and alive only this morning was dead. Suddenly Imani turned to him and buried her face in his shoulder. He massaged her back gently, wishing there was something more he could do. In the background, he saw the staffer wheel the body away.

Perry knew that several reporters waited outside to interview Imani on her way out, so he secured a wheelchair, put her into it, and took her out of the emergency entrance in a private ambulance. Afraid to take Imani to her apartment or her mother's home because of the press, he took her to his house and swore the ambulance driver to secrecy.

He spent most of the night in the chair by the bed, watching over her as she tossed and turned restlessly. He rubbed her back, held her hand, and stroked her head, determined to comfort her as much as possible.

About 4:00 a.m. Imani sat up, her eyes puffy, but clear. "Mama! Where's Mama, Perry?"

"She's gone." Perry took her hand.

"I thought—I hoped I'd only dreamed it." She squeezed his hand so hard it hurt.

"They say she died during surgery, so she never regained consciousness. She didn't suffer," he told her, trying to give her what comfort he could.

Imani shook her head negatively. "I've been thinking and thinking about Mama and I think she was hurting all day long. She knew she was going to die. I just didn't want to believe her."

"Maybe she did," he murmured, not knowing what else to say.

Imani turned onto her back and opened her arms. "Hold me, Perry, so I can sleep. I'm so tired I can't think straight."

She needed him. As he climbed on the bed with her, Perry knew he couldn't count on anything, but he felt as though he were coming home. Imani, his love, meant home to him, and it was all the better that they were in the house they'd had built last year and filled with the furniture they'd chosen. Pressing her soft form to his, spoon fashion, his only regret was that it had taken a devastating loss to bring them to this point in time. He closed his eyes, his soul at peace.

Imani awakened cold and shivering. Sunlight streamed in around the edges of the blinds, illuminating several of the photos Perry had taken and used to cover his wall. She was in bed alone. Dragging the covers up, she acknowledged just how comforting it had been to sleep in Perry's arms. She couldn't think about going home to her apartment or to her mother's house.

At the thought of her mother, a sharp pain stabbed her behind the eyes and she blinked back tears. She was going to have to get used to it, because Mama wasn't coming back.

Perry came into the room with a tray. "I know you didn't eat anything yesterday, so I brought you some fruit salad and raisin toast. Want some tea?"

"Yes," Imani sat up, allowing Perry to arrange the tray over her legs. "Thanks for taking such good care of me."

"It's my pleasure." The loving smile he gave her lit his entire face.

"And mine." The corners of her mouth turned up in a tentative imitation of his. She drank the rosehip tea he'd sweetened with honey and nibbled on the fresh fruit salad while he sat in the chair by the bed, one bare foot under the cover caressing her leg.

"Do you want me to go to the funeral home with you?"

She set down her teacup, her voice wavering. "Yes. Mama said she had it all arranged, but I have talk to them and pick a day for the funeral and put the notice in the paper."

He moved onto the bed and put an arm around her shoulders.

"I'll help you," Perry told her. "You can get through this."

308

Grateful, she laid her head on his warm chest and encircled his waist with her arms. She heard his heart beating steadily.

"Why don't you eat a little more?" he asked, eying the plate that still held more than half the food.

When she shook her head, he took her fork and ate some of the fruit. Then he fed her tidbits of pineapple, cantaloupe and watermelon. His soft lips came down on hers in a gentle, caressing kiss. "I love you, baby."

"I love you, too." Imani tightened her arms around his waist.

Shifting on the bed, he lifted the tray and placed it on the nightstand. "You should rest a little more. Then we can go over to the funeral home."

Obediently, she stretched out on the bed with him, dragging the covers up.

Imani got through the rest of the week in a fog. She vaguely remembered going to the funeral home with Perry and going through the arrangements her mother had made with the staff. Perry called the paper with her mother's obituary.

Four days later, she sat and cried through the funeral ceremony at her mother's church with Damon on her left and Perry on her right. Both men had worked together to make sure that everything went smoothly. The church had been filled with local dignitaries, neighbors, and friends. Imani could only remember a sea of faces and people whose voices came to her from a distance.

At the cemetery, she took one long last look at her mother in her favorite blue dress before they closed the casket and lowered it into the ground. Stepping forward, she dropped three red carnations onto the pearl casket and watched the crew cover it with dirt. "Good-bye, Mama," she whispered.

Afterward, Perry took her back to her mother's house where a friend of Damon's had catered the wake. People came to sit with her and talk about her mother. Even her mother's old friend Thelma came and hugged Imani, glad to hear that she and her mother had reconciled.

By seven o'clock in the evening, the guests and catering staff had gone and the house was quiet. Imani walked around her mother's house for the last time. She'd already removed the things she wanted to keep, her mother's jewelry, her Bible, and her important papers. Tomorrow the moving company was going to come, pack up everything else, and take it to a shelter for battered women and a for sale sign would grace the immaculate green lawn.

Perry approached her. "Let me take you home."

She nodded her agreement and saw that Damon was hovering nearby. As Perry took a moment to go and empty the trash, she went to Damon and gave him a hug. "Thank you so much for helping me through this. I can't tell you how much I appreciate it. You're a true friend."

"Do you know what you're doing?" Damon asked, his eyes strangely shiny. He evidently thought she'd chosen Perry over him and he was right.

"By letting Perry take me home?"

He nodded. "I could take you home."

In the past week both men had gone out of their way to provide unselfish love and support, but she'd realized early on just how much she loved and needed Perry. He seemed to know what she needed before she knew it herself and she'd felt lost when he wasn't around. She'd been incredibly needy, but he hadn't taken advantage of her, he'd taken care of her. Despite her grief she had known that it was a labor of love.

She looked up at Damon, her heart full of sympathy.

"That's not us, Damon. I don't think you should take me home. I've come to believe that my heart and my future are with Perry and maybe your future is with DeAndra."

Damon ran a hand over his face. "I can't explain or justify what's happened between me and DeAndra, but it can't touch what I feel for you."

"I know that," Imani hugged him again, her own eyes smarting with tears, "but no matter how much I've fought it, I've never loved anyone as strongly, deeply, or passionately as I love Perry."

"All right then." Damon caressed her hair and grasped her hand, his green eyes filled with sadness. "If you ever need me for anything, just call."

Imani squeezed his hand. "I will," she promised.

"Then I'll see you around?" He moved away from her.

"You're still my friend, aren't you?"

"Always." He strode to the door and opened it, turning to face her once more. "Good-bye."

"Bye." Imani watched him close the front door and heard his steps echo on the porch.

Perry came out of the kitchen. "Damon left?"

"Yeah." She didn't feel like elaborating.

"Are you ready to go?"

"Yes." She took one last look around and then turned the lights off for the last time.

Perry and Imani were both silent on the ride home. Imani was surprised when Perry actually pulled up in front of her apartment. As the doorman approached the car, she thought of her apartment and it seemed lonely and sterile. She could think of nothing she wanted less.

"Want me to come in with you?" he asked quietly.

"No. I want to go home with you," she answered honestly.

"Oh!" Perry chuckled with relief. "I thought you might want more time alone."

"I want more time with you."

"Good." Perry waved the doorman away and took off.

Two months later Imani sat up in the pale moonlight, unable to sleep. After a while she watched as Perry's sleep grew restless. Finally, he turned and sat up too.

"Imani?"

"Yes."

"Are you all right?" He put an arm around her and pulled her close.

"Yes." She snuggled close, her heart full of love. "Will you marry me, Perry?"

His chuckle held a note of self-deprecation and frustration. "Why buy the bull when you can get his services for free?"

Imani shook her head. Smoothing her palms down his clean-shaven cheeks, she answered. "Because I really love you and need you and I never have and never will feel this way about anyone else."

Perry gently tugged at her ponytail. "What about being a basketball wife?"

"I'll just have to learn to cope with it. I know you'll help me."

With his fingertip, he drew a line from the center of her forehead to the tip of her nose. "And trust?"

Imani spoke from her heart. "I trust you with my life. I can't imagine life without you." Closing her eyes, she pulled him tight against her.

"Hmmmh, I don't know," Perry whispered.

Imani's eyes popped open and she pushed back to scan his face. "Do you want to marry me or not?"

"I do want to marry you, I will marry you." Perry leaned forward and kissed her lips.

"You will? That's great!" She threw her arms around him.

He gave her an expectant look. "What about my ring?"

"Your ring?"

"Yes. When one person asks another to marry them, they're supposed to have a ring."

"Okay." Imani took off the delicate diamond ring she wore on her right hand and presented it with a flourish.

"I think we should have one of those long engagements," he teased.

"Oh no," she told him in a firm voice, "it took too long and we worked too hard to get back together. We'll get married within the next month or so because I'm not going anywhere."

"Yes, ma'am."

"And we're going to have at least two babies."

"Yes ma'am. Anything else?" Perry's eyes were glowing.

"Yes," Imani told him, "I'm going to love you forever."

The End

OTHER GENESIS TITLES

Passion	T.T. Henderson	$10.95
Path of Fire	T.T. Henderson	$8.95
Picture Perfect	Reon Carter	$8.95
Pride & Joi (Hardcover)	Gay G. Gunn	$15.95
Pride & Joi (Paperback)	Gay G. Gunn	$8.95
Quiet Storm	Donna Hill	$10.95
Reckless Surrender	Rochelle Alers	$8.95
Rooms of the Heart	Donna Hill	$8.95
Shades of Desire	Monica White	$8.95
Sin	Crystal Rhodes	$8.95
So Amazing	Sinclair LeBeau	$8.95
Somebody's Someone	Sinclair LeBeau	$8.95
Soul to Soul	Donna Hill	$8.95
The Price of Love	Beverly Clark	$8.95
The Missing Link	Charlyne Dickerson	$8.95
Truly Inseparable (Hardcover)	Wanda Y. Thomas	$15.95
Truly Inseparable (Paperback)	Wanda Y. Thomas	$8.95
Unconditional Love	Alicia Wiggins	$8.95
Whispers in the Night	Dorothy Love	$8.95
Whispers in the Sand	LaFlorya Gauthier	$10.95
Yesterday is Gone	Beverly Clark	$10.95

All books are sold in paperback, unless otherwise noted.

You may order on line at www.genesis-press.com, by phone at 1-888-463-4461, or mail the order form in the back of this book.

ORDER FORM

Mail to: Genesis Press, Inc.
315 3rd Avenue North
Columbus, MS 39701

Name _____

Address _____

City/State _____ Zip _____

Telephone _____

Ship to (if different from above)

Name _____

Address _____

City/State _____ Zip _____

Telephone _____

Qty.	Author	Title	Price	Total

Use this order form, or call 1-888-INDIGO-1	Total for books _____
	Shipping and handling: $4 first two book, $1 each additional book
	Total S & H _____
	Total amount enclosed _____
	Mississippi residents add 7% sales tax